Death in Twilight

Jason Fields

This is a work of fiction. Names, characters, places and incidents are products of the author's imagination, or are used fictitiously and are not to be construed as real. Any resemblance to actual events, locales, organizations or persons, living or dead, is entirely coincidental.

ISBN: 0615732097
ISBN 13: 9780615732091

Library of Congress Control Number: 2012922250
Ars Gratia Pecuniam, New York, NY
Cover photographs courtesy of Wikimedia Commons.

Dedication

For Martin Spett, survivor and storyteller

Prologue

A blow in the dark.
A body crumples to the pavement.
Leather shoes scrape cobblestones.
Stillness returns.

Chapter 1

Dawn's uncertain light reflected off a quickly freezing red puddle next to the head of a man in a threadbare winter coat. A yellow star was crudely sewn onto the coat's brown wool breast.

The little pool's source was the man's smashed skull, and its contents were a combination of his blood, bone and brain matter. Unstained by the blood, a uniform cap seemed carefully placed a short distance to the left of the body.

The cause of the blow was not immediately to be seen, though the force of the impact implied a weapon of some heft. No one stood over the body to claim credit for the act, nor was there anyone to grieve for the victim as a gray morning snaked through the narrow streets of the Jewish ghetto of Miasto, Poland.

At this early hour, only Aaron Kaminski was outside, and he wished he weren't. He kept to the shadows, hoping to avoid detection and a bullet. Breaking curfew was no small thing.

Unfortunately, Aaron was drunk and obvious. If there'd been a German observer, Aaron would have been dead.

Stumbling over his own feet and landing on the cobblestones face-to-face with the corpse didn't improve his situation. The fall pushed most of the breath from Aaron's body. The dead man's unblinking eyes startled him into gasping out the rest. It wasn't a good combination. Aaron nearly passed out.

Instead, he recoiled and sat up, examining the tableau with reluctance. He'd seen worse. Everyone in the ghetto had. Men, women and children dead from violence or starvation littered the ground of the enclosed district. It wasn't unusual to step over more than one body in the morning on the way to queue for rations.

And then Aaron noticed the dirty white cloth wrapped around the man's arm, the words *Jüdische Ghetto-Polizei* picked out in blue.

Everyone hated the Jewish Police, but nobody killed them. The men themselves weren't frightening, perhaps, but the Germans who they represented certainly were. To kill a Jewish policeman was to strike a blow against German authority, and that meant death — not only for the murderer, but also for the whole community of which he was a part.

It was time to go. Aaron struggled to his feet. He knew he didn't want to be anywhere near a dead policeman when a patrol came by. If breaking curfew brought the death penalty, being discovered anywhere near this body would likely mean torture bad enough to make him beg for the bullet.

What was your motive? Aaron's interrogator would ask. *Surely, you weren't acting alone …*

He knew the lines of questioning. He'd followed them hundreds of times with suspects of his own. But his time in the Polish national police — the Zendarmerie — hadn't given him any desire to be on the other side of the table.

Aaron backed onto the sidewalk and pulled in tight to the walls. He took one last look at the scene and found himself unmoved. He had his own problems, his own concerns. He had many jobs in the ghetto — everyone did — but the one thing he wasn't anymore was a cop.

Chapter 1

As the sun climbed and the curfew ended, the streets quickly filled with perilously thin men, women and children, all wearing clothes that would have been rags in another context. The months that had passed since the Jewish District had been walled off from the rest of the city had been cruel.

Everyone, whether on the street or cautiously peering out behind curtains, ignored the policeman's body. Curiosity wasn't a survival trait. Instead, people hoped for bread and dreamed of meat, unsure if their ration cards would get them either that morning.

The cards entitled each individual to 300 calories per day at a set price from the nominal Jewish authorities, the *Judenrat.* It was a joke, of course. Three hundred calories worth of food would have been a light snack for most before the war.

Mothers knew the rations would starve their infants, let alone their husbands. Some of them glared surreptitiously from under their hats as they passed the policeman's body. It was emaciated, but zaftig when compared with the bodies normally found dead in the streets at sunrise.

Within minutes, impromptu markets sprang up on sidewalks with people selling everything they had to others who had slightly more. The trade was often in barter. Money was tight and the Judenrat aggressively collected taxes in cash.

No one chose to haggle near the dead policeman.

Those who had come out in the cold for companionship or illicit prayer found other places to stand. Even the most fervent wouldn't say the Kaddish — the prayer for the dead — over the policeman. If anyone was struck by a charitable urge, it wasn't enough to make him willing to face a criminal charge for an overt act of worship. Not for this fallen man.

It was often said among the wise that Jews must possess greater powers than even they knew. Apparently, it wasn't enough for the Germans to wall them off from the world. To be safe, the Germans tried to erect a barrier to God, too.

Ordinarily, a murdered Jew would be of less interest to a German patrol in the ghetto than a public prayer. They left "justice" largely to the Judenrat and its street enforcers, the Jewish Police. Some of the men who wore the organization's special armband were forced into it, their lives and families held hostage. Others joined simply for extra rations or the opportunity to bully the people around them.

There was no way to tell what type of man lay in his own blood on Leopold Street. Was he one of the good ones, trying to arrest a criminal caught in the act? Was he trying to settle a domestic dispute when an angry husband or wife had caught him unaware? Or, perhaps, he'd been attempting extortion or rape when his victim turned on him?

An hour after sunrise, two shabbily dressed men with their own Ghetto-Polizei armbands and uniform hats walked slowly through the crowd, which ebbed around them. The men were dirty and unshaven. One wore glasses so thick it seemed possible light would give up the trip before it ever reached his eyes. They shambled, yet somehow conveyed a perverse cockiness. They displayed the pride of small men raised nearly an inch above their peers.

The cops arrived at the little clearing where their comrade's body lay. The circle around the men expanded as people retreated beyond what they hoped was the range of questioning. No one wanted to come under official scrutiny. No one wanted to bear witness where others could see them do it.

"Berson? Berson?" cried the officer with the spectacles.

The victim was easy to identify. The face was the only part of his head that retained its original shape.

Chapter 1

The second officer shouted at people to stop where they were, but civilians who had barely managed to crawl minutes before suddenly became gazelles.

Seeing it was useless, the shouter, whose name was Shemtov, turned to his partner.

"Check him, Finkelstein. Maybe he's still alive."

Hesitantly, the man with glasses moved toward Berson, knowing that the chances of finding anything other than a corpse were slimmer than the body itself.

Every Jew in the ghetto had become an expert on death and, for many, it had lost its sting. Still, Finkelstein felt reluctant to get closer to this corpse. He wasn't afraid of it, per se, but the fact that he was wearing the same marks of office as the dead man unnerved him.

Still, Finkelstein was a semi-professional — though a jeweler's apprentice before the war — so he leaned in close to the body. His examination started at the feet and was making slow, careful progress up the body when Shemtov brusquely interrupted.

"Just check his pulse," he said. "Then see what else you can see."

Finkelstein shuddered but reached up and placed his fingers on the corpse's neck.

"Yes, he's dead," Finkelstein said.

"Well, what were you doing with Berson's feet? It's not an ingrown toenail that killed him. Look at the wound," Shemtov said snidely.

Finkelstein hadn't started with Berson's shoes simply because he wanted to be thorough. He had no desire to stare into the gaping hole in the dead man's skull.

When he did look, he took away no clues. Finkelstein saw blood, bone and nothing else that meant anything to him.

"It looks like someone hit him very hard on the head," Finkelstein finally said.

"A brilliant deduction," Shemtov replied. "In another life, you must have been Sherlock Holmes."

Shemtov considered for a minute as Finkelstein stared down at his own toes.

"Why don't you try to drum up some witnesses?" he suggested. "Knock on a few doors, see if there's anyone we know who lives along here."

Anyone known to the police was likely to be either a criminal or a collaborator. Either would be susceptible to pressure, and Shemtov was willing to apply plenty of it. Better him than the Germans.

Shemtov understood that, revenge aside, no police force can ignore the death of one of its own without the threat of losing all credibility. In Miasto that principle was transitive. Though the Nazis had nothing but contempt for the Jewish power structure they had created, any defiance of it was met with deadly force.

Shemtov wanted revenge, but he was also a Jew.

The Ghetto-Polizei would have to take care of this mess quickly and quietly, he decided, otherwise the Gestapo would step in. That would mean bloody interrogations and the deaths of bystanders, even before collective retribution was meted out.

Shemtov stood staring into the middle distance for quite some time. He was a big man, and looked much stupider than he was. He'd hated that fact as a child, but in his new profession he found it useful — it put people off their guard and sometimes made them afraid. But intimidation wasn't going to get him anywhere with the Gestapo. This situation called for discretion and subtlety.

Chapter 1

It would be best if the Germans didn't find out that Berson was dead until his murder was solved. But how could he delay the news from getting to the Germans? If people were willing to give each other up for potato peelings, what would stop them from delivering a whole potato's worth of information?

Even if no one talked, police roll calls were held every day and the attendance report was handed to the Germans. There were only so many times a man could be marked down as sick before the Germans would get curious. If Berson was reported dead — from "natural" causes, of course — the Germans might ask to see the body.

Stare as he might, Shemtov couldn't think of a way to pull off the necessary miracles. More than that, he had no idea how to handle a murder investigation.

And that was his best quality, according to everyone he'd ever worked for: he knew what he didn't know.

Shemtov nodded to himself. It was time to gift-wrap the problem for someone higher up.

But first things first. Shemtov called to Finkelstein, who hadn't gone very far in his timid attempt to find witnesses who would speak to him.

"Put your coat over him," Shemtov ordered, pointing to Berson's body.

The air was frigid and Finkelstein looked at Shemtov as if he were the devil before doing what he was told.

"Well, at least the coat gives him a bit of dignity," a shivering Finkelstein said, though what he really meant was "Fuck him. Give me my coat back."

"I'm not worried about his dignity," Shemtov said. "We need to get him out of sight. Now. So, lift!"

Berson was light, but they had little strength to spare. Just picking up the body left them both winded.

"We won't be able to carry him far," Shemtov said, looking around.

"There's a cellar nearby, buried in some rubble," Finkelstein said. "My cousin used to live in the building above it before it was hit by a bomb."

Curtains twitched behind windows as the men carried their burden one block, then two. The street they turned down had been shelled during the initial German assault on the city. Several buildings had collapsed. One still had a rough staircase that led down to a basement formed from concrete. Finkelstein nodded toward it and the two men shambled over.

Climbing down into the basement with the body was nearly impossible. Both men were exhausted from the walk. Finkelstein, facing forward and holding Berson's feet, was the first down the stairs. He tripped twice, but didn't quite fall into the shallow darkness.

The space below was filled with shattered odds and ends of the former life above. Cracked china crunched underfoot; a child's jacks threatened to bring them down hard on their knees; everything was coated in coal dust. An unpleasant place to spend eternity, but Shemtov figured Berson was beyond caring. He found a little ledge, mostly by feel, put down his end of the body and ordered Finkelstein to do the same with his.

He then fumbled to remove Berson's symbols of office in the hope that anyone finding the body wouldn't think there was anything unique about it. Shemtov hid the uniform cap in his layers of clothing, while he concealed the telltale armband in a pocket.

Finkelstein took his jacket back from Berson and his teeth chattered as he put it back on. Shemtov leaned over and used a palm to shut Berson's eyes, but they were frozen open.

The men then bowed their heads and spoke the words no one on the street had been willing to, the Kaddish.

Finkelstein's teeth were still chattering. He'd been without a coat far too long. He looked longingly at the corpse's clothes. He and Berson were the same size — small to the point of petite. Another layer or two would be a wonderful luxury, possibly even a lifesaver.

"Do you think it would be okay if I took his coat?" Finkelstein asked. "He doesn't need it now. He can't get much colder."

Shemtov's face filled with disgust. It was bad enough to bury a comrade under a pile of rubble in an open cellar, but to leave him in his underwear? That was obscene.

"How warm are you going to feel, knowing where you got the clothes?" he asked.

"Warmer than I do now," Finkelstein said, unable to take his eyes off the stretch of wool in front of him.

"You're disgusting," Shemtov said, and headed for the staircase.

Tradition, propriety and sneering were no match for grim necessity — at least in Finkelstein's mind. The living must take precedence over the dead. Even the rabbis agreed on that. Fuck Shemtov and his judgment, his squeamishness. Finkelstein began his grim work.

When he touched Berson's skin, he shivered more deeply than he had walking around without his coat. But he kept on, awkwardly pulling on sleeves, forcing the body to sit up with its frozen, bloody head lolling to the side. Finkelstein, a lifelong nebbish, had transformed into an eager ghoul.

He came away from the "grave" luxuriating in his new coat. The pants were too pocked by holes and covered in nameless grime for even Finkelstein to swipe, so Berson kept them, along with his underwear and soiled shirt.

Reunited on the street, the little patrol turned toward headquarters, hoping for warm water they could pretend was tea and instructions on how to proceed.

As they walked, Finkelstein burrowed deep into his new clothes with what Shemtov thought was unseemly relish.

It was a slow trudge to the station. The wind lashed and flayed, laughing at Shemtov's old, worn coat. Finkelstein watched him cower against it and couldn't help a secret smile.

Icier than the wind were the stares of the people who parted around them. Contempt and fear rippled outward as if the men were stones dropped in a pond. The crowd was made up of people Finkelstein had gone to school with; men that Shemtov had done business with; members of their shuls. Now, a line had been drawn, and Shemtov and Finkelstein were made aware of the side on which they stood.

Shemtov told himself that he was just doing a job, and that there were damned few of those in the Jewish District. He'd seen the alternatives, aside from starvation. A few thousand Jews found work in "shops" — small factories inside the ghetto that made items useful to the Nazi war effort. The conditions were appalling. Between the short rations, grueling pace, long hours and violent beatings, Shemtov was happy to pass.

More worked outside the ghetto, in labor camps. Perhaps two thousand marched out of the Jewish District at dawn every day. At most, nineteen hundred returned after dark.

There were only so many jobs in soup kitchens or in stores with nothing to sell. Neither he nor Finkelstein had enough pull to get a better job in the bureaucracy ...

So he endured the hatred. He pretended to return people's contempt or ignore it. He showed no reaction when fleet-footed teens made catcalls. He walked gray streets lined with ruined buildings and worked hard to see none of it. He refused to acknowledge any role he played in the misery he saw on the ten-block walk to the Judenrat's headquarters, which now loomed ahead.

The sight depressed Shemtov. It always did.

German bombs had damaged the grand masonry of the former courthouse. Some of the stonework still lay where it had fallen more than a year before. The blocks were either too heavy to move or no one had felt it was worth the effort. But what depressed him most was the crowd gathered at the building's gates. People stood in a queue that never seemed to get longer or shorter. To Shemtov the line represented a precise balance between great personal need and near-perfect bureaucratic inefficiency.

Those in line were pitiful, even by the standards of the ghetto. Simply believing the Judenrat would be able to help — whatever your problem — made a person pitiful, Shemtov thought. He knew from the inside that the "authorities" had little charity to offer and even less justice to mete out.

He also knew that simply by joining the line, one stood a little taller than the rest of the grass, inviting the reaper's sickle.

Shemtov and Finkelstein pressed through the throng, elbows and curses flying. Not knowing who was behind them, people fought to keep their place. It looked like things might take a violent turn until the guards at the door recognized the policemen and got violent first, using clubs to clear the way.

Once inside the building, the doors closed behind them, the warmth of the entry hall struck Shemtov and Finkelstein. It was enough to make them gasp in relief.

Two more of their colleagues stood inside, the last line of defense should the petitioners decide to press their cases though means other than unflagging patience.

Beyond a second double door sat a clump of clerks moving paper or listening to people who they were apt to disappoint.

The petitioners stood shoulder-to-shoulder, back to front, front to back, held upright by the weight of their own numbers. The press of bodies brought the temperature in the room to nearly 80 degrees, but the petitioners unanimously refused to remove their coats, instead hoarding the heat for their walk home. Sweat dappled most faces.

The heat and close quarters had another, less pleasant, effect as well. Shemtov recoiled against smells the warmth brought out of hibernation. Soiled, sweat-stained wool, yes, but he bodies themselves were worse. No one wanted to bathe in cold water while surrounded by colder air. It could be dangerous and what was the point? There was no soap, anyway.

As the officers slowly bulled their way across the room to the safety of the Jewish Police offices, Shemtov caught snatches of the sad stories being told at each overwhelmed desk.

" ... But there's no more milk for the baby," a woman said, sobbing as she pointed to her own breasts. "There's not enough food ... my body has dried up. There must be some powdered milk somewhere. Please!"

"There's nothing. I have nothing to give you. I'd give you my rations, but I have to feed my own family. I'm sorry, but that's the way it is," the famished, bespectacled clerk said.

"Oh please! My baby ... "

Another voice, another desk, another supplicant.

"But they've taken up the wires! There's no electricity! Surely you can send some men around to fix it!"

"What do you think? You're the only one without power?" a heavily bearded clerk answered, incredulity in his voice. "What's wrong with you? People have real problems. Find someone else's time to waste."

Next into earshot, a small, elderly woman with an oddly jaunty hat clinging to her few remaining gray curls.

" … a new ration card. My son stole mine! I'll starve without it."

The clerk was young, his face was kind, but his answer was something else.

"Do you think I haven't heard that story before?" the man asked. "Do you think you're the first person who's tried to get a second ration card for themselves? Even if you're telling the truth, it's up to you to get the card back. You're his mother! There's nothing I can do."

There's nothing I can do. It was a phrase repeated a thousand times every day by every man behind a desk, Shemtov knew.

But then, as he continued his shoving, Shemtov heard something else.

" … I have heard that sometimes — sometimes — something can be done in such a case. Yes, perhaps something."

It was an older man talking. He was a stouter than the other clerks, though his desk was the same.

"Come back after we've closed. We'll talk then. And make sure to bring it with you," the clerk said.

It wasn't necessary for Shemtov to hear the particulars. As always, there were ways to get things done, even here. He'd learned that business, if not hope, survives even the greatest tragedies.

Finally through the crowd, past another guard and another door, the officers reached a short hall where they could breathe.

"Go get yourself something to drink and eat — if there is something. I'll join you after I speak to Captain Blaustein," Shemtov said.

Finkelstein looked at him nervously, but then finding a time when the man didn't look nervous — or at least shifty — wasn't easy. Finkelstein nodded and headed in the direction of the little room that served as an impromptu lounge for the police.

Shemtov turned to an unmarked door, knocked, and was told to enter by a man who was dressed only in shirtsleeves. In the small but uncluttered office a portable heater radiated warmth and a sense of better times. It was needed because the room's window was warped, making a proper seal impossible.

Blaustein was a large man. His face displayed shrewdness rather than intelligence. There was a subtle slyness that sat in his eyes and could be seen in the curl of his lip. He motioned for Shemtov to close the door behind him.

"So?" the Jewish Police's commander asked, meaning something more like, *Why the hell are you in my office?*

"We found Lev Berson this morning, on our patrol," Shemtov said, keeping his eyes down, his posture stooped.

"Found him how? I didn't know he was missing."

"I mean we found his body, sir. He was dead, in Leopold Street. His skull was cracked open and his hat was a meter away."

Shemtov took Berson's hat and armband from his coat and offered them to his superior by way of proof.

Blaustein made no move to touch them, so Shemtov laid them gently on his desk. For a moment, both men were trapped in an uncomfortable silence.

"Any chance he slipped and fell?" Blaustein finally asked, without much hope.

"No sir, no chance. You could see through the hole, all the way to his brains."

More silence.

Blaustein stood very still, his eyes frozen on an invisible something. Shemtov knew that Blaustein was working through all the angles he himself had thought of, and probably others that he hadn't.

After several minutes, Shemtov could see Blaustein's mind slowly making its way back to his office.

"Witnesses?" Blaustein asked.

"None who would speak to us, sir," Shemtov said.

That was little surprise.

"And where is Berson now?"

"I thought it was best if we took care of him ourselves, make sure there was no evidence in plain sight, sir," Shemtov said. "We moved him to a basement just a few blocks from where we found him."

"*You* thought it was best?"

"Yes, sir."

"And how did you come to that conclusion?"

"I thought you'd want to keep the Germans out of it as long as possible," Shemtov said, cringing under Blaustein's glare.

It would take no more than a word for Shemtov to lose his position, and that was something Shemtov couldn't face. He would miss the extra rations, but would probably miss what protection his armband offered even more. It wasn't possible to be a policeman and not make enemies, especially here.

Berson didn't get much protection from his armband, though, did he? Shemtov thought glumly.

But he needn't have worried.

"In this case, your judgment was right," Blaustein said grudgingly. "We have to keep the Germans out of this. Do you have any idea what happened? Do you know what Berson might have been doing last night?"

"No, sir," Shemtov said. "And there was nothing much to see at the scene. There was no sign of whatever hit him. No obvious reason why he was hit."

"All right, it sounds like you did what you could," Blaustein said, knowing just how poorly his men were trained. "Thank you, Shemtov, you did well. I may need to ask you more questions later on, so don't go too far. For now, you're dismissed."

Shemtov left the room, relieved to have shifted the burden onto other shoulders.

Chapter 2

Blaustein sat. After a minute he turned to the small heater at his side, shutting it off. He rarely kept it going for more than a few minutes — fuel was too expensive — but he always made sure to turn it on when he heard a knock at the door. The warmth served as a reminder of Blaustein's privilege and station.

This I didn't need, he thought.

Blaustein knew the investigation would have to be quick, subtle and, most importantly, wrapped up neatly with a bow before it was handed over to the Nazis. To best protect the Jewish community, there would have to be a clear villain and a non-political motive. Anything else and the Gestapo would launch its own inquiry, resulting in random sweeps, torture of the innocent and their eventual murders.

The key question then became who should run the investigation?

Blaustein considered his options among the men who worked for him. He knew most of them to be the bottom of the barrel, for the most part weak, cruel or not particularly intelligent. Some were all three in one delightful package. In fact, the more he thought about it, the more he realized there was no one on the force he trusted to do the job right.

The next option that Blaustein considered was appointing himself to the job. He quickly decided against it. Though he had contacts everywhere in the ghetto, he was no trained detective. Blaustein was a purely political appointee, previously known for his management skills and lack of scruples as a member of the Miasto city council.

He had always been a man to delegate work, especially if it was the kind of work that could lead him into danger. Blaustein could already foresee circumstances where the case's investigator would have to become a scapegoat. It wasn't a role he would volunteer for.

If only there was a way to play the whole thing off as an accident, to say that Berson had tripped and fallen. Blaustein had no deep desire to see justice. He wanted the case off his desk with as little damage as possible done to the people of the ghetto — especially himself.

But there were a few potential problems with labeling Berson's death an accident. If Shemtov's description of the body were accurate, the story wouldn't hold up for a second under the eyes of a Gestapo officer. It was also unlikely the Germans would buy the idea that the body had been quickly cremated. It was widely known that Jewish law didn't allow for cremation.

The other issue was potential informants. If someone took it upon him or herself to tell the Germans what had happened, any cover up would be exposed immediately. In that case, there was no chance Blaustein would survive.

Blaustein thought until he could no longer stand his own company and the closeness of his small, commandeered space. He stepped out of his office and headed for the lounge, struck by the change in temperature as he exited. The others in the hallway all had their coats on. Without the heat generated by the crowd in the main hall, the police offices were no warmer than anywhere else in the ghetto.

Today was a banner day in the lounge. Someone had found black tea and the samovar steamed with it. The smell spoke of days that had passed into oblivion — even the memories were fading. There was nothing to sweeten the bitter brew, but to ask for sugar was like asking for a personal visit from the beautiful Irena Solska. Or fresh pastry.

Blaustein poured himself a glass, savored the warmth in his hands, and brought the beaker up to his nose. For a minute, maybe more, he let the perfume of the Orient take him elsewhere and to better times. A single sip and the brown bitterness of inferior and ancient tealeaves shattered his reverie and made him shudder.

The only people in the room with him were Shemtov and Finkelstein, who had a guilty look, knowing he should be back out on patrol rather than sulking in comfort. Blaustein gave him a firm look that had him hastening on his way with a jerky nod.

Shemtov stayed where he was.

Blaustein gave him the evil eye, too.

"I'm sure there's some paperwork you need to catch up on," he suggested.

Shemtov gave a half-hearted salute and left the little lounge.

The tea provided Blaustein with little inspiration. In the end, all he could think to do was to follow Shemtov's example and take his problem up the chain of command and leave it with someone else.

The Jewish Police answered to the Judenrat, which, at its core, was comprised of a council of twenty-five elders. Their charge was maintaining order and allocating impossibly inadequate resources to sixty-five thousand people crammed into the ghetto.

The Jewish population of Miasto had been thirty thousand before the German tanks had arrived. A further fifty thousand Jews had lived in surrounding towns, villages and farms. Those who had survived the initial days of the occupation had been herded into a small corner of the city.

Many of the members of the Judenrat had been prominent men long before the Germans arrived, through religion, law or medicine. The occupiers merely confirmed them in their positions, some, literally at gunpoint. If given a choice, serving the Nazis was an honor most Jews, however venal, would have declined. The president of the Judenrat, and the man Blaustein needed to see, was Mordechai Zimmerman.

Blaustein headed into the main hall, the hand with his tea held high above the throng, as if he were a waiter at a busy French café. He worked his way carefully through the crowd and clerks, heading for a doorway adjacent to the police suite.

"You weren't next!" a voice cried out. "That lady was in front of you, and I was in front of her!"

Blaustein saw the person who had provoked the shout. It was an old man, pathetic in his threadbare religious garments, including a beaver fur hat that had balded badly.

There was a shove. A small shove, but the old man was frail and he stumbled forward. Everyone was packed so tightly they wobbled from the impact, though they had no place to fall.

The wavefront rippled outward, eventually reaching Blaustein. His cup tipped backward, tea spilled out on the tie he insisted on wearing despite the fact that no one was impressed.

Blaustein was instantly filled with rage. He growled and his body stiffened as if he was going to strike out.

But he didn't.

There was no target. Not the small, scarred woman who had touched him and now looked terrified. Not the man in black wool behind her who had tipped forward just enough to make her sway. Trace the line as far back as he liked, all he could see were victims.

Chapter 2

The officers from the front door hurried into the room to calm things. They looked bewildered at the chorus of accusations and counter-accusations, but quickly settled their interest on the old man who had stepped out of line. One of the officers grabbed the old man firmly and the other lifted a hand to strike him. He stopped himself as he caught sight of Blaustein, who simply shook his head. Instead of striking him, the officer spoke gently to the old man.

"Whatever business you have, you'll have to come back tomorrow. Things are bad enough without you making it worse," he said.

"I have no heat!" the old man shouted. It sounded to Blaustein as if the man was more deaf than agitated.

The officer spoke more loudly.

"Nobody has heat. Come back tomorrow, otherwise there's going to be a pogrom in here."

"I have no heat!" the old man said again.

Seeing there was nothing for it, the officer tightened his grip and pulled the man, now as confused as he was deaf, out of the room. All eyes followed the old man back into the cold. After a few moments the room returned to its sullen usual.

Blaustein carefully husbanded his remaining tea — less than half the glass — through the doors and into the offices of the Judenrat's president.

The rooms were luxurious by the standards of deprivation set everywhere else in the Jewish District. In the reception area, a lightly soiled Persian carpet lay in front of a desk made entirely of oak. Portraits of men in somber clothing with white beards hung on the walls. None of the frames were straight, and each was tilted in precisely its own way, leaving Blaustein a little seasick. He was unclear whether the men pictured were the ancestors of the man in the next office or just placed there to create an atmosphere of Talmudic wisdom.

Behind that oak desk was a man unremarkable in any obvious way. His yarmulke and studious look made him out to be observant but not so deeply religious as to remove himself from the world. The hair on his face and head was gray, and so was the man himself. Blaustein could easily picture him in front of King Solomon's Temple thousands of years earlier, filling in the blanks of papyrus scrolls.

"Mr. Kaminski," Blaustein asked. "Is Mr. Zimmerman available?"

Yitzhak Kaminski looked up from whatever form he had been filling out and peered nearsightedly at the police commandant.

"I'll check for you," he said, and was up and gone into the next office before Blaustein could blink.

It was several blinks before he returned.

"Mr. Zimmerman asks you to wait. He is on the telephone with the German officer in charge of the electrical supply," Kaminski said properly. "Please take a seat."

Blaustein took the short step to a wooden chair against the wall. At some point the green upholstery might have contained some padding. Now, it provided a thin veil over pointy springs.

He sat.

Blaustein was kept waiting just long enough to be reminded of his place in the scheme of things. At the right moment, Mordechai Zimmerman appeared in his own doorframe, his hand outstretched and his smile welcoming.

Zimmerman was a man who knew how to sell. Selling what or to who wasn't always clear, but the answer — whatever it was — had made him rich before the Germans came. And if someone could be rich in a ghetto, he still was.

Chapter 2

Zimmerman was well dressed. His suit showed no signs of wear. There was no fraying at the collar or cuffs of his shirt. His hair was held in place with scented pomade. Somehow the world had changed for everyone except Zimmerman. If he noticed how agitated Blaustein was, he showed no sign of it.

"What's that wet spot on your tie?" Zimmerman asked.

Blaustein brushed the comment aside.

"We have a bit of a problem," he said.

Zimmerman blinked.

"Come in then," he said.

The room Blaustein walked into was little like his own small office. It had the feel of a successful businessman's place of refuge, with polished wood and leather-bound books sitting patiently on shelves. There was another Persian carpet here. It was neither faded nor stained. There was a coffee table surrounded by comfortable-looking chairs, and a beautifully crafted, baroque cherry wood desk. Behind that sat a formidable leather office chair.

Zimmerman took one of the chairs around the table and pointed Blaustein to another. He poured himself tea and then offered the pot to Blaustein. Before pouring, Blaustein first gulped down the residue of his first glass so that it wouldn't contaminate the fresh brew.

Zimmerman then dribbled honey — honey! — into his own glass and offered that to Blaustein as well, who took it gratefully. Lastly, Zimmerman passed over a small plate of cookies. Blaustein showed enormous restraint in taking only two.

Even though Blaustein's business was urgent, he appreciated the excellent tea, the sweetness of the honey and the soft chair his ass was resting on.

When the head of the Judenrat said nothing but began to look impatient, Blaustein knew his brush with his boss' luxuries was coming to an end. He took a bite of the cookie. It was stale.

Zimmerman lifted an eyebrow.

"One of my men's been murdered," Blaustein said.

"What?" Zimmerman said. "Who?"

"Lev Berson."

It was clear from the look on Zimmerman's face that he had no idea who that was.

"Do you know who did it?" he asked.

"Not yet."

"You better know soon or the Germans will tear us apart!"

"I understand that, sir," Blaustein said.

Zimmerman took a deep, deep breath.

"So, what happened?"

Blaustein told him all that he knew, without gloss. Zimmerman might be a preening boot-licker, but he was also a sharp man, quick to see the ramifications of a problem.

"You have no one who can handle this?" Zimmerman asked.

It didn't speak well of Blaustein's command or the men in it, but he believed the circumstances made truth the best option.

"No, sir."

A strange smile appeared on Zimmerman's face.

"Lucky for us all that I'm not you, then," Zimmerman said. "Kaminski!"

The clerk came into the room so quickly that it was hard to believe he hadn't been there the whole time. He stood and waited respectfully to be addressed.

"Wasn't your son some kind of policeman before the war, Kaminski?" Zimmerman asked.

The clerk shook his head, but not quite in denial.

"He worked with the *goyim*, yes."

"But as a policeman?" Zimmerman prompted.

"He joined the Zendarmerie, sir." Kaminski said. It was clear he didn't approve.

Chapter 2

The words triggered Blaustein's memory. It had been a famous event in Miasto's Jewish community when a young man had joined the national police force that was better known for brutality against Jews than for hiring them. Blaustein was surprised he hadn't thought of Aaron Kaminski himself.

"But he's here now, with us?" Zimmerman asked his secretary, meaning inside the Jewish enclosure.

"Aaron was seconded to the army when it was clear the Germans were going to invade. He was captured, along with his unit," Kaminski said. "He was on his way to a prisoner-of-war camp nearby, but one of his 'friends' turned him in to the Germans as a Jew. So yes, he's here."

"Please bring him to my office, as soon as you can. We need him," Zimmerman said.

"We don't speak very often, sir," Kaminski said stiffly. It was difficult for him to defy Zimmerman in the smallest matter — he had been with him as clerk and secretary since long before the war — but still he hesitated. "Could you possibly find someone else?"

Kaminski meant another man besides Aaron, but Zimmerman took him to mean that Kaminski himself didn't want to run the errand.

"I think it would be fastest if you went. He wouldn't deny his own father," Zimmerman wheedled, "would he?"

Kaminski would have preferred the reunion to take place under less dangerous circumstances, and by his own choice, but he said nothing else. Instead, he turned and left the room to grab his coat.

Chapter 3

It was not easy to wake up hung-over in the Miasto ghetto in early 1941.

Alcohol — that miraculous liquid that can dissolve the fabric of reality — was one of the first resources to disappear after the district had been walled off. Still, for the enterprising, there are always ways to leave the world's troubles behind.

The return journey, though, tends to be on the painful side. Aaron Kaminski felt like yelping when his eyes squinted open. He stared into the all-too-bright murk of his small room, dreading a day that was unlikely to be better than the day before.

Aaron could feel a red-hot, electrified knitting needle slowly piercing his right eye. The only distraction from it was the unproductive nausea it brought along, almost like a side dish at the devil's dinner table. A thin whiff of vomit rose from near his tender head.

"Ayyyhhh," Aaron groaned.

He rolled onto his side, making sure to take the various scraps that made up his bedding with him. They were made up largely of the remnants of three military blankets he'd kept after being told he wasn't good enough to be a German prisoner of war. He had little else to show for his decade outside of the Jewish community, except for the warm coat he'd been issued when called to duty, and a pair of tough army boots.

Aaron shifted again and a bottle fell off the bed and into the gloom, clanking but not breaking. Aaron suspected from the sound that its final resting place was under the bed.

Deserter, he thought.

Aaron reached his hand out into the cold air, swept his fingers along the floor and finally felt the rectangular shape of a pack of cigarettes. If booze was rare in the ghetto — or at least hard to find — cigarettes were almost as precious as food. A family of four could have eaten for a week on the number of cigarettes that remained in the pack.

A little more fumbling and Aaron had a tube filled with tobacco clutched between his lips, waiting for the flame. More digging — he finally had to sit up — and he was able to find flimsy matches that required a number of frustrating strokes to catch fire. The light of the match hurt his eyes but, at last, Aaron was finally able to draw smoke deep into his lungs.

And choke. And splutter. And hack.

These were not good cigarettes.

The paper was stiff enough to be cardboard and the filling was execrable, likely 80-percent sawdust, Aaron thought with disgust. He took another deep drag. The smoke tasted of roofing tar and burning rubber.

But whatever the taste or quality, Aaron was grateful for his cigarettes. He'd worked hard enough for them. Sometimes he wondered if his addiction alone had led him to become a smuggler. There was no other way he could have afforded them. Or anything else for that matter.

Thanks to his skills and contacts — many of them developed in his time as a police officer — he'd brought more than a ton of illicit merchandise through the main gate at King Bolesłas I Chrobry (thc Bravc) Street. More had come over, under and through the weak points of the "wall" that surrounded the Jewish ghetto.

Aaron and the boys, girls, men and women who worked for and with him, knew the wall intimately. Well enough to know it wasn't a single wall at all, but a makeshift structure of boarded up buildings, concrete barricades topped with barbed wire, closed-off streets and the occasional machine gun nest. The holes in its boundaries were what allowed the ghetto to survive. Without links to illegal food and other supplies, the ghetto's privations would become even worse.

So, really, I'm doing a public service, he told himself when he needed to.

Aaron ran a hand through greasy hair that mixed dirty blond with sprays of gray. He kept it at a bristle length that would have done an angry drill sergeant proud in order to keep the ghetto's billion lice at bay.

There was a water tap in his small room. Aaron carefully placed his cigarette on the chipped rim of the grimy sink, turned a knob, and hoped for water. The pipes groaned, clanked and finally emitted a thin stream of brown liquid. He took a drink, brought a wet hand to his face, rubbed, and tried telling himself that getting out of bed would be worth it.

The water was cold, then just cool. Morning seemed to finally become a possibility.

A sharp rap on the door brought him to full wakefulness and sent him diving for a large knife that was tangled in his bedding. The knocking continued, became more insistent. Aaron expected the door to crash open at any second, the Gestapo to pour in after.

Instead he heard a small voice.

"Open the door, Aaron."

Aaron quietly crept toward the door and peered out through a narrow crack in the wood.

It was his father, and he was alone.

Shit, Aaron thought.

The elder Kaminski raised his hand to knock again. He was unlikely to go away. Aaron knew his father to be persistent, if nothing else.

Accepting the inevitable, Aaron removed the latch, another latch, a chain and a small bolt. Even then, it was hard to move the doorknob more than a few degrees without hurting his hand. If the only guest you're expecting is the secret police, there isn't must point in being hospitable, Aaron figured.

He stayed in the door's shadow in case he'd missed any armed men who'd accompanied his father. The possibility didn't seem out of the question. It wouldn't even have been much of a surprise.

For a few seconds, Aaron's father stared into the darkness. His son read some conflict in his body language, and saw the fear coupled with it. But it wasn't enough fear to keep the old man outside.

Yitzhak Kaminski's eyes needed time to adjust to the dark, even after standing in the dim hallway for several minutes. Slowly he was able make out the outline of his son's face. When Aaron finally stepped forward into the twilight provided by the open doorway, his father couldn't help but step back.

In front of Yitzhak was a large man with a deeply scarred face, relatively clean-shaven in a city hidden behind beards. The man's expression was hard and wary, and not like anything he'd seen on his son's face before. Ten years apart and his only child was nearly unrecognizable.

What Aaron saw was a small man who seemed to have gotten a little smaller. The light of humor he was used to seeing in the corner of his father's eye was extinguished. Despite the fact that it had been his choice to leave his family behind, Aaron suddenly hoped it wasn't his actions that had put it out.

"I wasn't expecting you," Aaron said, with a weak smile.

"Truthfully, I wasn't expecting to come."

Both men stood silently for a minute. Finally it was the good manners that Yitzhak had taught his son that won.

"Would you like to come in?"

"Thank you," Yitzhak said a little stiffly.

"Have a seat, if you'd like," Aaron said, pointing to the bed. There was no other surface available.

"I'm fine standing," Yitzhak said.

Aaron wasn't sure whether to be insulted or just realistic about how filthy his bed looked.

"A drink?"

Yitzhak shook his head.

"Aaron, the reason I'm here isn't social."

"I'm shocked!" Aaron said.

Yitzhak ignored that.

"Mr. Zimmerman sent me to get you."

"You still work for Zimmerman?" Aaron asked, not sure if he should be surprised. Yitzhak had worked for Mordechai Zimmerman all of Aaron's life. Still, he hadn't known that his father had followed the old man to his new job.

"Why would Zimmerman want me?" Aaron asked.

"Apparently, he remembers why you left Miasto," Yitzhak said sourly. "Now he needs a gendarme."

The older man's tone let Aaron know that nothing had been forgiven. Aaron's decision to join the world of the gentiles was still beyond the pale.

"He's got a whole police force of his own," Aaron pointed out. "Why in the world would he need me?"

"Because they're incompetent," Yitzhak answered. "Or at least that's what Mr. Zimmerman seems to think."

"And this has just become a problem now?"

"Someone murdered one of them. Now they need a real detective to find out who did it."

Aaron took that last part as a compliment, intended or not. "What makes you think I'd want to be a part of this mess?" Aaron said. "If we're talking about an officer in the Jewish Police, there's a whole ghetto that would want him dead. I'm not exactly broken up by the news, myself."

Still, he paused.

Saying the words brought back a vague, vodka drenched, memory of stumbling into a corpse just before dawn. Aaron's eyes widened, but he said nothing. Better to see how things played out, he thought.

Aaron began to fumble around, looking for the bottle that contained what was left of last night's booze.

"You've handled murder investigations before, yes?" Yitzhak asked.

Aaron stopped fumbling for a moment and raised an eyebrow at his father.

"What would you know about the kind of cases I handled?"

"You made the papers, sometimes. The Jewish detective solves a case!" Yitzhak said. "They always seemed so surprised."

"Well, flattery aside, I still don't see why I'd want to get involved."

"Mr. Zimmerman and Captain Blaustein — the police chief — seem convinced that the Germans would hurt people to find who killed the policeman."

"Sounds like standard procedure," Aaron said.

"Mr. Zimmerman thinks it would be better if we solved the case ourselves," Yitzhak said, then shrugged.

Aaron thought for a minute. Having the Germans rampaging through the ghetto would mean a lot of people would die, maybe even him. On the three occasions the Germans had flooded into the district in the last year, thousands had been rounded up and put on gray trucks. Many hundreds more had been shot out of hand. Sex or age had made no difference.

And now, in particular, was not a good time to have the Germans on high alert, as far as Aaron was concerned. There was important business he needed to finish over the next few days.

Success! Aaron found the bottle he'd been looking for. He walked over to a shelf above the sink that held a few dusty glasses and plates. He briskly wiped out two of the glasses and handed one to his father.

"Isn't it a little early?" Yitzhak asked.

"Is it ever early here? Even when the sun's up, it feels like midnight."

His father nodded and held up his glass. Aaron filled it generously, watching the clear trickle pour nearly like syrup in the cold. He was more sparing with himself, afraid of what his stomach might have to say.

After a large gulp, Yitzhak Kaminski felt a burning he hadn't for a long time. He savored it. Whatever the liquor was — and he wouldn't venture a guess — it reminded him of rough slivovitz, a Slavic favorite, or perhaps potato vodka, a Polish staple, or both or neither. It was terrible. Wonderfully terrible.

Aaron hoped the hair of the dog would help his stubborn headache.

After a few minutes, it did.

"Do you know the name of the officer who was killed this morning?" Aaron prodded.

"His name was Lev Berson," the elder Kaminski said. "He was young I think, but I can't remember his face, or even be sure I've seen him."

"I don't think I knew him," Aaron said.

"Why would you have known him?"

"I know a lot of people. Let's leave it at that."

The two men drank some more. Yitzhak contemplated the man his son had become. Aaron tried to decide what he would do.

Keeping away from the whole mess seemed the better bet. He dealt with the Jewish Police every day and felt little sympathy for them. They universally took his payoffs, but that hardly recommended them.

And what was the point of investigating one murder in a place where everyone was slowly being murdered?

Still, Aaron decided, it was worth a conversation. If he was careful, he would leave with more information than he gave away. He might even be able to find an angle that would lead to some kind of advantage. At the least, it wouldn't hurt to have the people at the Judenrat thinking he was on their side.

Aaron gulped what was left of his drink. He was already in his coat.

"Okay, finish up. Let's go," he said to his father.

Chapter 4

Mordechai Zimmerman, president of the Miasto Judenrat, stared across his desk at Aaron Kaminski, trying to see the Jew he had expected in the gentile who sat in front of him.

The Jewish gendarme looked nothing like his father and completely lacked that man's bookish air. Aaron's hard, scarred face connoted a certain brutality. His frigid blue eyes bored into Zimmerman and no doubt found him wanting.

The Jewish leader decided to keep the meeting brief.

He sighed.

"You understand what's at stake, right?" Zimmerman asked. "If we can't produce the person or persons who did this, the Nazis aren't likely to care much about guilt or innocence."

"I haven't noticed that being much of a priority for the Jewish Police, either," Aaron replied, his eyebrow arched.

Blaustein, the Jewish police's commandant, shot him a dark look.

"Whatever you think of them is beside the point," Zimmerman said. "We're all doing our best to live in an impossible situation."

"Some are living a bit better than others," Aaron said, staring around at the rich furnishings.

"Symbols are important," Zimmerman said defensively. "I can hardly expect the Nazis to take me seriously … "

"I think most of Europe knows how much they like symbols," Aaron said with heavy irony. "But no matter how many nice rugs you have, I doubt they take you very seriously."

Zimmerman's face passed pink on the way to red.

"I know no one else does," Aaron concluded.

"You little shit! The first chance you get, you abandon your community, forgetting everything about the people who made you, leaving your father alone?

"And now the Germans have reminded you of who you really are — shut you in with the rest of us Jews — and you still think that somehow you're better than us? Better than me?"

Zimmerman paused for breath, and Aaron's father stepped into the momentary void.

"I'm sure that's not what Aaron meant … " Yitzhak said.

"What the hell do you think the Judenrat does every day?" Zimmerman said, still thundering. "What the Jewish Police does? We're working with the Germans to keep people alive."

Aaron's stony expression hadn't wavered — despite the desperate glances his father shot his way — but he said nothing else. Zimmerman took a deep breath and steadied himself.

"My point is that you don't have to love the police to help find Berson's killer. You just have to care a little for your own people."

"Maybe whoever killed him had the people's interests in mind," Aaron said.

"See it however you like," Zimmerman snapped. "But should hundreds of innocents die for it? Is one Jewish policeman's death worth that high a price?"

Aaron had nothing witty to say to that, so he paused for a second. When did reply, there was a little more thought in his voice.

"Have you considered that you may be asking me to do the impossible?" Aaron said. "There's a whole ghetto full of suspects."

Zimmerman took this as another attack on his administration.

"You think you'd be better off with the Nazi death squads running things here, instead of the Judenrat?"

"Are you sure we could tell the difference?" Aaron replied with a sneer. "What we've got now are Nazi orders with a Jewish face."

"You wouldn't like to see the other face," Blaustein interjected.

"I have seen it," Aaron said. "Before my unit was captured, we passed through towns where the Germans had already been. They used machine guns instead of starvation. It's cruel, but quick. And you can't fault the honesty of the men doing the job."

"You sanctimonious fuck!" Blaustein yelled, taking a step in Aaron's direction.

Aaron's father moved between the two men.

"Aaron, this is getting us nowhere," Yitzhak Kaminski said. "You're either going to do the job, or you're not."

Aaron was undecided. However much pleasure he'd gotten from tweaking Zimmerman and the others, he understood the game. He knew that many served in the Judenrat only under duress. Some even deluded themselves into thinking they could heal the horrors of the ghetto if only they worked hard enough.

Aaron had heard that Zimmerman's second son had been tortured before the man had agreed to take his current job — though when Aaron looked around at the teapots and sweets, he wondered if that had been Zimmerman's only motivation.

In the end, though, understanding the system didn't make Aaron want to be part of it.

"Sorry," he said, getting up. "You're on your own."

Suddenly, Blaustein was chest to chest with him.

"I really don't think that's the way you want to go," Blaustein said, baring his teeth.

“Oh, I’m pretty sure it is,” Aaron said, pushing Blaustein back a couple of inches with a palm to the chest.

Blaustein leaned forward, shrinking the distance again.

“Let me explain,” Blaustein said. “I know what you do for a living.”

“And what’s that?”

“You’re a black marketeer.”

“Everyone still alive in this damned place is a black marketeer,” Aaron pointed out.

“Not everyone has such *diverse* business interests, though.”

“I don’t think I need to be penalized for my success.”

Aaron’s father couldn’t suppress a grin at that.

“Understand this: I can penalize you all I want,” Blaustein said. “I can take your operation apart piece by piece, until there’s nothing and nobody left. Then I’ll come for you.”

The man was breathing hard.

Aaron’s right fist was cocked. He was ready to let fly.

“Okay, that’s enough,” Zimmerman interrupted. “That’s enough!”

Blaustein took a reluctant step back, looking like he could spit.

“Blaustein’s not subtle, but I’ll back up what he’s saying,” Zimmerman said. “We can squeeze your business interests. We can squeeze you.

“So, the threats are on the table. The only incentive I can give you is the opportunity to be a mensch. So take the job and do it.”

Aaron looked inside for his reservoir of defiance, but it seemed to have developed a slow leak.

He believed every word Blaustein said. There was no reason not to. The Jewish Police could do what it wanted inside the confines of the ghetto, as long as a mass uprising wasn’t the result. What did the Nazis care if there were a few Jews more or less? Unless a Jew was on German business, of course.

Aaron knew he couldn't ignore this "request." A week from now, yes, but not today. He wasn't willing to give up months of careful work to stick it to the men in front of him.

Aaron sat back down in his chair, facing Zimmerman

"What can you tell me about Berson?" he asked with a sigh.

"He wasn't much," Blaustein said after taking a deep and calming breath. "He worked his shift, made no trouble for me," Blaustein said. "He always asked to partner with the same man — Martin Gersh — which isn't normal, but there was no reason to separate them."

"Do you have any idea why he was so devoted to Gersh?" Aaron asked.

"I assume they were doing some kind of business on the side," Blaustein said.

"And Gersh was with him last night?"

Blaustein looked uncomfortable.

"They left the offices together, but I haven't spoken to him, yet. He's not scheduled to be in until later. He and Berson always worked the night shift."

"Have you tried to reach Gersh today?" Aaron asked archly.

"I had a clerk call his house."

"He has a phone?" Aaron asked. Working telephones had become somewhat of a rarity in the ghetto. Few could pay the bills and there was no one to do repairs when something broke, or when the copper wires were stolen for scrap.

"His building has one."

"So did you reach him?"

"I would have said so, if I had," Blaustein said. "And watch your fucking tone. I suggest you take your astounding detective talents and go find him."

Aaron looked at Blaustein with incredulity.

"Do you realize you may have a second dead policeman out there somewhere? And that someone — even the Germans — might find the body, putting you right back in the shit?"

Judging from the blank looks on the faces around him, Aaron guessed they hadn't considered the possibility.

"Fine," Aaron said. "Is there anything else you can tell me about Berson? Anything at all? Did anyone have a particular grudge against him that you know about?"

"If I knew about something like that, I wouldn't need you." Blaustein pointed out.

"And Gersh? What about him? What's his background? Any problems with him?" Aaron asked.

"He's very smart. An educated man. Likes to work nights," Blaustein said.

"That's it?" Aaron asked. Something in Blaustein's voice told him there was more.

Blaustein shook his head and handed Aaron a piece of paper.

"That's got the basic information from Berson's file. Address, date and place of birth, when he was hired. Not much more."

Aaron folded the paper and put it in a pocket.

"Okay," he said. "I'll need to talk to the other 'police' to get details from the scene. So, who found Berson?"

Aaron saw there was no reason to make himself a suspect by mentioning that he'd seen the murder site firsthand. Besides, someone less drunk might have seen more.

"An officer named Shemtov," Blaustein said. "He's still here. I asked him to stay and tell you what he knows. If he's not at his desk, he'll be in the lounge, I'm sure."

"Fine, I'll start with Shemtov," Aaron said, shaking himself free of the deep chair.

Chapter 4

Before he could walk out of the room, Zimmerman wanted a final word.

"There's no way to know when the Germans may find out about this and begin their own 'investigation,' We'll put him down as sick on the roster, but I don't think there's much else we can do." Zimmerman said. "Please be quick."

"I'll do what I can," Aaron said.

As he walked out the door and into the hall, he could hear Blaustein talking to the other two still in the room.

"He doesn't give a shit."

"But he'll do it," Aaron's father assured them. "He's always done what he said he would. It's part of how he gets himself in trouble."

Blaustein actually laughed.

The smell of ersatz tea led Aaron to the lounge.

He thought of all the people in the main hall, waiting for their minute with a clerk who wouldn't be able to help them. If they could smell the tea, would there be a riot, he wondered?

The thought didn't stop him from heading directly to the samovar in the corner of the sparse and uncomfortably furnished room. Hard stools stood around nicked tables of horrible Formica that was peeling faster than an orange would in the hands of one the children outside.

There was only one other man in the room. He was nursing tea and what looked like a grudge. There was no way for Aaron to know that the man always looked like that.

"Shemtov?" Aaron asked, knowing the answer.

"So?"

A warm welcome.

"So, I'm here to find out what happened to your shit-dipped colleague," Aaron said. "And I'm told you're going to offer me every assistance. That's why you're here, yes?"

"Fuck you."

"Maybe later, but I need some information first," Aaron said.

"Fuck you, I said. And who the hell are you anyway?" Shemtov asked.

"That's more like it. Better to be introduced before you fuck someone, don't you think?" Aaron smiled.

Blustery men like Shemtov amused him. Blustery and tough were rarely synonymous, he'd found.

First, a lifting of the eyebrows, then, unexpectedly, Shemtov guffawed.

"No, you're right," he said. "An introduction makes it so much more romantic." He put out a hand. "Leon Shemtov. You must be the alleged expert I heard rumors about."

Aaron was just as happy not to have a fight, not least because his hangover hadn't entirely left him. He took the large hand he'd been offered and shook.

"Well, if spending a few years with the Zendarmerie makes you an expert in this kind of thing, I guess that's what I am," he said. "Aaron Kaminski."

"Never heard of you." Shemtov said, but without malice. "Have a seat."

He pointed to a stool next to him.

Aaron sat down and took a first taste of the tea. His face nearly exploded with disgust, making Shemtov laugh again, harder this time.

"We serve only the finest poisons," Shemtov said.

Chapter 4

Aaron had to agree with Shemtov's assessment. A fine and bitter poison indeed. The best the darkly amber liquid could do was crush the memory of what tea tasted like.

Aaron shunted the glass aside hoping that his stomach would be able to do the same with the drink.

"Well, I didn't come here for the tea," Aaron said.

"That's good," Shemtov said.

"Tell me what you saw when you found Berson."

Shemtov paused, brought together the scene in his mind and slowly began to speak.

"A body lying in the street," Shemtov said. "Leopold Street. He was sprawled on his back. His face was easy to see and not so damaged that you couldn't identify him immediately, if you knew him.

"Blood and brains had splattered out and to the right of his body. His hat was lying off to his right side, a meter or so away. The blood was frozen when we got there, so I suppose it had been a little while since he was killed. Since all the pieces of the skull and all that blood were right there, I'd guess he was killed in the street."

It all matched with what little Aaron remembered.

"And I'm the expert?" Aaron said lightly. "You sound as if you've dealt with this sort of thing before. Were you in the police before the war and no one told me?"

"No, but I read a little English," Shemtov said. "Dashiell Hammett."

"Who's that?" Aaron asked.

"An American. He writes about private detectives."

"Too bad he's not here to take the case."

"Yes."

Shemtov took another sip of the terrible tea.

"Did you find any witnesses?" Aaron asked.

"How much do *you* want to help our little police force?"

Aaron nodded his understanding.

"The few people Finkelstein could catch up with were studiously ignorant," Shemtov said.

"I had to ask. Berson worked nights?"

"My understanding is that he preferred it."

"Do you know if he was walking around alone?"

"Well, he shouldn't have been, but since his partner was out with a bad leg, maybe he was," Shemtov said.

"Wait, Martin Gersh wasn't with Berson on patrol?"

"No. I heard from someone else that he got hurt early in the evening, so Berson went back out alone."

"Do you know where Gersh is now?"

"I think he's in Breslaw Hospital. At least that's what I heard," Shemtov said.

"Okay. Well, I guess I know where I'm going next. Thanks," Aaron said.

"Sure."

"So, otherwise, how well did you know Berson?"

"We never worked the same shift, and I'd never met him before the Germans came," Shemtov said.

"But do you know anything about him?"

"He seemed nice enough the two or three times I spoke with him," Shemtov said.

"Really? *That's* what you've got for me? 'He seemed *nice*?'"

"Well … "

"You can do better than that," Aaron said in his best coaxing, just-between-us voice. "Was he a good cop?"

"Sure. Or at least I never heard anything."

"Really? Nothing?"

"Well, one always hears things," Shemtov said grudgingly.

Aaron waited.

"All I've heard was that he and his partner … "

"Gersh?"

"Yes, Gersh. All I heard was that they did a little more business than usual with the black market. Maybe that they didn't treat the citizens with much respect," Shemtov said cautiously.

"That's it?" Aaron asked. "Nothing more specific?"

Shemtov shook his head.

"What can you tell me about him personally?"

"That I truly know nothing about. I mean, I know he wasn't from Miasto originally, that he didn't have any family here. I think he was religious, but that's it."

Aaron was sure Shemtov knew more, but judging by the tone of the man's voice, he wouldn't get it out of him without inflicting pain.

"Anything you can tell me about Gersh, Leon?"

"Again, we didn't work the same shifts, but I will tell you that he's not someone who's easy to like. Actually, if I think about it for a minute, it might be impossible to like him."

"How so?"

"Well, to start with, he knows he's better than everyone else," Shemtov said. "Some people think it, but he knows it."

"Okay."

"Also, his eyes look like he borrowed them from a corpse. Nothing there at all."

"Well then, he has plenty in common with his friend Berson," Aaron said. "So, where is Berson now? Nobody's mentioned a coroner."

"We thought it best to get him out of sight as quickly as possible," Shemtov said. "We took him to a cellar a block from where he was killed."

"Where exactly?

"It's 331 Varlamow. He's in a basement under some rubble if you want to see him."

"It could be helpful, though I'm hardly a doctor," Aaron said. "Anything else you want to tell me? No, scratch that. Anything else I need to know?"

Shemtov smiled with sardonic sympathy.

"Other than who did it, I can't think of anything."

Aaron stood, then leaned over to massage his legs for a minute. He thanked Shemtov for the little help he'd been able to give.

Before leaving the building, Aaron turned and knocked on Blaustein's door. He got no answer and felt no urge to linger.

The cold was no surprise when he had walked through the miasma of the crowd, past the guards and back onto the heather gray streets, but it temporarily blinded him to his surroundings. He shook himself, raised the collar of his coat and started toward the hospital.

Chapter 5

Aaron Kaminski walked toward Breslaw Hospital under the gray light of noon. If anyone knew Berson's business, it would be his partner. People became intimate during long nights on patrol. Aaron knew it from his own experience. He remembered many nights spent bored to death, waiting for something to happen and hoping that it never would. Talk helped to fill the time and to deal with the nerves.

Aaron figured that Martin Gersh might not have witnessed the killing of his partner, but there was a good chance he would know what was behind it.

The only concern Aaron had was the severity of Gersh's injury. He assumed it was bad, only desperation drove people to seek help from the abattoirs the ghetto's hospitals had become.

Aaron was forced to make his way more slowly than he would have liked. His route led him straight through the ghetto's mostly lively district. Everywhere, despite the cold, clumps of men gathered to sell the literal clothes off their backs to each other. It was a race to the depths of poverty.

One pale man in a suit made up mostly of unidentifiable stains held up a small dressing gown made of fine satin, fit only for a child of fewer than two years. It was the kind of thing found in second-hand stores, sold or donated by parents whose children had grown.

"Our youngest died last week of typhus. She no longer needs it," the man told the prospective buyers, some of whom had a cynical look. It was impossible to know if the story was true or was meant to drive up the price through pity. It occurred to Aaron that the man may have stolen the dress and never had a child at all. No one in the ragged crowd was willing to part with even a groczy for the gown, so the seller moved on in search of a more biddable congregation.

Aaron pushed his way past the beggars' impromptu auctions, kept his chin tucked into the collar of his coat, his black hat tilted forward against the wind.

Other, less pitiful, wares were also for sale on Gdansk Street, which had once been a promenade of shops and cafés where people went to display their wealth. Signs of that recent past poked through the shabbiness of Nazi occupation. Little flecks of gilt remained in the names carved above storefronts. Flickers of light occasionally escaped the clouds, causing the gold to glitter gaily. Those flecks were stubborn. No one had yet been able to peel them and sell them for a bowl of soup or a thin piece of cheese.

A very few men and women that could be glimpsed inside café windows, something warm or warming to drink in their hands and, occasionally, laughter could be seen if not heard. The ghetto was not yet entirely a world of have-nots, though the divide had never been so sharp. Just a few doors down from a certain Café Bourdain was a bakery that had been turned into a soup kitchen. The line was long, the people pinched, their eyes either empty or filled with avarice for the steam they could see rising from the huge pots inside.

Many of the men and women, some with children clutched tightly by the hand, would be sickened by what they ate. Common ingredients included the dregs and spoiled leftovers of better meals enjoyed by others.

Those afflicted would quickly give back whatever nutrients they'd been able to take in. The truly unlucky would end up in a doctor's care, or worse, in a hospital like Breslaw.

Chapter 5

Aaron had been lucky, so far, and stayed healthy. But he'd seen inside, either visiting people he knew or selling supplies. It was a desperate situation.

Since the entry points to the Jewish quarter had been cauterized from the body of Miasto and its inherently superior inhabitants, medical care had deteriorated to a nearly medieval level, though even leeches were inaccessible to the doctors. There was no flowing water to fetch them from.

Medical centers were set up in former storefronts, and doctors' surgeries were converted to small hospitals by the Judenrat for the common good. There was no lack of doctors or nurses; though nearly everything else, from medicine to bandages, was in short supply.

Before the war, Breslaw Hospital for Mental Defects and Diseases — where Aaron was headed — had functioned as an asylum for all of Miasto. Polish sufferers of retardation and schizophrenia resided cheek by jowl with Jews with similar diagnoses. The Poles interned had not been separated out when the Germans came because they were no more welcome in the New Order than Jews were. Similar patients who had been housed at other facilities were consolidated into Breslaw, if they hadn't simply been shot.

Now, a wretched place that had always been crowded was reduced to a mass of stinks and screams. With no soothing medications, little food and no hope of ever being rid of lice or dysentery, it was hard to know who had less hope, the inmates or their watchers.

Added to Breslaw's burdens was the need to care for the physically ill. There had always been a small emergency clinic for residents of the area. Now many people had nowhere else to go and Breslaw refused to turn anyone away.

As Aaron turned the corner past what had once been another bakery and onto Breslaw Street, named for the hospital, he was stopped dead by the sight of at least half a dozen gleaming black vehicles. Cars such as these would hardly have caused comment just a year before, but today there was menace behind their headlights; the growl of their engines keyed fear in those who heard them rev. The sound meant death. The machines carried the Gestapo.

The Gestapo was Aaron's worst fear. It was everyone's worst fear.

Officially named Section IV of the German occupying authorities, the Gestapo was given the responsibility of quelling dissent within the Reich and conquered territories. Jews were, of course, a threat by the very definition of Hitler's regime.

There was nothing else to be but brave. Aaron continued walking toward the hospital, trying to look invisible in plain sight. Just another dark coat with a white armband and blue star. Nothing to catch the eye, nothing to remark on.

Only the drivers were left in the cars, the back seats were empty, the men who had ridden in them were nowhere to be seen.

Just keep walking, Aaron told himself, keep walking.

The granite entrance to the hospital was close, perhaps one hundred meters. Aaron could see the elaborate façade, carved into stone, the many windows, all of them barred.

Forward, forward. Don't look at the cars. Don't not look at the cars. Forward.

The wind picked at his collar, trying to reveal his face. Aaron wanted to give these men nothing to remember, so he pulled it closer again.

Aaron was almost surprised when he wasn't stopped, when he walked past the gleaming Mercedes-Benz without hearing a hard voice call him over. Perhaps the men were more interested in the warmth of the cabins than in a Jewish man walking by himself in the one part of his city that a Jewish man could walk freely.

The hospital's massive door didn't move easily and Aaron felt eyes on his back as he struggled. A few seconds more, a heave and he was inside. A few seconds after that, he wished he weren't.

The Gestapo men in their black leather coats were inside the hospital's arched front hall, along with perhaps a dozen soldiers whose Schmeiser MP40 submachine guns seemed pointed everywhere at once. They looked nervous. A meaty giant, in a leather coat that would have required several cows to make, was talking to a frightened man — a doctor from his once-white coat and tangled stethoscope — who seemed to be denying everything, whatever everything was.

"I'm sorry doctor," the giant said in a voice that sounded as if it had never been touched by regret and was as deep as the man was tall. He spoke in German. "A decision has been made. These are hard times. There are great shortages and we all do our part. Every man must give his all to ensure victory."

"But how does this get you any closer to your victory?" the doctor asked in his own stilted, schoolboy German. He was as angry as he was afraid.

"Arbeit macht frei, doctor. Arbeit macht frei," the Gestapo man said. "Please have everyone ready to be moved to the work camp within one hour."

"But many can't walk Herr Clausewitz!"

"I'd like to judge that for myself, if you don't mind, doctor. Just bring out those you consider ambulatory and we will visit with each of the rest to make an assessment."

The hospital's gray-faced guardian pitched his head down in despair.

"You know doctor, your skills would be of great use in the work camp, too," the devil in the black coat said.

The doctor was broken. He turned to an attendant at his side, who Aaron hadn't noticed before, and said what he had to in order to begin the evacuation.

"Thank you, doctor. I'll leave a few men here to help you. You'll forgive me if I disappear for a little while to ensure the transports are on their way."

The German doffed his hat sardonically and headed for the door, which Aaron was unintentionally blocking.

"Excuse me," Aaron muttered, his eyes cast down.

The German didn't move past.

"What did you say?"

Aaron had spoken in Polish without thought.

"I'm very sorry, mein herr," Aaron said in bad German.

"I'm sure you are," the Gestapo man growled. "Look at me."

Aaron looked. He saw eyes the pale blue of an Arctic dawn. Behind them was nothing.

"What's your name, and where do you live?"

Aaron began to pull his official papers out of his pocket.

"I have no time for that, or for you! Just give me your name."

Aaron considered giving a false name, but if the Gestapo officer changed his mind, Aaron's papers would betray him.

"Kaminski," he said. "Aaron Kaminski."

"Kaminski. Good."

The Gestapo man turned to the clerk behind him. "Make a note."

Then he was gone.

He left behind mere anarchy.

Chapter 5

There was nothing for it. Aaron burrowed through a mass of people who were running in no obvious direction. It was as if they hoped that motion would save their lives.

The hospital director was at the center of the chaos. He was trying to give orders to a staff that was looking for direction. Instead, everything was confusion. The man tried to shout but his voice couldn't cut through the competition.

A woman who also wore a stethoscope began to shout for him. Her voice would have cut through the hull of a tank far more effectively than the Polish artillery had the year before. She began to bring order to the crowd.

"Zeitel, take charge of the people on the third floor … Maurice, the second floor … " She turned to one of the nurses. "Do what you can to help the patients from the medical wing. Use crutches, wheelchairs, roll them out on beds … Whatever you can think of."

The nurse apparently demurred because the next thing Aaron heard was, "Do you think they'll be better off staying here? Didn't you hear the Gestapo man? What do you think he means by a 'visit?'"

The hospital personnel began moving off in the required directions. The female doctor was speaking more softly to people nearer by, trying to organize the evacuation of the main floor. Aaron walked briskly into the circle surrounding her, using his elbows to make progress.

"Lekarska, doctor … " was all he had time to say.

"What the fuck do you want?" she said, barely glancing at him.

"I'm looking for a policeman who was hurt and was taken here. His name is Martin Gersh." Aaron kept his gaze level and his tone was calm.

"So look for him. But I suggest you make it quick. There'll be no one here in an hour, one way or another."

She turned away.

Aaron tried again.

"Where are emergency cases treated?"

"What other kind of cases do you think we have here? Go!"

The doctor gathered some of her people and was gone.

All that left for Aaron was a dash down fetid hallways throwing open doors. After only a few meters he realized his task was impossible. A deluge of people was beginning to flow against him. Some hobbled, swathed in blood-soaked bandages. Others were being wheeled out by attendants. Some were so emaciated Aaron had a hard time believing he wasn't seeing the animated dead. Many of those patients were doubled over with dysentery, wearing shit-stained robes or blankets.

"Martin Gersh!" Aaron shouted into the din. He wouldn't give up. "Martin Gersh!"

All that got him was a few stares. Many of those who passed and pushed him were beyond answering, anyway.

A few in the crowd were surprisingly well dressed. A woman in what must have been her own wheelchair — it was made of burnished wood — had a fur draped over her. The man attending her may have been her own, as well. He brutally blazed a path for her. But Aaron saw that she hadn't been able to buy what she needed most from the hospital — her health. She was as pale and thin as any of the others.

"Martin Gersh!"

Men, women, a few children. Thank God not many, Aaron thought. There was a separate facility for them. He hoped it was nothing like this.

As he found himself herded further into the main hall where the staircases converged, Aaron began to see the hospital's other type of patient. Telltale signs of retardation on faces, limbs that had never grown right, uncomprehending moans.

Shaking and rocking; incomprehensible shouting and screaming. It was an immovable wall of madness being struck by an unstoppable force of desperate suffering.

"Martin Gersh!"

There was no answer but the noise of the crowd.

Aaron found himself battered by an endless stream of shoulders crashing into his own — left, right, left, right, sometimes both at once — pushing him closer to the door.

"Martin Gersh?"

"Here!" called a voice.

At first Aaron was unable to spot its owner in the crowd, but after a minute, the speaker became resolved into a bearded man in his forties wearing nearly rimless spectacles. He was neat and smooth. He was reasonably well fed. Aaron was surprised that he hadn't noticed the man on that basis alone.

And there was another factor — Aaron knew him, though not by the name Martin Gersh.

Under the name Tamislaw Jaruzelski, he was a Pole in the import-export business. The importing was made up of trafficking potatoes and other necessities and frills though the walls of the ghetto, working from the Polish side. The exporting came in the form of the people who were occasionally smuggled out either in the hope of escape or just for an afternoon's work. Those who worked hoped to bring home enough zloty to add an extra bit of bread to a meal of thin soup.

The two men eyed each other for a second before Aaron forced himself into a quick decision.

"Martin!" he called out, as if greeting a long-lost friend. Then more quietly, "We need to talk."

"I guess we do," the other man replied heavily.

Aaron took him by the arm and began pulling him against the crowd, knowing that they would have no trouble finding an empty room as everyone else tried to flee. Aaron quickly realized that as he dragged "Gersh," the man himself was dragging a leg twisted and covered in bandages soaked through with blood. "Gersh" was leaning on what could only be called a crutch in charity. It looked more like a bent piece of plumbing.

Now was not the time for mercy, though, and frankly, Aaron didn't care much about the other man's pain. He pushed on, through the crowd, which began to thin after only a few steps. In a minute it was possible to see the institutionally dirty white walls again, and finally an office. The two men stumbled inside and Aaron closed the door behind them. The office had a window and a draft came through it. The fog of their breath began to fill the room.

The man with at least two names propped himself on the desk, trying to find some comfort for his leg, or at least prevent further damage by taking his weight off it. The bluff confidence he had always projected as Jaruzelski was replaced by a twitchiness that was near panic. There was still something central to the man that Aaron had been able to spot in the crowd, but now, "Gersh" looked like a Gersh, not a Jaruzelski. He was Semitic in a way that his alter ego hadn't been on the other side of the wall. It was a striking transformation.

"You're Berson's partner?" Aaron asked.

"I wouldn't say partner, but we did work together," the man replied.

"As Gersh or Jaruzelski?"

"It doesn't have to be one or the other, you know."

"What should I call you today?"

"Well, Gersh would make more sense here, I think," Gersh said.

"All right. Let's try it," Aaron said, reaching for his second cigarette of the day. He offered one to Gersh who looked down at the package, trying to catch a glimpse of the label.

"What are these? They're not the ones I sold you," Gersh said, taking one with a hint of suspicion. "Those were Pall Mall, weren't they?"

"I'm glad to say you're not my only supplier. Otherwise I think I'd be in a little trouble now, what with you nursing that leg," Aaron said. "And on the wrong side of the wall, too."

"Was that why you were looking for me? For a little business?" Gersh asked. "But of course not, you weren't even looking for me. Or at least you weren't expecting to find me when you found Gersh.

"So what is it you do want? I think we may be a little pressed for time here."

Aaron acknowledged the point with a nod.

"Lev Berson is dead," he said.

Gersh did not look shocked at the news. In fact, other than a tightening of his perpetual squint, it was hard to see much of a change at all.

"All right," was all he said.

"I'm looking for whoever killed him, and I've been told that you were supposed to be with him last night," Aaron continued.

"Who told you that?"

"Your commander, Blaustein," Aaron said with a certain amount of irony. "Who does he think you are, by the way?"

Gersh ignored the question, instead asking one of his own.

"Why are you here, asking about Berson? I wouldn't have thought a dead Jewish police officer would be high on your priority list," Gersh said. "Don't you have anything else to do? Or is business just that bad?"

"We can talk about my motives some other time."

The noise in the hall was starting to fade. The evacuation was nearing completion.

"Not much time left, so smoke up and just tell me what you can about last night."

Gersh squinted and took a deep drag on the thick, black smoke, and in a gesture as Gallic as his counterfeit cigarette was supposed to be, he gave a shrug of surrender.

"Last night we were supposed to be patrolling over by Morawica Street. There's a new hole that's been dug through the wall. A hundred kilos of potatoes were scheduled to be coming through," Gersh said. "Not a lot, but worth the usual risk."

They heard shouts in the hallway. Orders in German as well as Polish.

"Especially if you're employed on both sides of the deal," Aaron pointed out.

"Just so."

"But Berson wasn't found on Morawica Street," Aaron said.

"No reason he should have been. The deal went fine, and it was done by 9 p.m.," Gersh said. "After that, the boys were off with the goods. Berson and I went our separate ways.

Aaron heard banging on doors and the sounds of a struggle nearby.

Aaron pointed to Gersh's leg. The bloody bandages had been soaking through as they spoke. Red splotches began to appear on the floor.

"So where did that come from?"

"This? An unhappy customer in another part of town," Gersh said wryly. "Not your business. Not Berson's either, for that matter."

"What else was Berson involved in? I'd never heard of him before today," Aaron said. That was neither surprising nor unsurprising. Smuggling was a major employer in the Miasto ghetto and it would be impossible to know everyone involved.

Chapter 5

"Funnily enough, he was a very religious man," Gersh said. It was clear from the way he said it that Gersh had very little use for God, himself.

"What does that mean? So are at least 75 percent of the people trapped in here."

"In his case, it was a bit more than that ... " Gersh said. "He seemed particularly devoted to his congregation, and he'd gotten himself deeper and deeper in debt with me to get supplies for them."

"You were fronting him the money?"

"Some of it anyway. Which, may I point out, gives me a very good motive for not killing him," Gersh said.

"Maybe," Aaron said. "But you'd hardly be the first partners to have a falling out."

Gersh's mouth opened but Aaron never got to hear his reply. Something or someone smashed into the office door from the outside.

"Raus! Raus!"

The door shook in its frame.

Aaron quickly turned from Gersh and grabbed the handle, opening the door just as a soldier with lightning bolts on his collar lifted the butt of his rifle to slam the door again. The Nazi saw no reason to stop his swing. Only the target changed. Aaron gasped and nearly fell to the ground as the breath rushed out of him. Thanks to his thick coat and the half dozen other layers he was wearing, the blow was cushioned substantially.

"Raus! Schnell!" the German shouted again. *Out! Move it!*

There was no more time for questions. Gersh immediately started hobbling out the door. Aaron gathered himself and followed, quickly overtaking the wounded man.

They joined a thin trickle of others exiting the front door out onto Breslaw Street. A German officer glanced at each person as they exited the building and motioned them toward one of two piles of Jews. Aaron was sent to the right. When Gersh limped out the door, his foot pointing at an unnatural angle, he was sent left.

It soon became obvious to people in both groups how they had been divided.

On the left were the injured, sick, deranged or mentally incompetent. Some lay on the ground in stretchers, having been borne out by orderlies. Others were holding their wounds, were obviously feverish or, more commonly, had their own shit covering their gowns because of dysentery. No one was dressed for the cold, though a few had managed to grab the soiled blankets off their beds.

The other group — a much smaller gathering — was somewhat better off, though they hadn't been given much time to grab warm clothes, either. All of the people in Aaron's group were relatively healthy, if emaciated, with no outward signs of mental defect or insanity. No obvious wounds or disease. Mainly they seemed to be doctors and visitors rather than patients or inmates.

Both groups were lined up in front of the hospital. Open vehicles with machine guns mounted on their backs had joined the black sedans that Aaron had seen on his way into Breslaw.

A needle-sharp man wearing a black greatcoat was inspecting each of the sick and wounded. He had the air of a schoolmaster and a red, white and black armband. Every patient received individual attention and the schoolmaster called out notes to the giant who had confronted Aaron in the doorway of the hospital earlier. Clausewitz, Aaron remembered. In turn, the big man passed along the comments to his own aide-de-camp who followed behind them both with a notebook, carefully capturing every thought.

Chapter 5

The ominous inspection was endured by the patients until one man, who had appeared catatonic, broke free and ran. It was as unexpected as a figure in a photograph taking life. It took an eternal fraction of a second for the rest of the world to catch up. And then it did all at once.

Aaron's gaze tracked the fleeing man just a few steps before blood bloomed on the back of the patient's whitish gown. It seemed to Aaron that he saw the wound even before he heard the pistol shot. He looked for the source of the bullet and saw the schoolmaster, steady hand on the grip of a Walther P38, smoke rising from its barrel.

The patients began to scream.

With a sigh and a signal to Clausewitz, the schoolmaster walked back to the line of German vehicles. Clausewitz nodded his head to one of the soldiers dressed in gray. The soldier, an officer, raised a black-gloved hand. A beat, and then he dropped it again.

The machine guns began to spit.

Chapter 6

Bullets ripped apart men and women; the sick and the mad; the holy fools and the simple souls. It was a leaden rain that became a torrent.

An impossible amount of time passed but the barrage didn't stop. Aaron began to believe it would never stop. The booming rattle of gunfire returned Aaron to the trenches outside Warsaw as the Germans advanced on the city. Then, it had presaged the earthquake of tanks that would crush Polish independence. Now, it spoke of immediate death, unadulterated by hope.

Aaron waited to be killed along with everyone else. He did nothing. He didn't make a run at the guards. He didn't scream. He didn't even try to duck down out of the way. As a gendarme, he'd been trained to take action, to protect people, but as the machine guns spit he felt no urge to do so. He stood where he'd been told and witnessed the flowers of evil bloom.

He watched bodies fall, heads explode in blood, heard the cries, pleas and screams. He felt something other than human.

He turned to watch the killers at their work, curious when the barrels would shift to take his life, too. The machine gunners' faces held no expression. They were concentrating on their work, focused on stamping out a clear threat to National Socialism.

The commander — the academic — had a small smile of satisfaction as he watched a job well done. The other Gestapo officer, Clausewitz, looked close to sexual climax. It must have been all he could do to stop himself from grabbing a burp gun out of one of the soldier's hands and joining in the fun.

The final shot was fired. The work was done. Gray, cold death spattered with red blood, burst brains, children's dolls and tortured faces was all around. The last echoes fled the confines of the killing ground.

And Aaron realized that he'd been spared.

The next sound came from the schoolmaster's boots as he stepped in front of the living to give a eulogy for the corpses.

"We can no longer afford to carry the weak," he said. "This is war and sacrifices must be made if the strong are to remain that way. To survive, we must all work to our capacity. We can no longer afford parasites."

He nodded once and walked to a black car. Clausewitz opened the door for him and they drove away. The other vehicles fell in behind, leaving only a few soldiers to keep an eye on the survivors.

The orderlies and doctors among the living made their way over to the dead, fruitlessly hoping they would be able do some good. Aaron joined them, not looking to help, but for a single face. It wasn't long before he found it.

Gersh, Jaruzelski — whatever his true name had been — was dead.

Aaron stepped back as hand-drawn and horse-drawn carts pulled onto Breslaw Street. There were wagons from the three Jewish mortuaries that ran an ever-growing business within the walls of the ghetto, as well as others manned by conscript labor.

The laborers had been drawn from every walk of Jewish life. Former yeshiva students mixed with men who had worked with bricks and brooms in the days before the ongoing apocalypse. The blunt point of a gun now united men who would only have come together at worship, if at all.

Chapter 6

Aaron watched as the bodies were awkwardly lifted. Soon the impromptu morticians looked like butchers after a hard day's slaughter. If those who had died had possessed dignity in life, it had gone with their souls. Gravity made fools of them as their limbs flopped about under the ungentle ministrations. Wet, squelching sounds came from the pile. Workers stepped on one body to reach for the next. Hands and whole arms came away at a tug, bullets having cut through tendon and bone. The remains were laid on wheeled beds of rough wood.

The dead wouldn't mind a few splinters Aaron guessed, as he stood rooted to the horror. He knew he should move. The Germans had packed up their big machine guns, but the remaining soldiers looked ill at ease, even jumpy.

"Who will visit our unmarked graves when the last of us is gone?" a voice muttered.

Aaron turned to look, but couldn't be sure who had spoken.

The words freed him from his trance. He turned and quickly retreated the way he'd come. German eyes followed him, watching for any sign of resistance or even emotion.

Once he was well out of view, he began to shake. Aaron's numbed fingers clawed at his coat, seeking the cigarettes he knew were in some pocket. When he couldn't immediately come up with them, he sought out his flask instead. That was easier to find because of its weight.

His fingers weren't any more nimble with the cap than they'd been with his pockets. When he finally got the flask open, the cap spun away. He heard it fall but couldn't see where it landed.

Fuck it. Just fuck it.

He managed to get the flask to his lips. He poured the liquor down his throat so fast that he choked. Some of the liquid sprayed up into his nasal cavity, burning away the stench of cordite, urine and voided bowels.

Most of the schnapps went down, though. Lava spread from his throat to his stomach and out to his extremities. It was welcome. He put the flask to his lips again and breathed in the fire. Another minute and the artificial calm had spread to his fingers, letting him pull the tattered cigarette pack from his coat. The cigarette trembled at his lips, but he was able to light it with the third match.

A deep breath of nicotine and then another. As the chemicals pushed their way through his system, Aaron's mind put what he'd seen into a box he'd never open outside of his nightmares.

His eyes itched and when he put a hand up to rub them, it came away wet with freezing tears. He wiped them off on his coat and tried to turn his mind back to the case. It offered him the opportunity to consider just a single murder instead of a massacre.

Jaruzelski hadn't added much to what he already knew, and Aaron wondered if he could trust even that much. If Jaruzelski had witnessed Berson's death, he had little incentive to talk about it. Even less if he'd been the one to kill Berson.

That speculation, though, led to a dead end and Aaron decided to push it aside. Instead, he would play along and take Jaruzelski at his word; that Berson had been a smuggler for God, trying to steal as much as he could for his congregation. And that was all.

It wasn't much and it didn't bring Aaron closer to the answers he needed in any obvious way. He was, however, more aware than ever of the price of failure.

Chapter 6

Aaron walked back the way he'd come, but now the streets were abandoned. The gunshots' echoes told the ghetto that the Germans were out for blood.

When Miasto had first been taken, the Germans had carried out a massive purge, using machine guns and house fires to kill not only Jews, but prominent Poles as well.

Days of killing had taken place in a Jewish cemetery, with death only stopping to reload. More than ten thousand people had died before the rest had been ushered into their new "homes." Then came the edicts governing Jewish life: the curfews, the armbands, the rationing, the Judenrat and the Jewish Police.

Many people who heard the shots outside of Breslaw Hospital were survivors of other mass slaughters. Many had planned ahead for the day when the killing would begin again, when the next roundup would come. In minutes they became invisible, having gathered their children and aging parents into the safest places they could imagine. Some hid under floorboards, others up in attics, still others crouched down in sewers or lay on top of shingled roofs.

Aaron felt himself floating ghostlike through a realm of shades. Everywhere were closed shop fronts and bolted doors. In front of the American Jewish Joint Distribution Committee soup kitchen there was no line. A normal day meant a queue that stretched for blocks beginning the minute the ghetto's curfew was lifted and lasting until it fell again.

Despite the cold and fear that Aaron felt, he wandered aimlessly at first. He found his direction only when he discovered that he was out of cigarettes. He walked two more blocks and then took a sharp turn down an alley so narrow it could only be seen by someone standing directly in front of it.

The wind funneled into Aaron's face. His shoulders brushed the bricks on both sides of the alley and he was forced to advance like a fencer. Light was fast disappearing. A frigid stink grew and formed a wall of its own for Aaron to push through. Ahead was a low window partially covered by random junk.

Aaron tapped on the junk, his rhythm confident. A voice called out, a code word was exchanged, and the odds and ends revealed themselves as a door of sorts. It was pulled aside, allowing Aaron to climb down into a dim, cluttered room.

"We weren't expecting you until later," said a gruff voice from the shadows, speaking in Yiddish.

"I wasn't expecting to see what I just saw, either, Lech," Aaron said. "A cigarette, please."

A flame sparked in the darkness and an ember glowed. Lech Teitel, a rough man in a workman's clothes, handed the cigarette's unlit end to Aaron, who took it gratefully.

"What happened?" Teitel asked, motioning Aaron to a chair that sat mostly empty.

"I was at the hospital," Aaron began and, inhaling tobacco smoke with nearly every breath, he told his business partner everything he'd just seen, including Jaruzelski's death.

Teitel knew the name through Aaron and had met the man more than once. It was Aaron's contacts in the wider Polish community that helped bring the supplies into the ghetto. Teitel organized the manpower and distribution once they were inside. Before the war, Teitel had been a grocer. He saw no reason why a wall should force him to change professions, especially as demand had never been greater.

"We saw it coming," Teitel said a few minutes after Aaron had finished. "It won't be the last massacre, that's for sure.

What were you doing at Breslaw, anyway? You weren't looking for Jaruzelski, were you? And what was he even doing there?"

"He said he'd been injured in some deal that had nothing to do with us. And I wasn't there looking for him. Except it turned out that I was."

"Very cryptic."

"I was looking for a man named Martin Gersh, supposedly a Jewish policeman," Aaron said. "Turns out that Gersh and Jaruzelski were the same man."

"Hmmm … " Teitel paused. "Well, I can see how that could be useful. Being both a smuggler and the man who is supposed to catch him."

"I thought the same thing," Aaron said. "But it must have cost him quite a bit. A lot of people would need paying off. I can't imagine he was regularly showing up for his shifts. He must have been fairly busy on the other side of the wall."

"Yes, if it was me, I'd only work the shifts when I had a shipment coming in." Teitel nodded to himself. "Interesting that he was willing to do deals with us but never offered us the protection he had for himself."

"Maybe he knew we had our own arrangements."

"Maybe," Teitel said. It was clear he wasn't convinced.

Aaron wasn't sure it mattered much anymore.

"Okay, next question," Teitel said. "What were you doing looking for a Jewish policeman named Gersh?"

"Slivovitz?" Aaron asked, instead of answering.

There were crates and boxes behind Teitel, who reached around and pulled out a bottle of the sharp liquor. He opened it and poured the contents down his own throat for one second, two seconds, three seconds …

"I don't know why I didn't think of that myself," Teitel said through a burning throat, after handing the bottle over. "So, why were you there?"

"One of the Jewish Police was killed sometime between midnight of last night and dawn. Head bashed in. No witnesses, of course."

"Well," Teitel said, grabbing back the bottle of slivovitz. "That's a reason to have a drink."

He tipped the unlabeled bottle into the air, drinking deeply in celebration. He was surprised to see the grim look on Aaron's face when he looked to pass the bottle.

"Is this a problem somehow?" Teitel asked.

"He was Jaruzelski's partner. A man named Lev Berson."

"You mean Gersh's partner?"

"Right," Aaron said.

"Okay, but I'm not sure why this is your problem. Or mine, for that matter."

"It wouldn't be, usually, but it is today," Aaron replied. "I have to find out who bashed in the cop's skull."

"How is that your job?"

"The Judenrat is making it my job."

Teitel raised his eyebrows and waited for more information.

"I was called into Mordechai Zimmerman's office this morning, out of the blue," Aaron said, not bothering to mention his father. "When I got there, they dumped this on me."

"Why you?"

"Because I was a gendarme, moron!" Aaron said sharply. "How many real police do you think we have in here? How many men here have ever conducted any kind of murder inquiry?"

"I see your point," Teitel said, taken a bit aback by Aaron's tone. "But why did you say yes? I know I wouldn't want to get involved in this."

He paused.

"Actually, please take that as a request. Don't get me involved in this."

"You are involved, though," Aaron said, shaking his head. "Anyway, after a brief appeal to my better nature … "

"A failed appeal, I imagine."

"Right. After that, though, he threatened to shut us down," Aaron said. "Blaustein, the head of the police, was in the office with him and they seemed to have at least some idea of what we're doing."

"You thought they could do it?"

"I thought they could put me in a concentration camp, and probably you, too," Aaron said. "Even if they just took us out of action for a few days, it was the timing that worried me the most."

Teitel nodded.

"So, does that mean anything for tonight?" he asked. "Do we still go ahead?"

"Even if we wanted to stop the delivery, I'm not sure how we'd do it this late," Aaron said. "We go ahead. I'll meet you at the house on Kozikowska Place after curfew. In the meantime, can you ask around and see if you can find anything out about either Berson or Jaruzelski?"

"Aaron, this is not something I want to get involved in," Teitel said. "I'm not a detective. If you have to do it, then *you* do it. It's not my battle, and I think I might desert if it was. Whatever happens to the Judenrat or the Jewish Police, it's a good thing.

"And if you haven't learned the lesson from today at the hospital, let me tell you what it is: The Germans are coming for each and every one of us. They will not be happy until every Jew in Miasto is dead. Every one of those bastards that's helping the Nazis? Let them go first."

Teitel's face was red as he finished.

"Fine. Don't help," Aaron said. He wasn't pleased.

"I'll see you tonight."

Aaron turned and twisted to get out by the same door he'd come in. He felt a hand grab his coat and looked back down.

"You'll need this," Teitel said, handing him a pack of cigarettes.

Aaron nodded his thanks.

When Aaron pulled himself up into the alleyway and dusted himself down, he felt a hard lump in each of the front pockets of his coat. He reached in and found potatoes. He pulled out the one from his left-hand pocket and bit into it raw. The taste of the starch wasn't wonderful, but there was no way of knowing where his next meal would come from, so he swallowed it down.

Chapter 7

Aaron's stomach wasn't happy with the raw potato that it had to digest, bathed as it was in a sauce of 120-proof slivovitz. He felt both bloated and hungry at the same time. Another cigarette might have helped, but they were far too precious to waste in such quick succession.

At least the alcohol gave him a false feeling of warmth as he made his way back out of the alley and onto Wadowice Street. A few people had returned to the sidewalks, talking quietly, sharing whatever gossip and misinformation they had about the events in front of Breslaw Hospital. Cold never overpowered people's need for news, and it wasn't likely the massacre would make it into tomorrow's Nazi-approved newspaper.

Word of mouth — rumor's pretty cousin — was the language of Miasto. A quiet word was often the only way to find a supply of food or fuel, or to avoid German soldiers looking for a good time in the ghetto by beating, raping or killing Jews.

On Wadowice, Aaron could hear snippets of conversation. People who knew nothing asked others who knew less whether today's massacre meant the entire ghetto would be liquidated. People spoke of relatives missing and rumors of entire Jewish settlements being erased by a mix of bullets and flames. What difference was there between Miasto and a shtetl, other than size? Obviously, the Germans weren't intimidated by scale; they had invaded the whole world at once, after all.

The more optimistic argued that the Germans needed the Jews for their labor, that their slavery was their salvation.

Otherwise, why concentrate them all in one place and work them so hard? Killing Jews was just wasteful.

As Aaron passed the small groups of men huddled in the street, he heard the rationalizations, the "guarantees" of safety. Reasons why these men would never face the guns.

"I can still work my sixteen hours every day. They need me," one man said.

A few steps later …

"Those people were sick. All they were doing was soaking up food," another said. "Killing them even makes sense in a kind of sick way."

A block further on …

"If we just work harder, surely … I mean, they may be evil, but even Germans aren't crazy. They've always been thrifty people."

Aaron understood the need for rationalization, even hope. What advantage would there be for people to believe they were doomed?

The men and women of the ghetto were not fighters, by and large. They had been merchants, doctors, sellers of junk, manufacturers, seamstresses, lawyers and more than a few religious scholars. The scholars were the most useless; men who refused to take any unnecessary part in the life of the body, instead devoting their lives entirely to study and to teaching.

Give them guns and watch them shoot themselves, Aaron thought.

Aaron was one of the few men behind the walls who had ever held a rifle, let alone a grenade.

That needs to change, Aaron thought.

He shook himself and shook off the words he'd heard. He entered his own state of denial, which allowed him to focus on the task at hand and let him believe there was a purpose behind it.

Again, he brought his focus back to the case.

With Gersh/Jaruzelski dead, Aaron decided that his next avenue was to look into Lev Berson's life outside of the Jewish Police. To begin, all Aaron had was Berson's address.

Berson lived on a street that had been quite posh a half-century before. Now, Krawcy Boulevard was lined with tenements and small factories making cheap clothes. Aaron wasn't looking forward to the long walk to get there.

Even though the ghetto was small compared to the rest of the city, Krawcy was at least twenty-five minutes away by foot. The cold had retained its knife-edge, and the wind was relentless. Aaron suspected that the sun's feeble showing was intended as a purely ironic touch. He decided to find an alternative to his gum-soled boots.

Not long ago, Wadowice and Krawcy had been joined by a streetcar line that made the trip between the two stations in less than 10 minutes, keeping its riders warm on the way. But streetcars had been constricted along with every other aspect of the life of the Jews of Miasto. Before the ghetto had been completely enclosed, people with Star of David armbands were forced to ride in separate cars from the rest of the passengers. The stated reason was the same as that for the construction of the ghetto. The civil authorities, under instruction from the occupying military authorities, proclaimed Jews to be carriers of disease — particularly typhoid. It was a sensible precaution to make sure they traveled separately.

That hadn't been enough in the end. Eventually, it became clear that the only way to safeguard the Aryan and Slavic populations was to ensure that Jews were kept within the boundary of the ghetto as much as possible. An exception was made for Jewish laborers on their way to and from factories or labor camps. On those occasions, Jews were either marched out en masse, or carried out in gray, open-topped trucks. There was no longer a reason for streetcars to stop in the Jewish district at all.

The cars still passed through, though now it was more like a bobsled run, with the tracks' path acting as the chute. The route was lined by makeshift walls to keep any illicit contact between the district and the city to a minimum.

Still, the end of regular trolley services was not the same as the end of industry. An older form of transport had come back into vogue. Horse-powered buses now ran down a few streets. They were makeshift things, and it amazed Aaron that the horses hadn't been eaten and the vehicles pulled apart for firewood. He would've been less surprised had he known the companies behind the buses were German and the Jewish fares ended up in their pockets.

An enclosed bus drawn by an enormous, though emaciated, horse pulled up in front of Aaron and didn't quite stop. He swung on and one or two patrons climbed off. The vehicle wasn't crowded, and the heating system, unfortunately, depended solely on the density of bodies aboard. Aaron moved forward, handed two zloty to the driver and found himself a seat. He had hoped to simply watch the streets roll by and say his thanks for getting out of the wind, but another passenger had a different plan. A woman stood up in the middle of the cabin and began to beg.

"Please," she said. "I have a dying child at home. Every day he's thinner and more pale … "

Aaron had no desire to look at her, but for some reason he did. In that, he was unique among the riders. The woman was young, she had been pretty, and if she was acting, she was truly excellent.

A voice answered the woman's plea.

Chapter 7

"Who do you think you are to beg from us? Do you think we don't go home to the same place you do? To the same circumstances?"

It was an elderly woman who spoke, a woman who wore fur around her neck and the remnants of a once-fashionable hat. It was slightly frayed, but must have cost her hundreds of zloty when she'd bought it.

"If you can walk, you can work!" the old woman continued.

"There is no work … Please … " the younger woman replied.

Aaron knew it was true. Unemployment was as high as 80 percent, leaving the 300-calorie ration cards and charity as the only sources of sustenance for most.

"There's always work for a pretty one like you."

The beggar began to cry. She headed to the back of the bus and the exit, seeing only her own feet. No one's eyes followed her. As she passed Aaron, he slipped his second potato into her pocket without her noticing. He said nothing.

The entrance to Krawcy Boulevard appeared on his left and he made to stand, turning so that his elbow slammed into the back of the old woman's head. Her hat fell off and her forehead hit the glass of the window she was sitting beside. What Aaron muttered as he climbed out of the bus may have been an apology.

Eight Krawcy was on the left as Aaron walked down the street from where he had jumped from the bus. There was little to distinguish the building from those around it. It was five stories tall and it was neither attractive nor strikingly ugly. It was as gray as everything seemed to be in the ghetto. The glass in the windows was unbroken and some of the apartments were lit.

There was an electric bell in the entryway, but it didn't work. The locked door had several glass panels, allowing Aaron to see that the hall beyond was filled with people. In the cold, with most schools and synagogues closed and large gatherings prohibited, the hallways of tenements had become the focus of social life. Many buildings had transformed themselves into communes.

Aaron knocked and a woman holding a half-naked 3-year-old boy — it was his bottom half that was bare — put the child down and came to the door. She saw the military cut of Aaron's coat and hesitated for some moments before opening it wide enough to ask him what he wanted.

"I'm here about Lev Berson," Aaron said.

The woman frowned at him and began closing the door while at the same time saying, "He's not here."

She was a little surprised when the door wouldn't close fully, eventually looking down to see Aaron's foot wedged in the doorframe.

"I'd be surprised if he was," Aaron said. "But I'd like to speak with anyone who knows him."

"Why?"

The woman wasn't budging. To resolve the situation, Aaron put his weight on the door, which gradually inched open. The woman leaned against the other side, but wasn't heavy enough to stop him.

"I'm happy to talk with anybody," Aaron said, using his best cop voice. "But if you like, I can start with you."

The woman's defiance was brittle and shattered as Aaron gave a final little push.

"I don't know him very well," she said meekly. Then with more strength, "Who are you? Why do you want to know about Lev?"

It was a good question. Aaron had thought about what he would say when people asked. Announcing that he was working for the Judenrat was not the way to gain people's trust. And telling them that he was investigating Berson's death was hardly the best way to keep it a secret.

In the end, he said, "I arrived from Serca about a week ago, and Lev Berson is the only name I know in the city. I figured that since he works for the Judenrat, he might be able to help me get set up here."

Serca was a village not far from Miasto that had once had a thriving Jewish community. Aaron had met several men from there who had been forced into the Miasto ghetto at literal gunpoint. The village also wasn't far from where Berson had grown up.

"Well, I don't know how much help he can be. He hasn't done very well for himself."

The woman moved back from the door and picked up the toddler who had never stopped clawing at her worn and modest dress.

"How do you mean?"

"Well, you have eyes. You have a nose. He lives here."

She punctuated her words with a roll of her eyes and a dismissive sniff.

Aaron sniffed, too, in sympathy, and immediately wished he hadn't. The miasma was composed of all the stinks of the ghetto brought together in a single lungful. There was the rot of old food, the rot of unwashed bodies living on top of each other, the rot of illness and the loose shit that comes with it.

The woman saw his expression and her answering look shouted, "I told you so," with a wicked gleam.

"I get your point, but I'd still like to talk to him," Aaron said. "I haven't been able to find him and they're so disorganized at the Judenrat that the only thing they could give me was this address."

"Well, I certainly don't know where he is, or what he does with his time," the woman said.

The toddler was now nibbling on some hair he'd been able to work free of his mother's tight bun.

"Does he have roommates?" Aaron asked as he tried to maneuver himself around the woman.

"Who's so rich that they don't have roommates? My baby and I live with two other families. It used to be my apartment. And it was small then," the woman said bitterly. "Lev's apartment is on the fifth floor. Do what you want."

Her voice was flat. She had no more time for Aaron.

"One more question: Does he get along with the people here?"

"What's that supposed to mean?" she asked.

"Anybody have a problem with what he does for a living, let's say?"

"People do what they have to. Who can judge anyone else these days?"

She turned away from Aaron, and with her child at her hip, sorted through a pile of cloth lying nearby, looking, it seemed, for something to use as a diaper.

His way cleared, Aaron moved further into the building. From behind one door he heard the sound of prayers. From behind another, the sound of a husband and wife arguing about whatever married people argue about. Loudly.

Children were using the stairwell to play with marbles. Men perched above them and watched, some making wagers. They called down hints and suggestions that sometimes sounded like orders. No one moved aside as Aaron worked his way up the staircase.

Wash lines were strung from the bannisters and the array of clothing and rags that hung from them was colorful if pitiful. Circumstances left no room for modesty concerning ladies' undergarments.

On the third floor landing a kind of tent was set up, made from ropes and blankets. The blankets billowed gently and small sounds of hushed lovemaking filled Aaron's ears, turning his cheeks crimson. He quieted his steps and continued upward.

There were more tents set up in the fifth-floor hallway by people looking for the pretense of privacy. Aaron decided to start his inquiry with the floor's original apartments, complete with solid walls and doors.

He started on the right side of the hall. A knock on the first door brought him nothing but a groan. Aaron then pounded more loudly, but with the same result. He decided to move on. He could always come back if he had to, he figured.

The next door opened at the first tap, and a young, somewhat elegant young man peered out.

"I'm looking for Lev Berson," Aaron said by way of introduction.

"Well, he lives here, but he's not here at the moment," the young man said. "May I ask who you are?"

Aaron saw no reason not to be friendly. He put his hand out.

"Aaron Kaminski. Damn. I could really use his help."

"How so?" the man asked. "I'm Manny Cohen, by the way."

"Do you mind if I come in?"

Cohen started a sweeping gesture of welcome, but stopped half way through, obviously thinking twice about his impulse toward hospitality. In the end though, politeness won out.

"Please do, though I have nothing to offer you, I'm afraid."

"Well, a place to sit will be much appreciated," Aaron said, as Cohen moved aside to let him into the room.

And that's all it was, a single room, a squarish box really, with one window and a radiator that looked as if it would clank brutally if there were any steam coming up through the pipes.

Little fear of that, Aaron thought to himself.

There were no beds, per se. Seven cots took up what space there was. Some were neatly made, others had bedclothes tussled together with other personal objects all in a stew. There were no closets, no armoire, no dresser or shelves. Apart from the radiator, the room would have made a perfect closet. The only amenity that Aaron could see was an electric hotplate resting on top of the radiator. A slice of bread sat on the hotplate, which appeared to be on, surprisingly.

Cohen shrugged apologetically and pointed to one of the neat bunks in an invitation for Aaron to sit.

"I know it doesn't make much of a chair, but at least I can promise that it's clean," he said. "It's mine."

Cohen wrinkled his nose as he looked around at the other cots.

Aaron sat.

"I'm happy to get off my feet, actually, so thank you." Aaron was doing his best to mimic Cohen's smooth and educated tone. Clearly, it would not do to appear a savage in front of this young man.

"So, how can I help you?" Cohen asked.

"Well, I was hoping you might be able to give me an idea of where to find Lev when he's not at work," Aaron said truthfully. "The Judenrat and the Jewish Police weren't any help, really."

"Oh, I know! When the Germans took my family's home — it was outside the ghetto, unfortunately — the best the Judenrat said they could do for me was to put me up here, in this rat hole," Cohen said, his voice bleak. "The Germans wouldn't let me take anything from the old place. All the furniture, my mother's jewelry, my father's paintings … "

Cohen stopped himself, with an effort.

"I mean, I shouldn't complain. I've certainly seen many people who have it worse."

"I'm in much the same situation," Aaron said, nodding. "I was forced here from Serca. Lev's family knew mine. It's not easy getting along here, and I figured a friend hooked into the authorities could only help."

"You can probably tell that Lev doesn't have much sway," Cohen said, looking around. "You're catching me at a rare moment. There's almost always someone else here. There are seven men assigned to this tiny little space."

The smell of burning bread began to fill the room.

"Oh God!"

Cohen rushed to turn off the hotplate, grabbing up the bread and bouncing it from hand to hand to avoid getting scorched. Finally, the toast was cool enough for him to hold. He gave a slight smile.

"Well, not too badly singed," Cohen said and lifted it to take a bite. Again, his better angels intervened. "Would you like some?" he offered with a certain noblesse oblige.

Aaron returned the smile and said thank you, adding one of the polite lies commonly told in the ghetto, "I've already eaten."

No one had ever eaten enough.

The words were barely out of Aaron's mouth before the toast was gone. Cohen then turned his attention to his fingers, looking for crumbs.

"How do you all get along, cramped in a place like this?" Aaron asked.

"Well, people have things to do that take them outside," Cohen said. "I know that a couple of the other men work in the shops. Of course, I'm still looking for work myself."

"How do people get along with Lev, do you think?"

"He's not here very much. That makes any roommate more attractive," Cohen said. "He doesn't snore, he doesn't smell — more than the rest of us anyway. Other than with religion, he's quite private."

"Religion?"

"He's always trying to get us to come with him to that synagogue of his." Cohen looked annoyed.

"Which synagogue is that?"

Cohen looked toward another neat cot.

"Actually, I think he might have some sort of flyers here. He has fits of giving them out."

"Do you mind if I check?" Aaron asked.

"I probably should, but frankly, there's so little privacy in here anyway, I'm not sure what difference it could make."

Under Berson's cot, Aaron found a small stack of prayer cards and nothing else. The paper the cards were printed on was so thin that a breath of wind would carry them to Moscow.

"I have to tell you, the stack used to be larger," Cohen said. "But everyone takes a few with them when they go down the hall."

Aaron quirked his eyebrows.

"You know. To use the facilities? It's impossible to get tissue paper, you know."

"Cleanliness is next to godliness," Aaron said with a smile, making Cohen laugh out loud.

"I'd thought that myself," he said.

Aaron looked at the sheet he was holding. He had expected some tout or overt plea for money. Instead, what he saw was in Hebrew, not Yiddish or Polish. As he slowly worked his way through the words — it had been years since his bar mitzvah and he wasn't a religious person — he began to see that it was the Shema, the fundamental words of Jewish faith.

Shema Yisrael, Adonai Elohainu, Adonai Ehad!

"Hear, O Israel! Adonai is our God! Adonai is One!"

Below the poorly printed words was an address. Nothing else.

"Do you mind if I keep this?" Aaron asked.

Cohen laughed again.

"I think I can say with complete assurance that Lev would very much want you to have it."

Aaron thanked the young man, said his good-byes and did what he could to prepare for the cold that waited for him outside.

Chapter 8

Aaron could see the light fading through the windows of the stairwell, so he picked up his pace. Curfew was coming and he didn't have much time to get where he was going.

He smelled boiled cabbage as he swept down the stairs to the fourth floor. It reminded him immediately of his mother's best dish, stuffed cabbage, which he'd enjoyed regularly as a kid. The sauce had been both sour and sweet, and the aroma filled the house for the entire afternoon, as it was prepared.

Most of the ingredients for that homely meal were either absent entirely from Miasto, or were well beyond the means of a middle-class family, such as Aaron's had been. Aaron was hardly a good enough smuggler to assemble the whole recipe.

The third floor's stench held no pleasant memories. The pleasure tent that he had noticed on his way up was still and quiet now, its occupants sated or elsewhere. Below that, he passed through the men who gambled and shouted over the marble game on the ground floor, then out to the sidewalk and fresh, cold air.

Snow had begun to fall, but it was a pretty drift of flakes rather than a blizzard. Aaron was glad to see it and hoped that it would get worse, keeping German night patrols gathered by heaters rather than looking for Jews who might have missed curfew.

He was headed for a building that was only a few streets away, but he could now see that he'd misjudged the sun in the overcast. He had very little time. Again he pulled up his collar, buried his face in it and tried to walk quickly, though not conspicuously.

But it's hard to be in a subtle hurry.

Even as he kept his head down, he heard a voice calling to him from the curb.

"I hope you're close to home. Otherwise there's no way you're going to make it," a black-haired man in a gray uniform said. "Actually, I don't hope that. I hope you've got a long way ahead of you. Shall we, perhaps, walk together, untermenschen?"

Aaron didn't understand every word. His German wasn't very strong, leaving him to translate it into Yiddish in his head. But he gathered that he had not actually been stopped, since he had not heard the word "Halt!"

So, he made a mistake. He kept his eyes down and continued to walk, saying nothing

"Halt!"

There was no choice. Aaron stopped and waited as the German caught up the few steps he'd fallen behind.

"Do you not speak German or are you just stupid?" the scharfuhrer, *troop leader*, asked.

Aaron could understand that.

"I speak only a little German," he replied. His accent held a world of Yiddish inflection.

"Well, I'm sure you know what curfew means," the SS man said.

Aaron nodded.

"I'll put this in small words. When it is dark, I will shoot you. You understand that, right?"

Aaron nodded again.

"Say it out loud. It's very funny when you people try to talk."

"Ja."

"No, no. You forgot to say 'sir.' We can't allow that, can we? Let's try again." There was a delighted malice in the man's eyes and a hint of alcohol on his breath. "Say, 'I understand that when it is dark, you will shoot me, sir.'"

Aaron was easily insulted. He'd been in many fights because of it. He liked fighting. He suspected that if the urge to fight hadn't been born into him, his life would have followed a very different path. Perhaps he would have studied the Torah and God's laws, or been a baker or a bureaucrat. But he hadn't and he wasn't.

He was a Jew, however, and had spent enough time in shul to know that life was sacred above all. The scholars agreed that virtually all of God's laws to could be put aside if a life was at stake. A man can set aside the rules of kashrut if starvation is the other choice. A man must not steal, unless not stealing would mean death.

Bend, do not break.

Aaron kept his head down, perhaps even dropped it a little lower than before, doing his best to mumble out the words.

The German bellowed with laughter.

"Excellent!" the man said. He gave Aaron a friendly, though forceful, slap in the face and said, "You've been a good sport. I tell you what, why don't you run, and if you make it home, good for you. If you don't, well, I've already told you what will happen."

Aaron began to walk swiftly, but he refused to run, which made the German laugh.

"So proud! Well, use your time the way you want. It won't make much difference, really. I'm sure I'll see you soon."

A turn at the corner, another turn. The laughter faded and Aaron's sense of purpose returned. He broke into a trot when he was sure there was no patrol to see him.

Two more blocks; two more turns; another block; the light fading all the time; his sense of danger growing with the darkness.

Aaron reached a street that looked no different from the others he'd passed. A few shop fronts, mostly closed up — either for the night or forever, who could say? — apartment buildings of three to six floors, composed of brick and stone, indistinguishable in the dimness but for the street numbers. The building he was looking for had a number that he knew well. Over the last few weeks he had been a constant visitor.

An engine growled not far away. Aaron couldn't tell what direction it was coming from, but it sounded like it was getting closer. He began to run, each footfall sounding like thunder in his ears.

The door he needed was just in front of him, perhaps twenty meters away. He closed the distance at a pace that he couldn't have kept up for a second longer, reaching the doorway, entering and gasping, coughing, choking all at once. Lights from a car filtered though the glass in the top half of the door above Aaron. He lay on the floor unmoving.

The car passed.

Aaron's heart restarted.

He slowly rose to his feet and stepped down the building's unlit corridor, feeling for a door that led to darkened stairs and the basement.

He turned, closed the door behind him, and walked down toward a glow. After a few steps, he heard the bolt of a rifle snick.

"It's me," he said. "Put the gun away."

In lieu of an answer, the gun's barrel was pointed in a different direction.

Teitel was waiting there for him with three other men and lanterns. Behind the men was a ragged hole that had been ripped into the Aryan world.

Or more precisely, a short tunnel dug through brick and dirt that led into a small space below a warehouse that had been closed to prevent smuggling. Now, unbeknownst to the authorities, the warehouse was back in business, under new management.

"Things look good?" Aaron asked Teitel, who was smiling.

"You can see for yourself," he said proudly. "Everything's clear, thanks to the help from your friends on the other side."

"Friends might be a little strong. They didn't do it out of good will. They're hoping for a little return on their investment," Aaron said, lighting a cigarette, breathing the smoke deeply. "Do we have enough to pay for the shipment?"

Teitel pointed to two steamer trunks and a small satchel that sat in the dirt of the unfinished space. The lack of dust on them betrayed their recent arrival.

Aaron walked over, reached down and undid one of the clasps on a trunk, and then another, releasing the lid and allowing some of the lantern light to penetrate the box. The contents glittered in reply.

It was a strange collection of wealth. A kind of wealth only available to the poor. It was everything that could be stripped from a person while leaving the owner alive. Silk from a mother's wedding dress, a candelabrum that had passed generations in the same family, a necklace that had adorned the throat of a woman on a forgotten evening at the opera. A trunkful of such things.

"And the other trunk?" Aaron asked.

"Furs," one of the other men replied, "and the special package."

"And cash in the satchel?"

"What there is. And a little gold, mostly in coins, but a tooth filling or two, also," said the same man, whom Aaron knew only as Boris.

"Let's hope it's not a biblical trade," laughed a squat man with an unintended beard. His name was Dov.

When nobody else laughed he added, "You know, from the Torah. An eye for an eye? A tooth for a tooth?"

Thin smiles all around.

Aaron looked directly at Teitel.

"And the special items?"

"At the bottom of the second trunk. When are we expecting your friends?" Teitel asked Aaron.

"They don't have the same curfew. They may want to wait a while longer, until it's been dark for a while and people have settled in for the night."

"Well, it's okay, I brought cards," Teitel said. "And this."

He pulled out a bottle of slivovitz that had been hit hard already. Probably the one he'd shared earlier with Aaron.

The group gathered around one of the trunks, using it as a table, and Teitel dealt cards as the bottle passed from hand to hand, mouth to mouth. The air in the little space grew stale as they played and drank, its only escape through the hole in the wall.

A sound of something scraping on brick or rock caught Aaron's attention and his gaze snapped toward the wall. Another scrape was followed immediately by a metallic click that Aaron knew was the sound of a gun safety snapping off. That sound came from his side of the hole, so Aaron kept his eyes locked in front of him, poised to leap forward or fall to the floor depending on what he saw or heard next.

Chapter 8

Dust settled down into the lanterns' light. A boot, a leg and then a second boot followed it quickly. Next came a voice.

"May I come in?" the woman in the boots asked.

The voice filled Aaron with relief and a joy that he kept entirely from his face and his voice.

"Please do," Aaron said evenly.

The woman who was revealed when she ducked under the ledge belonged on a propaganda poster drawn to Goebbels' personal specifications. Her eyes were Arctic blue, but more sympathetic than that. Her cheekbones were high, but not so high as to give her a Slavic look. Her lips pouted just a bit, sensuous. Her brow was high and clear, her hair edged toward the platinum side of golden, drawn back in a businesslike fashion.

Goebbels' only quibble? Perhaps she was a little short of his ideals, standing 5-feet 3-inches tall. It was a fault that most men forgave her easily.

"Good to see you, Yelena," Teitel said, walking over and kissing both of her cheeks.

"You, too, Lech," she said, putting down the messenger's bag she carried.

The other men nodded their hellos but said nothing. They continued to stare.

"Where's everyone else?" Teitel asked.

"They're being careful, taking different routes. Something has the Germans stirred up," Yelena said. "But I doubt it'll be too much longer. It's fine, though. Gives me time to work out some details with Aaron."

She turned to face him.

"And I have a message to pass on, as well."

She picked up her bag again.

"We can use one of the rooms upstairs," Aaron responded levelly, though his pulse picked up a beat or two. "I've got a few things stored there. The rest of you can stay down here in case Yelena's crew shows up with the supplies."

Teitel nodded. The right corner of his mouth twitched slightly. Aaron chose to ignore it and led Yelena out of the basement, leaving behind the smell of rotting cement.

The building they stood in was less crowded than most and, perhaps because of the darkness of the halls, everyone had retreated behind their doors for the night.

Aaron felt ahead for the door he wanted. A hand snaked its way into his other palm. He gripped it tightly, its slight warmth enough to thaw out the part of him that remained frozen between Yelena's visits.

He found the metal door and opened it smoothly and quickly with a key from his pocket. He had to drop Yelena's hand for a few moments while he did it. Once they were inside, he replaced that fingers' touch with his arms, his lips, his body. She pressed back against him and their combined weight shut the door more loudly than they would have liked, startling them and forcing them apart for a moment.

Yelena recovered first.

"Damn. My nerves didn't need that."

"Don't worry too much, everyone here is used to our banging by now. It's hard to take down a wall quietly, even if it's in a basement," Aaron said, and now he smiled. He was pretty sure the last time he'd done so was more than a month before, when he'd last seen his wife.

"I hope you're right. Every time we do this, I'm scared from the minute the planning starts until … Actually, I'm not sure when I'm not scared anymore."

There were several cots in the room, she picked one and sat. Aaron sat down next to her. They could both feel the wooden rails give a little, despite her small size and Aaron's ever-shrinking weight. He held her. She held him.

"If I'm not worried about the Gestapo showing up at my door, then I'm worried about you in here," Yelena said. Aaron could feel her shaking her head, negating everything she'd seen and felt over the last year and a half.

"How are things outside the ghetto?" Aaron asked, trying for a lighter tone, though he didn't feel light.

"It all looks the same, but everything feels different. It's all so empty, the shelves in the stores, the streets themselves."

She shook her head again.

"But, speaking of the world outside, I brought you some things I think you probably need."

She reached her hand into her bag.

"I'm sure I need them. I can't think of a single thing I don't need," Aaron said with a bitter laugh. "Neither can anyone else I know."

Yelena pulled out a thick sweater, two warm shirts and even a few pairs of underwear.

"You would have made a terrific Jewish mother," Aaron said. "Bringing underwear to the ghetto."

He pitched his voice to a gravely falsetto. "'At least when the Germans shot him, he was wearing clean underwear!'"

She picked up the tone.

"'If he wasn't, I'd have died of embarrassment.'"

They laughed softly together. It was a comedy routine they had shared since they'd met in a bar years before, when Aaron had begun his training in the Zendarmerie, far from Miasto.

Yelena Gorska had been bored but well educated. Aaron had been handsome and exotic — at least by the standards of the small town where they found each other. There were a thousand things they shared in common and more that divided them. All of it was entirely beside the point. Within hours, it was obvious to both of them that they were in love.

Yelena got an apartment with Aaron's pay and he visited as often as he could during training. They called each other man and wife though no ceremony was ever held, socialized little and told only their closest friends. By then Aaron was estranged from his family. Yelena's parents had both died young.

His training complete, the couple took a small house in the town where Aaron was assigned as a gendarme. A few years later it was there that the war found them.

Aaron became a soldier and told Yelena to go to Miasto, which seemed far enough from the front to offer some protection. She moved into a neighborhood he knew well, though he'd never lived there. When Aaron had been dumped into the city's ghetto, he was able to contact her through a mix of bribes and telephone calls.

It was a strange business, but even as the walls had gone up, some lines had been left uncut. Everyone assumed that either they wouldn't last, or they were monitored. Aaron had worked the phones carefully, using only the homespun code that had developed over the months of German occupation to ask his questions.

Aaron didn't understand where Yelena's courage came from. It was Yelena who had suggested that they work together to get supplies into the ghetto. It was she who bought favors from the Blue Police — Polish constables who had been co-opted by the Nazis. Many of the Blue Police liked the Germans as much as the Jews did, and they were more than happy to be corrupted by the beautiful woman who cried so pitifully about her husband.

Such long and lonely nights she must have, they thought.

And, at least until the tightening noose utterly strangled the Jews, the operation was highly profitable. Yelena learned that she had quite the head for business, making it grow and bringing in ever more supplies.

The smuggling would have been impossible if the Germans themselves were less corrupt. Even now, there was money to be pillaged from the Jews, so Nazis at all levels pitched in where they could, sometimes by looking the other way, sometimes by selling military stores. Greed, it seemed, made a better motivator than hatred.

Yelena was hardly the only one in business on the Polish side, of course. Men like Jaruzelski/Gersh had their own angles, and the competition was, at times, violent.

But the fact was that Yelena thrived, and because of it, Aaron and others survived.

This evening, so far, that meant clean underwear, and later there would be potatoes, bread, liquor, cigarettes, maybe even some meat. Oil for cooking, a little fuel for heating, perhaps.

And special tonight, something a little more dangerous: guns.

"Maybe I should try the sweater on," Aaron suggested. "See if it fits."

"Maybe you should."

Of course, in order to make sure the fit was right, he needed to remove his coat, and then a layer or two more. It was enough to reveal the shape of his body, even though there was hardly more than starlight filling the room.

"Oh my God," she said. "How can you possibly look thinner than the last time I saw you?"

Aaron felt slightly ashamed, though he knew she spoke only out of concern.

"I eat better than most," he said. "Thanks to you. Let's not talk about it, we haven't much time, anyway."

She reached for him.

Afterward, it was a matter of quickly putting back on the few clothes they'd taken off. The room was freezing and there was no time to spend drowsing in each other's arms.

As Aaron reached for his coat, Yelena surveyed him one more time in the dim light. She thought she saw something in his posture beyond the hunger, the pressure and the unrelenting grimness of the life he lived while she was on the other side of the wall.

"Got something on your mind?" she asked, trying to keep her tone light.

He laughed.

"What, you mean besides the ghetto and the Nazis?"

"Besides that."

"I can't think of anything."

He smiled.

"Come on. I can see it," she said.

"We should get back downstairs. No way to know when the others will arrive," Aaron replied.

She grabbed his arm as he turned toward the door.

"You might as well tell me. What am I going to do, worry?"

Aaron couldn't think of a way to argue against that.

"The Judenrat's got me investigating a murder," he said.

Yelena looked genuinely shocked.

"A murder? In the middle of this massacre?"

"One of the Jewish Police turned up dead late last night, maybe early this morning. I actually stumbled across him on my way home. Anyway, my father apparently told Zimmerman what I used to do for a living," Aaron said. "So, they dropped it in my lap."

"So what? Why would you care?"

"I don't, but their ultimatum was pretty good. They threatened to shut us down." He took her hand and squeezed it. "There are a lot of reasons I wouldn't want that to happen."

"Me, too," she said, squeezing back.

"Actually, you might be able to help, if you're willing."

"Willing is such a strong word … "

He pinched her and she yelped.

"Okay, okay," she giggled. "What do you need?"

"I'm told the man who was killed — his name was Lev Berson — was involved in some kind of smuggling," Aaron said. "He was partners with Tamislaw Jaruzelski, who turns out to have also been named Gersh."

"What? I don't think I get all that."

"It's confusing the hell out of me, so I'd be surprised if you did. Turns out the Jaruzelski we were dealing with was also a man named Gersh who worked in the Jewish Police," Aaron said. "I have no idea which identity came first."

"Why don't you ask him?"

"He's dead. Just a few hours ago."

"Killed by the same person?"

"No, and that's one thing I'm sure of."

Aaron explained what had happened at Breslaw Hospital.

"Jesus," Yelena said. To Aaron, she sounded nearly out of breath.

"Yeah, it's been quite a day."

"Jesus," she said again. "I have to say, I was wrong. You look remarkably good for a day like that."

She paused.

"Aaron, I think it's time for you to leave Miasto," she said. "Come with me, tonight."

"You know I want to," Aaron replied. "God knows this is the last place I want to be."

"So, come with me."

"I can't yet. Soon."

"Soon?"

"I promise," Aaron said. "Let's finish what we started, then I'll go."

He sat up.

"Are you sure Andrusz will be here tonight?" he asked.

"He promised," Yelena said.

"And we need him? I would have preferred to keep this to just the normal crew."

"Unfortunately, he's the one with the connections," Yelena replied. "If you want guns, you need him."

"Okay, I trust you."

"I should hope so!" She played affronted. "I don't know many other women who would do something like this for their husbands."

"I didn't mean it that way!" Aaron said quickly, not getting the joke. Words stumbled out of his mouth. "Life behind this wall ... it doesn't make any sense. The good guys are the bad guys ... Hell, there aren't any good guys. Nothing, nobody is ever clean."

Yelena reached for his hand.

"I love you, Aaron," she said, trying to quiet him. "Don't doubt that."

"I don't. I love you, too."

"Even when you don't need something?" she said, teasing again.

He took a deep breath, even laughed a little.

"Even then," he said.

They took one more moment for themselves, slowly breaking their embrace. It was time to re-enter the war.

Chapter 8

When Teitel saw them come down the stairs to the basement, he didn't bother to hide his somewhat mocking smile.

"Were you able to agree on the terms?" he asked.

"Yes, I think everything worked out quite satisfactorily," Yelena said.

"Oh. That sounds a little disappointing. I always hope for better than satisfactory with most of my deals," Teitel said. "I guess you take what you can get in wartime."

The others chuckled. Aaron colored slightly. Yelena's skin retained its normal whiter shade of pale.

"No signal from anyone, yet?" Aaron asked.

"We haven't heard anything. Not a peep," Boris replied.

"Why don't we get comfortable?" Aaron suggested, huddling down against one wall.

Teitel brought out a second bottle, schnapps this time. Yelena passed around a pack of cigarettes. Everyone smoked and drank quietly for a few minutes.

"I should have brought sandwiches," Yelena said.

"It would have been nice. Or a kielbasa. I haven't had a decent kielbasa in a million years," Boris said, licking his lips.

"Treif!" Teitel said.

"You'd really quibble over a little pork at this point? What's wrong with you?"

Boris' eyes were wide in mock amazement.

"Don't mock a holy man," Aaron said. "Even if he's a holy hypocrite."

Teitel struggled to lean over far enough to swat Aaron, but couldn't quite make it and gave up.

The room was quiet for a little while. One of the lanterns sputtered and went out.

Aaron turned to Yelena.

"How much longer until we should be worried?" he asked.

"Soon," she said.

One more round of cigarettes, and then came the distinct sound of rubble crumbling under boots. A voice called out.

"Yelena?"

"Here."

An enormous man bent nearly double and poked his head through the hole. Seeing no obvious signs of danger, he came under the ledge and stood up in the dim room.

"Everything good?" he asked.

"We're fine here. Start bringing the stuff through," Yelena said.

The tall Pole climbed back up and soon returned with several others who carried sacks containing flour and potatoes and even onions. A short queue of wheelbarrows followed with more produce, beets, turnips, parsnips. All and everything was welcomed by the Jews in the basement, their eyes nearly as ravenous as their stomachs.

Finally, luxury items. The cigarettes, the booze. Tins of meat, some of it no doubt spoiled. It would be eaten anyway.

Last and most dangerous, guns.

Not many. Rusty rifles with a few rounds of ammunition each. The Polish Army hadn't been the best equipped in Europe in 1939 — it contained many brave, gallant cavalry officers, after all — but the weapons that entered the basement looked as if they'd been old in the previous war.

"No muskets?" Teitel joked.

"Don't worry. These are just as likely to blow up in your face," replied one of the Poles who was going back up for a last load.

Finally, the procession ended and the room was nearly full.

Chapter 8

Yelena and two of her men came and stood over the chests the Jewish team had assembled. Aaron handed her the satchel with cash first.

"How much?"

"All told? About one hundred thousand zloty. Plus the gold," Teitel said. "I can't give you a better number because I don't know what gold's worth in the real world, anymore."

Yelena spilled the gold out into her hand. Teitel hadn't been joking earlier; along with coins of several sizes, there were a few teeth with gold and silver fillings.

"Good," Yelena said. "And the trunks?"

Teitel opened them.

Inside one was the gold menorah, some other gold items and many that were silver. The menorah might have come from a rich family's house or been taken from a synagogue as Jews fled the German advance. Every item bore unreadable memories that stretched back over generations.

Inside the other chest was the rich pile of furs, stoles and coats. Enough to keep the cold at bay even on a journey to the North Pole. Most of what was there could have been mistaken for new. The labels were all from the best Jewish furriers.

Everything had been given to Aaron's gang a piece at a time, to pay for a few potatoes, maybe enough flour for a week's worth of bread. People bought what little they could with everything they had.

Yelena nodded.

"This is fine, though I think I could probably live without the furs."

"Oh, please, even members of the master race need to stay warm," Teitel said. "But there's one more item I want to show you."

He pulled back the bottom fur and picked up the glittering thing beneath. Aaron nodded as he saw it.

Yelena and the other Poles were transfixed. It was a gold plate suspended from a chain as if it were a necklace, except this bauble was the size of a small breastplate from a suit of armor. It was encrusted by gems of many kinds, and Hebrew letters were picked out in gold filigree.

"Holy shit!" one of the Polish men said.

"Very holy shit," Aaron said wryly.

"What is it?" Yelena asked?

Teitel explained.

"It's a ceremonial covering for a Torah. This one was made a long time ago in a town that might not even exist anymore," he said. "Gorgeous, isn't it?"

"Well, thank you for throwing it in!" a huge blond Pole — Andrusz — said, laughing.

"Not exactly," Aaron said. "This is a separate deal. This isn't just for a few groceries and a some rusty carbines."

"You need those groceries," the Pole pointed out, while Yelena stood quietly aside.

"Yes, but this is special. There isn't anything else like it in the whole ghetto," Teitel said, speaking directly to the big man.

"Okaaaay." Andrusz tortured the word. "What do you want for it?"

"Guns," Aaron said. "Real guns. Ones that'll fire more than two shots without jamming. And ammunition that's more of a danger to the Germans than it is to us," Aaron said.

Yelena nodded.

"I spoke with Aaron about this before you got here, Andrusz," Yelena said. "I thought you might be able to help get this done."

"Very hard to find," Andrusz said, thoughtfully.

"Impossible?" Aaron asked.

Andrusz concentrated for a second.

"Not impossible," he said slowly. "No, not impossible, but nearly. How many would you need?"

"Fifty."

"No way. Maybe ten. Maybe."

"Thirty."

"I might be able to make it twenty-five, but it's going to cost more than one nice piece of gold," the Pole said, though his eyes wouldn't leave the object.

"We didn't mention that it comes with two matching crowns that sit on the handles of the Torah scroll?" Teitel asked. He loved to haggle and always kept something in reserve.

"You didn't," Andrusz said, considering.

"Do it," Yelena said.

"I'll need some time," Andrusz said.

Aaron nodded, but betrayed no emotion.

"Good!" Teitel said. "Tomorrow."

"Tomorrow? You're insane."

"I might have forgotten to mention that there's also a cloth-of-gold covering that goes over the whole scroll. It has rubies on it." Teitel smiled openly now. He loved to see the avarice on a mark's face.

"Tomorrow," Andrusz said. He nodded very slowly to himself. "It should be possible."

"Good," Aaron said. "Same time."

"Same time," he agreed.

There was nothing else to be said. The Polish men picked up the trunk with the menorah but left the furs and sacred items to be collected the following night. Yelena kept the satchel.

Everyone shook hands all around, and if Yelena's hand lingered briefly in Aaron's, no one was willing to acknowledge it.

Chapter 9

Aaron woke with a start at the first pale rays of dawn.

He reached out his left hand and shook Yelena awake.

"What?" shouted the surprised voice of Lech Teitel.

Full consciousness hit Aaron like a derailed boxcar. With it came the knowledge that Yelena was once again on the other side of the city.

"It's light," Aaron said gruffly, trying to hide his embarrassment. "We should get moving."

Teitel turned red-rimmed eyes to Aaron and then to Boris and Dov, asleep in the other cots. His eyes slammed shut again and he rolled over onto his other side. Aaron kicked him and then leaned in the other direction and shook Boris awake.

When the man's black eyes blinked open, all Aaron said was "Sun's up."

Boris kicked Dov in turn.

Cigarettes and a dash of plum brandy usually dispelled the men's grogginess. But today they were able to add recently fresh bread to their usual "Balkan breakfast." In fact, to celebrate last night's success, Teitel suggested opening a few tins of a mystery stew that had been intended as German field rations.

Dov voiced concern when he looked down into the can after its top had been removed.

"Do you think if I say a brucha over it, it'll become kosher?" he asked.

"Try it and see what happens," Teitel said. "But if you decide that's not good enough, I'll be happy to eat yours."

Aaron stuck two fingers into the gray glop and scooped something unrecognizable into his mouth. His taste buds were no help in unraveling the ingredients in the enigmatic mush, but the solidity of the food as it hit his stomach was both gratifying and a little nauseating.

Aaron spared a moment for guilt at eating so well while surrounded by so many hungry people — but just a moment. He knew plenty of others who lived better in the ghetto by doing worse — collaborators, extortionists, thieves and murderers.

Some of his best clients were men and women who still enjoyed tattered remnants of their lives of plenty, or had become "rich" through the positions they'd wrangled for themselves at the Judenrat. They took bribes from the poor for everything from ration cards to jobs.

Aaron didn't love them, but he took their money just like everyone else's. He used the prices he charged them to help subsidize everyone else, as well as to provide for his own comfort. What he charged a rich man for a bottle of slivovitz was enough to bring in kilo after kilo of bread.

And being rich, or even corrupt, didn't necessarily make someone stupidly selfish. The Torah raiment that was being exchanged for the guns came from a thief who understood that money wouldn't be enough to save his family from the Germans.

Aaron knew that the twenty-five rifles he expected tonight wouldn't make much difference against the Werhmacht, but it was better to have them than to be completely defenseless. What he'd seen the day before at Breslaw Hospital added to a certainty that had been growing for several months. Though the ghetto might seem like Hell, Jews would not be spending all eternity here. The ghetto, with its starvation and terrors, was merely a stopping point on the way to the real thing.

Chapter 9

So, the twenty-five rifles Yelena brought would, he hoped, become one hundred in week, two hundred in a month.

In two months?

Aaron had no idea. By then it might be entirely too late. The battle might have been fought and lost. Still, he hoped each rifle would kill a German soldier and send a message to the Reich. Like the Roman emperor Titus at Masada, Hitler would learn that Jews do not go quietly.

Would providing weapons to a doomed resistance save his soul from the sin of eating while children starved? Aaron knew it wouldn't, but he worked hard to convince himself otherwise.

The curfew had ended at first light. By the time Aaron reached the building's front door, several hand carts and other conveyances were waiting. It was important to get them loaded and on their way quickly, before the operation was spotted by the authorities.

Aaron looked at his young couriers; grubby boys who sat on bicycle rickshaws, all of which had been built out of spare parts. To earn what amounted to loose change, the boys moved any cargo they could find from one side of town to the other, including passengers.

Aaron was familiar with most of the boys who greeted him, either from working with them before or seeing them around the neighborhood. Some were working as the only support for their families, he knew, and many were simply orphans who had found a way to survive. They were all, without exception, dirty. They wore tweed caps and clothes that were raggedly patched with varying degrees of success. They seemed bright-eyed and eager in the early light, knowing that they would be fed some of what they transported.

"Chaim, you're first," Aaron called to the boy nearest. Dov had come up behind Aaron and the two men quickly loaded several sacks aboard the rickshaw. When everything was set, Aaron handed over a thick slice of bread to the driver and asked, "You know where you're going?"

"Thirty-two fifty-one Lezno Street."

"Good. Go."

The next rickshaw pulled up and was piled high. The driver got a different address to go with his slice of bread.

And then the next.

And the next.

"Police!" cried the boy who was the furthest away from the makeshift loading dock. He mounted his bike and, in a panic, began to pedal. Other boys tried to follow suit but got tangled together before they'd made it a hundred feet. Curtains were drawn in a hundred windows, with only a corner left open for spying.

"Germans?" Aaron shouted to a boy who could see around the corner.

"Jewish."

Aaron could feel himself relax somewhat. He was comfortable that the patrol would be happy to take a bribe. Especially from the man who was supposed to be finding the killer of one of their own.

Aaron was even more confident when he saw that the man leading the patrol was Shemtov, one of the cops who had found Berson's body. A personal connection would work even better than greed.

Shemtov took his time as he walked up the block with an officer who Aaron didn't recognize. The big policeman made a show of studying each young face he passed. He nodded slightly and in a way that told each of them that they would be remembered.

Finally done with his hard looks, Shemtov walked straight up to Aaron, who stood on the stoop of the building.

Shemtov showed no sign of having met Aaron before.

"What's going on here?" Shemtov asked, speaking in the exact same manner as every other cop down through history.

Aaron had used that voice many times himself when he was a gendarme. It was a tone that could make a saint feel sinful and a newborn want back into the womb.

"I'd be happy to explain, officer," Aaron said.

"Of course you would."

"Perhaps we could speak privately?" Aaron suggested. There was a form to be observed, after all.

Shemtov nodded.

"Ciarnakow, stay here and make sure everyone behaves."

"Yes, sir."

Aaron imagined he could see the second officer licking his lips at the promise of a bribe. What would it be? Cash? Something even better?

Shemtov took Aaron roughly by the shoulder and dragged him halfway down the block. Aaron noticed curtains twitch to get a better view of the action. But if the people behind them were hoping to hear anything, they were disappointed. Both men spoke in near whispers, their heads close together.

"Have you found him?" Shemtov asked.

"The man who killed Berson? No."

"Well, what have you been doing since yesterday? I figured if you were back to your usual business — yes, I know what you do — you must have found Berson's killer already."

Shemtov hadn't released his grip on Aaron's shoulder and now tightened it.

If Aaron felt the pinch, he didn't show it. When he replied, his voice held no strain.

"A prior engagement that had to be kept," he said evenly. "Nothing I could have done overnight, anyway."

The grip stayed tight.

"Did you find Gersh?" Shemtov asked.

"I did," Aaron said. "He said he wasn't with Berson when it happened, of course. And he said he was injured in another incident entirely, meaning that he left Berson alone for the rest of the shift."

Aaron saw no reason to reveal Gersh's alter ego as a Polish national.

"Did he say anything else?" Shemtov asked.

"He didn't have much of a chance before he was taken outside and shot."

"He was killed at Breslaw?"

Aaron reached for a cigarette from the inside of his coat. When he opened the top buttons he realized his fingers weren't frozen and that the air allowed inside the coat felt almost warm. After offering the pack to Shemtov, who took three, Aaron slowly nodded.

"Shit," Shemtov said quietly.

Aaron agreed and helped light one of Shemtov's cigarettes. Both men drew deeply.

A minute passed.

"Any progress at all?" Shemtov asked.

"Some. You know anything about Berson's rabbi? I found one of these flyers in his room."

Aaron handed it over.

Shemtov looked at it carefully. His lips followed along silently as he read the prayer.

"Amen," he said, and after a pause, "I've seen a few of the flyers around the station. I'm not sure it was Berson who brought them in, though now I guess it must have been. From what I've heard, the congregation is run by some kind of holy man from the hinterlands. His people were transported here from the back of the beyond. Very strict sect, a little secretive."

"And they're reaching out for new parishioners?"

"I guess so," Shemtov said with a shrug. "Maybe they don't have enough for a minyan anymore. They wouldn't be the only ones."

"I guess not," Aaron said. "They're my next stop. If Berson was so religious, his rabbi might know what he was up to."

"I guess it's worth a shot."

Aaron turned to go.

A rough hand stopped him, grabbing the same shoulder it had so recently released.

"One more thing."

"What?"

"This," Shemtov said, pointing to the boys and the pile up of their vehicles. "I can't just let you go without paying the tax. People would be suspicious."

"Seriously?"

"Well, I guess I could just let it go, and we can tell everyone here that you're working with us."

Shemtov's smile was ugly.

Aaron sighed.

"Take what you want then."

The two men walked back to where the second officer was standing.

"We've reached an agreement," Shemtov told the other man.

"Oh?"

"Yes, it turns out all of this is part of Mr. Kaminski's charity work," Shemtov said. "He's known around town as quite a humanitarian. I'm surprised you haven't heard of him."

“Very surprising.”

“He’s very, very generous.”

Shemtov slapped Aaron on the back. Aaron gritted his teeth and displayed them in a smile filled with so much acid that it could have burned through the armor of a German tank.

After one more slap, the two officers borrowed a cloth sack and began to go shopping. In a few minutes, the sack was full and some of the most precious commodities, including a dozen eggs and two cartons of cigarettes, were in it.

But still they didn’t leave. Instead, the policemen walked to opposite corners of the block and stood looking out.

“What are you doing?” Aaron asked Shemtov.

“We’re a full-service department,” Shemtov said. “You get value for what you pay for, which in this case is safe passage. So, get this stuff out of here quickly, before I have to be somewhere else.”

The bicycle rickshaws had finally been untangled and, seeing how things were, the boys began to line up again to pick up the supplies.

Dov and Boris did most of the loading now, while Aaron sat on the stoop thinking about his next move.

Sacks and cartons were placed on the rickshaws as quickly as possible. The ritual was repeated until there were no more rickshaws and the supplies were running thin. Only the rusty rifles hadn’t been moved from the building. There were some things even the Jewish Police would have a hard time overlooking.

As both a thank you and a plea for silence, the smugglers left a large pile of supplies, from flour to fuel, in the hall of the building they were using. Aaron trusted the woman who led the building’s house committee with ensuring everything was parceled out fairly.

After the boys were gone, Shemtov offered Aaron a mockery of a salute, grabbed his bulky package and walked off with his partner. Not even 8 a.m. and he'd already done a good day's work.

Aaron took his leave of Teitel and the others with the promise they would rendezvous back at the building that night. Dov would stay in the basement, guarding the guns they already had, as well as the Torah vestments.

Aaron took a small sack of the remaining goods for his own, intending to ingratiate himself with Berson's rabbi by way of an offering. If he walked quickly, he would arrive just after morning prayers.

Chapter 10

Berson's shul was located on a street without a synagogue. Instead, it was lined with stables and funeral parlors. The mix was no coincidence. The primary use of horse-drawn carts in the Jewish district was to haul away bodies.

It was later than Aaron had hoped it would be when he arrived. The walk had taken longer than he'd anticipated, and the streets had filled early with hungry people hoping to find something they could afford from the various vendors. The selection, as ever, was poor, with bread made partly from talc and sawdust to make up for a shortage of flour.

Aaron had noticed a stand or two where his own runners had already made their deliveries. He received a wink from several of the proprietors and returned a smile. In more than one case, he was shocked to see how much the prices for his goods had been marked up. But then, a carrot that showed hardly any sign of rot was a true rarity in the ghetto.

Starvation and malnutrition in Miasto weren't caused solely by lack of quantity. Just as serious was the quality of the bread and produce. The Judenrat was responsible for using money collected in taxes to buy in supplies. They placed orders with both Polish and German contractors and, often enough, the food would arrive.

The problem was that the food delivered was made from the scraps of the German empire: turnips that were unripe or overripe, misshapen or too small, flour that wasn't entirely flour. Worse, entire shipments were often spoiled or contaminated in some other way.

The challenge to the ghetto's cooks, stomachs and doctors was considerable. Many people ended up on the street where Aaron now found himself because of contamination and spoilage.

Sheinin & Sons was the biggest of the ghetto's funeral homes. Aaron could see that business was good. Hearses and carts were queued up and a funeral procession was just beginning its journey to the large cemetery on the border of the ghetto.

The cemetery was no longer just a place for the dead, but, as the only open space now permitted to the citizens of the sealed district, it was also used as a park. Unfortunately, its capacity was limited and the supply of newly dead did not seem to be. It would not be long before bodies would need to be piled on top of each other, in addition to the mass graves that had already been dug for those who died in total anonymity.

Still, the rituals were carried out with care for those who could afford them. The group in front of Aaron put on a fair show of mourning. Both men and women wore respectable black, the men's lapels were torn to demonstrate their grief, the women's heads covered. The family was not, perhaps, overly religious, as none of the men had side locks and the women wore their own hair. Still, it was a distinctly Jewish affair in that the men, women and children were humiliated by wearing the armbands the Nazis had forced on them even as they buried their loved one.

An old woman — perhaps now a widow — was at the center of the procession. She was supported by those around her, including a middle-aged man who Aaron decided was her son. The woman herself appeared to have crumpled under the weight of her grief. She would be joining her husband soon, Aaron thought to himself.

Chapter 10

A beautifully appointed hearse led the procession. The wagon was constructed largely of engraved glass with the Star of David prominently etched into it, along with a few words of Hebrew prayer. The rest of the wagon was black, of course, the casket inside a simple pine box — the most elaborate coffin allowed under Jewish law. Drawing the hearse was a horse in shockingly good condition. Certainly not fat, but neither were its ribs prominent. It was brown with a white star on its forehead, and clearly somebody loved it very much.

Aaron was also fairly certain it would be a good advertisement for business. Everyone who saw it would remember.

After the funeral had passed him by, Aaron checked the number on the mortuary's building. It wasn't the one he was looking for. Next-door was the stable where the still-vigorous horse probably spent its nights. From what Aaron could tell, they must have been lonely ones. There was hardly a whiff of manure on the air as he walked past.

He had to peer carefully at every structure on the street. None of their numbers were prominently displayed. When he reached under his coat for a cigarette, he was surprised to find sweat under his arms. The wind had been defanged, swirling well above zero degrees centigrade. Even the gray of the sky was a lighter shade — brighter than the gray of German uniforms. It was weather that boded better times soon to come. Aaron willed himself to believe it, but failed.

Finishing his cigarette, he reached into the bag he was carrying and tore himself off a crust of bread. Young eyes caught the motion and followed hand to mouth. Faster than thought, short legs sprang to action, propelling a girl toward the sack Aaron carried at great speed. As she ran past she snatched it from his lightly clenched hand.

His reflexes were good, though. One of his arms shot out and grabbed the girl before she had a chance to get out of reach, catching her by the collar of her coat. She tried to shrug it off but, luckily for Aaron, it was buttoned, holding her up just long enough for him to wrap an arm around her middle.

She struggled for another minute, quickly exhausting herself. He looked down at her and saw that she couldn't have been much more than eight years old. Her hair was dirty, stringy, even matted in places. The eyes in her smudged face stood out, piercing green. To look at her, it would have been impossible to judge her either Aryan or Jew. And yet here she was on the Jewish side of the wall.

Aaron found himself somewhere between fury at the little thief and pity for the little girl. As his adrenalin cooled, the pity won out. He reached into the bag and pulled out what remained of the small loaf of bread.

"This what you wanted?"

She didn't speak. She simply looked numb, defeated. She didn't try to move, she didn't reach for the bread. She waited to be punished.

"You have parents? Brothers or sisters?"

No answer except the beginning of tears.

Aaron was not in a position to help every little girl in the ghetto. The Judenrat itself was in no position to do so. There was simply not enough of anything and the need was beyond knowing.

But that was the larger view and the girl in his arms was very small.

His firm grip turned into something else. Tears reached his eyes. It was too much. It was all too much. Perhaps his soft reaction was because of his lack of sleep or the hunger that gnawed at him despite his lavish breakfast. Maybe it was the funeral procession, which trailed behind it the reminder that death had once been treated with respect. Whatever it was, all he could think of was how close this little one was to her own funeral.

And why?

No why.

He knew the outcome of the girl's struggle on the streets was inevitable. But he could delay it a little.

He put the child down. She did not move.

He took the sack and put it in her hands, deciding to keep the loaf of bread he had already pulled out. She sagged a bit with the weight.

Finally, her eyes met his and she said one word.

"Thanks."

She ran.

Feeling both infinitely better and worse, Aaron continued looking for his address. He didn't bother to see where the girl went. His solace was another cigarette pulled from his jacket and sucked down in just a few breaths.

He found the place he was looking for in just another minute. Rather than one of the funeral homes, it was a simple stable. The sign above a wide doorway — clearly intended for wagons to pass through — read "Hershkowitz & Sons." Horses harnessed to a cart were painted to the right of the owner's name. The paint was fading but the image was still clear, with touches of bright color still to be seen in the team's tack. It had no air of a religious place, any hints of holiness cleverly hidden from the casual eye.

Up close, Aaron finally found what he was looking for. Synagogues were traditionally proudly marked, inscriptions and holy symbols welcoming in the congregation. But this was a sign for a different time, pride giving way to discretion.

On a human-sized door to the right of the larger one, Aaron saw shallow carving. The words were the same ones he had seen on Berson's flyers; the Shema, the declaration of God's existence and singularity in the universe He had created. A statement of belief and words of courage.

There was no one outside the building and both doors were closed tight. Aaron approached slowly, giving anyone behind the windows a chance to see him and decide that he was neither German nor an obvious threat. He knocked on the smaller door and waited. A minute, two. No sound from inside. He replaced his knock with a bang and waited again. One minute, two. He saw no one come to the window, he heard no sound from inside.

Should he stay? Even with the relative warmth, the sweat under his arms was beginning to cool uncomfortably. Aaron stamped his feet and thought again. If he was stymied here, what should his next step be? There was no time to question every member of the Jewish police. Germans that Berson might have encountered on the night of his death — who might have caused his death — were unavailable for questioning. Perhaps he could return to the building where Berson had lived and hope to find additional roommates with a grudge. Or maybe he should canvass the neighborhood where the body was found.

After another half hour, Aaron felt he couldn't wait any longer.

As he turned to leave, he caught the sound of a cane on cobblestones. Using it was an older man with a white beard and every sign of deep religious faith in the mode of the small towns and villages of the Polish countryside. Of course, since borders were known to be fluid in this part of Europe, he could also have been from the Ukraine, Russia, Lithuania, Estonia or Latvia.

Chapter 10

The rabbi — he could be no one else — wore a black hat made of beaver fur and the silver hair beneath it shone. Payos hung over the stems of the glasses perched on his nose. So perfectly did the glasses reflect an air of study, they seemed almost an affectation. He peered over them to examine Aaron.

"No service this morning, rabbi?" Aaron asked.

The man didn't bother to deny what he was.

"I am sorry to say that you missed it. We begin early, as the sun rises," the rabbi replied. "I'm on my way back from breakfast with my wife."

The voice matched the man in every regard. It was rich, it was full, it was filled with Yiddish, even as the words were Polish. It reflected a lifetime of deep thought.

"You are certainly welcome to join us tomorrow morning, if you wish," the rabbi said, a little more warmly. "We would be very pleased if you did."

"Actually, rabbi, today I'm just as happy to find you alone," Aaron said. "I'd like to talk to you about a man in your congregation."

"And who is that?"

"Lev Berson," Aaron said, his voice giving nothing away.

There was less than a moment's hesitation. If Aaron hadn't been looking for it, he was unlikely to have noticed anything amiss. As it was, it seemed to the former gendarme as if the rabbi considered claiming not to know Berson at all.

Instead, the old man shuddered as if a cold wind had struck him, though the day was perfectly calm.

"Hmmm. Well, there's no reason to talk out here, in the cold." the rabbi said. "Come. I think I can manage a cup of tea. At least we can agree to call it that, yes?"

Now he smiled and felt in his coat pocket for a key. Finding it, he inserted it into the lock, turned and pushed on the door with a shoulder. Grudgingly, and only under a persistent assault, the door yielded.

The barn was cold and empty, some straw was scattered about on the floor and in the vacant stalls. A few chairs filled the center of the space in a horseshoe pattern — an ironic touch, Aaron thought, since there obviously hadn't been horses here for some time. A table was set up at the open end, and a few books lay on it. Aaron and the rabbi passed through the room quickly, with little time for Aaron to see that the books were from the Talmud, the accumulated wisdom of the Jewish people, compiled over the course of more than a thousand years.

The air that greeted the two men in the rabbi's office was considerably warmer than any Aaron had felt for a while, even in the Judenrat's offices. A coal stove had been left burning while the rabbi enjoyed his morning meal. Aaron wondered at the extravagance.

The rabbi took a seat behind an ornate desk, motioning Aaron to a simple chair in front of it. The younger man found himself looking up at the older one, though they had been equally tall when standing. The rabbi rooted in his desk for a minute, giving Aaron a chance to take in his surroundings beyond the remarkable coal stove.

Shelves lined three walls. They were roughly cut and assembled, with every inch taken up by leather-bound volumes — some of obvious antiquity. The books behind Aaron were simply stacked, apparently not deserving shelves of their own. The spines identified the contents sometimes in Hebrew, sometimes in Yiddish.

In one case, Aaron suspected the words might have been in English, but he wasn't sure he would know. Languages had never been his strong suit. He spoke only four, and just Polish and Yiddish with fluency. His Hebrew belonged to a child of thirteen, mainly because after his bar mitzvah he had no interest in studying it further. His scraps of German came seemingly out of the air and from the vocabulary that overlapped with Yiddish.

The rabbi had finally found what he wanted, which turned out to be a leather notebook and a fountain pen. He opened up the little book and scribbled something down before lifting his eyes to Aaron, who wondered idly if the stove had been left burning simply to keep the ink liquid.

The two looked at each other for several minutes without speaking. Aaron was attempting to use the old police trick of silence in the hope that the rabbi would feel compelled to fill the void and perhaps give something away.

The rabbi had apparently invented the trick. He might as well have been a painting of a revered religious figure.

Okay, then, Aaron thought, and gave in.

"Was Lev Berson a member of your congregation?" Aaron asked again.

"Yes."

Silence returned.

Aaron decided to try another tack as he became uncomfortable under the old man's gaze.

"I'm sorry, rebbe," Aaron said deferentially, and using the more intimate form of the Jewish term for teacher. "I know nothing about your congregation — or you yourself for that matter. Could you tell me a little?"

"I think, first, it's only fair to ask who you are, and why you want to know about us," the man replied. "Excuse my caution, but … "

The rest didn't need to be said and the rabbi didn't say it.

"I've just arrived here from Serca … At the Germans' invitation," Aaron said, with small, bitter laugh, which was met by a twitch of the rabbi's lips. How else could a Jew travel anywhere, now?

"My family knew Berson's, and I was hoping to find him in the city after I got here," Aaron continued. "I was hoping that he might be able to help me set up here. There doesn't seem to be much other help available."

"No, not from the Judenrat," the rabbi agreed, then said nothing further.

"Anyway, I haven't been able to find him yet, and people spoke about his connection to your congregation, so I was hoping you might be able to help. And also that this would be the right place for me, as well."

The rabbi sat back and pondered. It was obvious to Aaron that he was wonderful at it. After a few moments, the old man nodded to himself and turned his gaze back to Aaron and dropped a bomb.

"Thank you, Mr. Kaminski," he said. "I enjoy stories very much. Much of how we learn is through stories, either those handed down to us from our fathers — or those told to us by our *friends.*"

Aaron looked into the cupboard of his mind where the words usually were, but found it empty.

"Some stories aren't true, but they are parables that teach us something," the rabbi said. "Some stories are just lies, like this one. We've known about Aaron Kaminski the smuggler for as long as you've been in business. We may not seem very worldly, we Hasids, but it's always good to pay attention."

"So why ask me who I am?" Aaron asked, both annoyed and embarrassed.

"As I said, all stories have value, even those without truth," the rabbi said, raising his thick eyebrows a little. "Your story tells me both that you don't want me to know the reasons that brought you to me, and that you have no idea who I am."

Bold seemed the only way left to go.

"Okay then, who are you?" Aaron asked.

"Rav Schmuel Levinsohn of Krozni."

The way the words dropped, Aaron was obviously supposed to have heard of the man, but he hadn't. He did know enough about the Haredim — the Jews who had refused any invitation to join in the modern world — to know that many followed individual religious princes in their villages, and that the principality was usually passed from father to son. By including the town name in his title, the man was announcing himself to be an important figure, a tzadik, a righteous one.

Aaron, who had become almost entirely secular, had a hard time figuring out exactly how he felt about tzadiks. On the one hand, they seemed a little bit like cult leaders; on the other, he had been brought up to believe they were men of great knowledge and wisdom.

The man in front of him fit nicely into both categories, having wrapped an unwilling Aaron in a cocoon of charisma, and giving the impression of having read every word in all the books around him.

Frankly, Aaron was impressed.

"And, if I can be honest with you, I would greatly prefer to be in Krozni. But unlike the man in your story, I truly was 'invited' here by the Germans some time ago," Levinsohn said.

"And here, I have tried to continue to do what I have always done, which is study and, if I can, help others to do the same."

"Thank you for that, rebbe," Aaron said. "If I'd known who you were, I never would have … "

"Oh spare me, Mr. Kaminski," said the rabbi. "What do you want Lev Berson for? I assume it's related to your work, since he's a policeman?"

Bullshit was clearly getting him nowhere. Time for something else.

"Berson's dead."

"What?"

For the first time, the furry brows pulled back far enough for Aaron to see the clear blue of the eyes that lived under them.

"I'm sorry, rebbe. I hate to bring you such news."

The rabbi's head bowed toward the blotter on his desk in evident sorrow.

"I understand that this is difficult, but I need to know anything you can tell me about him," Aaron said, careful to keep sympathy in his voice.

"Why would *you* need to know anything?" the rabbi said, once again meeting Aaron's eyes. "I don't understand. What happened to Lev?"

"He was found dead yesterday before first light. He was murdered, his head bashed in," Aaron said. "I've been asked to find out who killed him."

The rabbi shook his head.

"You? Why you?" he asked.

Aaron was surprised to find himself a little insulted by the rabbi's tone.

"Before I became a smuggler, I was a gendarme," Aaron said. "Unlike most of the so-called police around here, I've actually run a murder investigation. A few, in fact."

"I see," the great man said. "And you don't know who did it?"

"That's why I'm here. I need to know more about Lev; what he did when he wasn't working; who or why someone would want to kill him," Aaron said.

Chapter 10

The rabbi looked down at his notebook where he had occasionally been jotting something down. It was a beautiful little thing, hand-bound, the paper thick. Aaron wondered if the rabbi was perhaps looking at the name of the murderer, but thought not.

"I can't imagine anyone would want to kill him for any personal reason. He was a very reserved person. Very devout," the rabbi said. "But he could smile sweetly, too. He was a good young man and would have been a good father, I think."

Aaron nodded. Among the Haredim, it was the duty of every man to marry young and father many children.

"Did you ever speak with him outside of services, perhaps about personal things?"

"Sometimes, yes," the rabbi said. "He was deeply concerned about how to perform his job as a Jew. Was he, at root, helping the Nazis or helping his people?"

"I can imagine that was quite a conflict," Aaron said, shaking his head in sympathy.

"It's not a Jew's duty to stand against civil authority," the rabbi said. "It's his duty to listen to his God."

Aaron could hardly have disagreed more, but he couldn't see how saying so would help him with the rabbi.

"I worked hard to help him see the good he was able to do in his position, and that without order, people here would be far worse off than they are, even now," the rabbi said.

"Was there anything in particular that bothered him?" Aaron asked.

"He felt ashamed of the privileges he was given for his work, the extra food rations. He hated having to turn men who seemed to have good hearts over to the Germans."

The rabbi paused and shook his head.

"He did, though?" Aaron asked.

"It was his job," the rabbi said, as if the explanation was a good one.

"And, of course," he continued, "Lev hated the names he was called. It's a hard thing to be hated by your own people."

"I'm sure it can't be easy," said Aaron, thinking of his present assignment and the scorn he'd sometimes suffered as an officer in the Polish police.

"It was not. And Lev was a sensitive person. I'm sure if there had been a job open as a clerk, he would have taken it.

"Still," the rabbi shrugged, "I told him, above all else, even the Laws, God values life. Like the rest of us, Lev had to eat."

Aaron nodded sympathetically again.

"Did you give him any other advice?" he asked.

"Well, I suggested he could share his extra rations with others in need, if he was concerned. We work together among our community, doing our best to make sure everyone is taken care of." The man paused. "I told him to bring whatever extra he had here, and I would help him distribute it."

"And that helped ease his conscience?" Aaron asked, lifting one eyebrow.

"Well, with the amount of food he brought, I have no doubt it must have."

"How much did he bring?" Aaron asked. "The police don't get that much more in rations than the rest of us, do they?"

"I certainly don't know any specifics as to what his work entitled him to, but I have no doubt that what he gave to our community was above and beyond that," the rabbi said, raising a hand to show some large amount.

"Were you at all worried about where he might be getting that extra?"

"I assumed, Mr. Kaminski, that he came by the food much the way you come by your own living."

The rabbi sighed and looked back down. When he spoke again, his voice was softer than Aaron had heard it.

"We were certainly in no position to turn it away, wherever it came from," he said. "It is hard to bear God's judgment."

"Is that how you see this?" Aaron asked, meaning the war, the ghetto, the death all around them.

"Nothing happens without God's hand," Rabbi Levinsohn said with certainty. "Our people have been drifting away from God, becoming no different from the goyim. They have forgotten our unique covenant with the Lord."

A sermon had brewed up in front of Aaron, and he steeled himself invisibly to weather the storm.

"Coming to the cities. Dressing as the goyim do, eating as they do! Even marrying their women, if the men marry at all! Turning to Karl Marx for their salvation, rather than the Torah and the rabbis who have always led them.

"This judgment comes as no surprise! It is the inevitable fruit of our actions!"

Aaron knew this was the time to shut up, to sit still, but it was simply impossible for him.

"And what about your followers?" he asked, acidly. "Those who eat and dress just the way you like them to? If this is God's judgment, why are they dying, too? And they are dying. I see the bodies of the Haredim, same as everyone else. I see them stumble and limp and starve. Is that a fair judgment?"

The rabbi was back to his calmly contemplative form.

"It is God's judgment."

Aaron breathed deeply.

"May I smoke, rabbi?"

"Only if you're willing to share," the rabbi said. He raised the corners of his lips.

Aaron handed the old man a cigarette and then leaned in closely over the desk to light it. He stole a glance at the notebook. He couldn't make out any words, though there was something about the binding that caught his eye.

"Lev was a good man," the rabbi said reflectively. "I don't know why someone would kill him."

He exhaled smoke that was the same color as his beard.

"There was no one in the congregation who had anything against him?"

"He wasn't here long enough for anyone to develop a grudge, I don't think. Besides, most of his time with us was spent in study or prayer. Neither is much of a way to make enemies," the rabbi said.

Aaron offered a slim smile.

"Back to the food. Do you know anything else about how he was able to get it?"

"I didn't want to know. And he didn't want me to know. I think he believed it would protect us somehow."

"Nothing else?"

"Well, he once suggested I could offer a prayer for his partner, if I wanted to," the rabbi said.

"Gersh?"

"I think that was the name."

Right back where I started, Aaron thought to himself.

Having finished his cigarette, Aaron carefully snuffed out the butt. He made a habit of saving the ends in order to roll them together when he ran out of fresh cigarettes. He pushed his seat back a little, causing a squeak he wished he hadn't, and stood, reaching his hand across to the holy man.

"Thank you, rabbi, for your time," Aaron said. "I may have to come back with more questions."

"You are welcome. And what Jew doesn't have questions?"

Aaron couldn't help chuckling, as he was meant to.

The rabbi saw him out to the street and bid farewell. No tea had ever been offered.

Aaron walked without direction for a while, not noticing the more purposeful small feet that followed him.

Chapter 11

Aaron wandered slowly away from the stables and mortuaries, into the dying heart of the Jewish District. As he walked, he sifted through his conversation with the larger-than-life rabbi, trying to find some kernel of information that would count as progress in the case.

It wasn't likely that his conflicted soul had bashed the young policeman's head in. But knowing that Berson had struggled with his conscience helped Aaron to build a picture of the victim in his mind. Even if it wasn't immediately helpful, he hoped the image might help him recognize clues later on.

It was also interesting to see what kind of group Berson had involved himself with. The rabbi had made an impression Aaron was unlikely to forget any time soon. He might look like a kindly grandfather, but there was no mistaking his zealotry. Aaron guessed unquestioning loyalty would have been one of Rabbi Levinsohn's chief demands from his flock.

Did he also demand tribute? Is that how Berson had gotten himself involved in smuggling in the first place? The rabbi had made it sound as if it were the other way round, that Berson had already had a small piece of the action.

Aaron stumbled on a cobblestone, which forced back into his immediate surroundings. He discovered that his feet had dragged him toward one of the half-dozen official checkpoints between the ghetto and the world. Six men representing three nations stood around the small hut and pinioned barrier arm.

Two Jewish policemen huddled close together, their special armbands and other symbols of office marking them out. Two Poles, members of the Blue Police created by the Nazis, were clearly trying to ingratiate themselves with the final two, who wore the gray of the all-conquering Reich.

Aaron knew them all for what they were: tumblers in the lock that kept the door to the pantry closed. It was a lock easily picked with skeleton keys cut from gold. The Germans required the lion's share, two-thirds of the bribe. Poles took two-thirds of what remained, leaving the Jewish Police with a crust, payable occasionally in literal form.

Surely, if Berson had stood guard here, he would have taken his share when a load of goods came through. From what his rabbi had said, it sounded as if he cared more about charity than cash, but what does anyone tell his rabbi?

Aaron turned away from the checkpoint before he caused the guards to perk up. A proper destination finally suggested itself. It was time to take a closer — sober — look at Berson's body, Aaron decided.

He was no kind of forensic expert, but over the course of a dozen murder investigations, he'd developed a keen eye. He wished that eye had not been quite so blurry when he stumbled upon Berson the morning before.

Aaron paused for a moment and tried to put himself back at the scene. No fresh details came to mind. Maybe having the body in front of him would help bring back a clearer picture, Aaron thought. He turned his feet toward the cellar where the body was hidden.

As he walked, he tuned out his surroundings. He'd already seen his daily ration of suffering. He lost himself in thoughts of Yelena and an imaginary sun-swept plain where no menace could be seen or felt.

Chapter 11

Unexpected music brought him back to the gray streets. He was only a few blocks from the blasted basement where the body lay, but the pure sound of a violin stopped him flat. He looked around for the source.

A cello joined the violin and then a viola. Others were as transfixed as he was, but Aaron could see no one on the street with an instrument. It wasn't until he followed the eyes of the crowd to a tenement roof that he saw the three musicians. They were dressed as if for Warsaw's finest concert hall. No stains marred their white shirts or bowties, their coats were immaculately brushed.

The men played something lively, even cheerful. The bright music battled the dreary landscape. And won.

Aaron couldn't identify the piece. He knew nothing about music. He couldn't identify the musicians, either, but a young woman who held the hand of a younger man loudly whispered that the trio had performed for Jozef Pilsudski himself!

Presumably prior to his death, Aaron thought. Before the war he never would've imagined missing the country's strongman. *Now, he looks pretty good.*

It was not the first impromptu concert that Aaron had heard since being confined in the ghetto, but it was the most lovely. Aaron admired the trio's defiance of reality, their desire to create beauty instead of accepting horror.

He turned away after a few minutes, long before the others around him. Aaron understood the urge to stay, even if he didn't share it. Free entertainment was hard to find and any diversion was welcome here. Plays and even movies were sometimes available, but they cost money.

The crush thinned once again as Aaron neared the abandoned building and its half-collapsed basement with Berson tucked inside. Aaron spun around 360 degrees, hoping to catch out anyone who might have been watching him. He saw nothing, but it was an odd nothing. Staring and listening revealed only more nothing.

It must be paranoia, he told himself, though he didn't believe it.

Perhaps another trip around the block?

He decided it couldn't hurt, but in the end it didn't help, either. He found himself again staring down into the hole in the crumbled cement, no wiser than he'd been before his stroll. He took the broken steps down, one at a time.

Aaron hadn't brought a lantern, and he hadn't seen a flashlight for quite some time. Instead, he saw Berson's body in flashes as he struck one match after another. Blood on the head, the clothing hard in patches where the blood had frozen. The face of a young man, the expression on it meaningless.

It was impossible to lift the head and keep a match alight, so Aaron settled for probing the wound with his fingers.

His examination added little to what he'd seen the morning before. He felt shattered bone piercing frozen gray matter and bits of scalp that hung loose from the wound. It had been a very hard blow indeed, and from behind. But the gash had nothing else to say to Aaron, who, though no medical expert, was a veteran of blows to the head.

He was running short of matches but what he had to do next would work just as well by feel. He began his search of the rest of the body at Berson's hands, carefully coaxing open the fingers of the left and being disappointed when a telling clue failed to fall from the dead man's grasp. The other hand was open and equally empty.

Berson's coat was gone, taken by one of the policemen who had found him, but his pants and the pockets in his stained wool sweater remained. Aaron got no joy from reaching into them, feeling the hard skin of the frozen man under his fingers, but it had to be done.

The sweater contained a handkerchief that itself contained nothing else. The pants, on the other hand, held both a wallet and a folded piece of paper. There was no way to read the note or examine the contents of the wallet in the dim basement, so Aaron put them aside and began a more intimate search of Berson's body, tracing his arms, torso, pelvis and legs. Nothing else presented itself.

Aaron decided his work in the makeshift morgue was done, and that it was time to leave Berson to his uneasy rest.

Back aboveground, Aaron found a sheltered doorway to examine his prizes.

First the wallet. It was of surprisingly good quality, considering the condition of the rest of Berson's clothing. The leather was somewhat worn, yes, but it had been quite expensive when purchased. Unfortunately, the contents failed to live up to the wrapper.

Identification, a few zloty, a ration card, a photograph of an older woman — likely his mother, Aaron decided. Not anything that even vaguely resembled a clue, let alone evidence. It was what Aaron had expected, but certainly less than he'd hoped for.

Carefully re-packing the wallet's contents — minus the zloty, which Berson certainly didn't need — Aaron turned to the scrap of paper. It had been folded in quarters and was wrinkled and dog-eared as well. The edges were ragged along one side.

The words on it were crabbed and hard to read, with the ink heavy and splotchy, as if the writer had failed to blot it properly before folding the note. Perhaps he had been in a hurry?

Aaron stared for a while and eventually turned toward the sun to see if brighter illumination would help him to puzzle out the words. And it did, if only to the extent of revealing that the note wasn't in Polish, but German. After minutes of wrinkling his brow and squinting his eyes, he was able to pull out a few individual words, but not enough to make sense of what was in front of him.

Aaron decided that he would have to show the note to someone who read German more fluently — and maybe had better eyes. There were plenty of candidates. He was trapped along with some of the best-educated people in Eastern Europe, and besides, many people had dealt with the Volksdeutsche — the diaspora of German-speaking people — all their lives.

The translator had to be someone he trusted, or at least someone who owed him a favor. If the note contained anything germane to the case, Aaron would have to be able to rely on the man's discretion.

Aaron knew just such a man, and he knew where to find him at this hour of the day — at a soup kitchen for writers, founded by the guild for the betterment of its members.

Everyone who could afford it — few — contributed what they could to put ingredients into one another's soup bowls. Most of those who could afford to pay in were men and women who wrote either the cheerful propaganda of the official newspaper of the ghetto, Gazeta Zydowska, or those who still occasionally published in scholarly journals in the West.

While Aaron wasn't a writer, he figured his role as the primary supplier to the kitchen entitled him to entry and perhaps a bowl in addition to his friend's help.

Chapter 11

Aaron turned into the breeze and began to walk again. He was tired. There had been little sleep the night before and every minute he was awake, Aaron felt the weight of Berson's body pressing down on him.

It seemed farcical to be looking for a killer in a graveyard — to seek justice for one murder among thousands. After all, no one would ever pay for the hundreds killed at Breslaw Hospital the day before.

Soon Aaron had to stop and rub his brow with a cold hand. He could feel a sick headache building, but knew there was no time for it.

A 12-year-old boy pedaling a bicycle rickshaw spotted Aaron's distress and decided to take advantage of it for at least a few groczy.

"Hey," the boy called. "You look like you could use a lift."

Aaron wasn't too proud to take it. He climbed on the front of the makeshift vehicle and told the boy to head to the main street. He relaxed his neck muscles and pulled his hat over his eyes to ease the pain caused by the dim light of the Polish winter. The headache was building and the rickshaw's rocky ride was no help with the nausea that came along with it. On any other day, Aaron would have taken to his bed and stayed there until the pain passed. Today that wasn't possible.

"Stop at the nearest druggist," Aaron told the boy.

While true medicines were scare and dear in the ghetto, patent solutions could be found on every corner. These home brews sometimes did exactly what the proprietor said they would. Sometimes they did nothing. Sometimes they were dangerous.

Aaron doubted any concoction's side effects could be as bad as the headache he had already. And if whatever he took killed him, so be it. Aaron doubted the headache would be able to follow him into death's realm.

The boy stopped at a storefront that had the traditional strange bottles in occult shapes and shades in the window. Admixtures and alchemy. Potions and placebos.

"Do you want me to wait?" the boy asked.

"I think I can walk the rest of the way from here."

The boy looked disappointed, but Aaron decided he had reached the day's limit on charity. He gave the driver a few zloty and told him to scram.

A bell jangled cheerfully as Aaron walked into the store. He found it a pleasant reminder of better days and full shelves, but the store itself was, unfortunately, a more accurate reflection of the times. There was little for sale, and what there was had been made in the ghetto out of God knew what. The wrappers around cough drops, candies and medicines alike had been labeled by hand or been badly printed by presses using the lowest quality ink and paper. Still, each wrapper was an attempt at normal life, and as cynical as Aaron was, the naiveté touched him.

"Can I help you, sir?" asked a surprisingly pudgy man who had appeared behind the counter.

"Headache," Aaron said.

"Bad one?"

Aaron glared in lieu of an answer.

"There's not much, as I'm sure you know. Even the bandages aren't bandages. They're just old clothes that couldn't be patched together again," the pharmacist said.

Aaron, truly, sincerely, could not have possibly cared any less.

"I do have something that I make here. It's aspirin, more or less. It's not very expensive."

Aaron reached for his wallet.

"Unfortunately, it's also a little uneven in its effect," the pharmacist continued. "Some people have been very pleased … "

He left that hanging.

Finally, Aaron took the bait.

"You suggest something else?"

"It's a little expensive, but there's no doubt it works."

"Yeah?" Aaron said, starting to get angry at how long the pitch was taking.

"I've managed to get my hands on some morphine," the plump man said slyly. "Would you be interested?"

Aaron had been given the drug before to treat his headaches. Even when the pain hadn't disappeared entirely, it had retreated an indefinite distance. He was tempted.

"How much?"

The pharmacist named a price that was enough to feed a family of four for a month — on real rations, not sawdust and rotten beets.

"How do I know it's real?" Aaron asked. He had the money in his pocket.

The man ducked below his counter, returning with a small, sealed box bearing the label of the Bayer pharmaceutical company.

"Check the labels and seals for yourself," the pharmacist offered.

Aaron did so, but remained unconvinced. If it was profitable to smuggle drugs into the district, it was far more profitable to fake them and reuse boxes from the real thing.

So, it was a gamble, and an expensive one.

But the headache was somehow getting worse.

"Give me the entire box at that price, and one shot right now and we have a deal," Aaron said.

More haggling, but shortly Aaron had his coat on his lap and the sleeve of his shirt rolled up. When the druggist opened the box, Aaron saw ampules that were properly filled, which boosted his confidence. The druggist prepared a syringe and needle. Aaron waited to feel the prick and the relief it would bring.

It was quick. So quick.

A cool wave broke over him, a release. His eyes closed. He rolled his shoulders and made to stand.

Then something hit him just below the neck, rocking him forward. His eyes flew open.

Aaron spun around to see a very surprised pharmacist with a heavy, blue-tinted bottle in his hand. The man clearly had no idea what to do with an Aaron who was on his feet and not unconscious.

Aaron, on the other hand, didn't hesitate. One hand shot out to grab the druggist's right wrist and strip the bottle from his grip. The other found the pharmacist's neck and began to clench and then clench further.

"What the fuck were you thinking, fat man?" Aaron asked.

The man choked in reply.

"Get me high and rob me?"

The man's eyes widened as fear filled them.

"Figured if I could pay your price for the shot, I must have more on me?"

Another choked garble.

Aaron took that as a yes and used his free hand to punch the strangling man hard enough in the face to draw blood.

"Fuck you," Aaron said.

The pharmacist passed out.

Aaron took his money back, took the full box of drugs, kicked the other man hard in his guts and walked back out onto the street, his headache much improved.

A few blocks away was a tenement with a large public space where the Writers' Guild had set up their meeting room and mess hall. The final stage of Aaron's walk was pleasant. The wind had no sting and he could even see hints of the beauty his city kept hidden beneath a veil of grit and defeat.

It was still there, he wanted to tell the people he passed. Not everything was death and pain. Life still pulsed through the district. It could be seen in the face of every hawker, vendor, pedestrian or even policeman. It's not over, yet! We can still fight! We can still win!

The morphine told him it was so, and for the moment, Aaron took the joy he was offered.

He said nothing to anyone else, though. A part of him must have known better. And if people along his route saw him smile, they simply assumed he was mad.

The drug delivered him safely to his destination. The building had a welcoming courtyard that had gone to seed. People sat outside, either on benches or perched on planters, enjoying the relatively mild weather. Aaron noticed one thin old man who was smiling himself. He made sure to catch the man's eye so they could share the moment.

The older man ducked his gaze, clearly disturbed by something he'd seen in Aaron's face. Instead, the altacocker gathered himself up and turned away, limping toward the entrance of the building.

Aaron shook his head, too high to take what the old man had done personally. Instead, he took the man's place and stared up at the bright, watery disc that hung in the sky behind only the thinnest veil of cloud.

He sighed and stayed still until he felt himself descending from the drugged peak. Once his feet were firmly on the downslope, he headed inside.

At the far end of a long hall, Katrina was busy making perpetual soup from nothing.

Aaron walked over and kissed her.

"How's the soup today?" he asked.

She smiled.

"Better than it would have been if your boy hadn't come around this morning. Before that, I was considering using scraps of paper for stock and ink for color. Maybe flavor, too. Fucking writers."

"Well, it's our pleasure to serve," Aaron said.

"It's your pleasure to get paid," she said in return, but she was still smiling slightly.

"That, too."

"So, what are you doing here, today? We paid in advance, didn't we?"

"It's not payment, though I'll take a bowl of soup, anyway," Aaron said. "There's someone I've got to talk to. Works for the newspaper."

"Thinking about taking out an ad for your services?"

"Not the worst idea I've heard," he said.

Katrina ladled soup into a bowl and handed it to Aaron, who thanked her and headed to one of the tables where he saw a youngish man whom he recognized.

"Mind if I take this seat?" Aaron asked.

"No, it's fine," the man said, without looking up. All of his attention was in his bowl.

Aaron sat down and considered his dining companion. The man's hair was a strikingly average brown, and thinning. He wore a patched sports coat — the patches were not an affectation, but a necessary part of keeping the garment together — and brown pants so nondescript as to be indescribable. The shoes might have been made from cardboard. The overall impression given was of a poor man who cared very little for the world outside his head.

Aaron sat and picked up his spoon. The broth wasn't hot enough to need blowing on, so he dug into the mixture of parsnips and mystery without hesitation. The only flavor he could identify was salt.

Aaron's neighbor looked over after he'd practically dug a hole through his own bowl.

"Aaron, how are you?" he asked.

"Good, good. You?"

"As good as a man who tells lies for a living can be."

"So dramatic! You're hardly Josef Goebbels, Horowitz."

"Now there's a natural talent," Horowitz said almost admiringly. "Imagine if we had someone like that on our side."

"I doubt any words could have stopped the invasion," Aaron said.

"Maybe not," Horowitz answered. "Maybe not."

"Anyway, what you write for the Gazeta Zydowska is as pretty as fairytales," Aaron replied. "I have trouble sleeping in anticipation of the next edition."

"It burns well, doesn't it?"

"And leaves you feeling fresh and clean."

Aaron turned back to his soup for a minute. His friend didn't bother him, though the look on his face somehow conveyed his hope that Aaron wouldn't finish the bowl. Aaron knew the look and remembered it from long before rationing. Even when they were boys, Horowitz had always had a remarkable appetite.

"Are you eating here to flatter me?" Horowitz asked.

"Of course not," Aaron said through a final slurp. "I need a small favor."

"Small?"

"Yes, actually. The only biggish part is that you can't talk about it, and I'm not sure I'll ever be able to tell you what it was all about."

"You know, I was a real newspaperman once," Horowitz said.

"Once."

"Right. But your favor would have hurt me then."

"Now?"

"Not so much," Horowitz said. "Hit me."

Aaron pulled out the note he'd found on Berson and passed it to Horowitz.

"You speak German, right?"

"How could I collaborate like I do if I didn't?" Horowitz said. The wry look was intended for himself.

"So true, though I'm not sure hundreds of recipes for stone soup are much help to the enemy."

Horowitz took that seriously.

"I'm not sure," he said. "Is keeping our morale up good for us or them?"

"Despair wouldn't help anyone," said Aaron, trying to be positive for the sake of someone he'd loved practically since they had met as infants.

"But are we easier to control if we have hope?" Horowitz asked rhetorically. "I don't think there's any doubt that we are."

"I'm not going to argue with you. I'm not even sure what side I would take," Aaron said. They'd gone down this road before. "I need you to focus on the note."

"Okay, okay."

Horowitz adjusted his glasses, which were on the thin side for an intellectual.

He studied the note, first on the tabletop, then up against the thin light in the room. He made little noises, tapped on the table, then readjusted his glasses.

Aaron started to think he might have to hurt his second person of the day when Horowitz finally spoke.

"The handwriting's terrible, but what it says is pretty simple.

"It's basically an offer to become an informant for the Nazis. See, here," Horowitz said, pointing to the paper. "It's addressed to someone named Clausewitz, who works for something called 'Section IV.'"

"That's the Gestapo," Aaron said.

"I know. Who doesn't know?" Horowitz said. "Below that, it says 'Following on our previous conversation, I believe we can reach an agreement that would be beneficial to us both. I will be able to provide you with a list of names on an ongoing basis in return for the considerations we discussed at our meeting.'"

"That doesn't sound good," Aaron said.

"No, it doesn't, does it? Want me to continue?"

Aaron nodded.

"'As a show of good faith, I have included the names of three men I know to be members of a resistance cell,'" Horowitz read, then stopped himself.

"Holy shit, Aaron! Where the hell did you say you found this?"

"I didn't," Aaron said.

"So this is where you change your mind and fill me in on all the details, right?"

"Nope. But thank you," Aaron said, standing up.

"Come on. This is important!"

"Maybe someday."

"And we all know someday isn't coming." Horowitz sighed, disgusted. He paused, then said, "Good to see you anyway."

"You, too."

Aaron walked out. The breeze had freshened, but he didn't feel it. He was deep in thought. He didn't know any of the names on the note, but that didn't stop them from being there. Three human beings delivered up to the Germans, with a promise of more.

But who was behind the note? Was it Berson himself? Had he written it? Had someone found out about him, and was that why he was killed? Or had Berson somehow discovered the note? And if he had found it, what had he planned to do with it?

Whatever the answers were, one thing was certain, the Germans wouldn't like them. Either, one of their collaborators had been killed, or, through the search for the killer, one of their prize informants would be revealed to the Jews.

Aaron had never felt more sober.

Chapter 12

Aaron walked while he tried to sort through the implications of the note. He became ever more distracted from his surroundings, and his sense of the streets fled. The earlier feeling that he was being followed faded deep into the background.

So did the person following him.

He tried to break the puzzle into indivisible pieces. Find the facts obscured by the noise. What did he know for sure? The only incontrovertible fact seemed to be the death itself, the only obvious clue the note.

The note, however, begged questions and offered innuendo, not more facts. If he could figure out who'd written it, he would know far more about Berson's role in the game: author, conniver, messenger or even avenging angel.

Aaron had no idea what Berson's handwriting looked like, nor did he know if Berson could write in German. The Judenrat offices, he thought, would likely have answers to one or both questions

The ersatz Jewish government was as bureaucratic as the Polish civil authority it had officially replaced, but more so. That meant paperwork, which in turn meant reports filed by every person in every department, including the police. Finding a sample of Berson's script was unlikely to present any difficulties.

It was also possible that he would find something in Berson's files that would point to his killer, though Aaron doubted it.

He wasn't far from the former courthouse and was able to make the trip in less than five minutes. When he reached the Judenrat headquarters it was mid-afternoon. The lines for permits and ration cards were as long as they had been the day before. Every person who stood in them was a unique and special case. Each man and woman thought his or her story or need was as individual as a snowflake. The clerks inside vehemently disagreed with that assessment, and all the while the queue slowly lengthened toward infinity.

Aaron had no sense of uniqueness anymore. His time in the Zendarmerie and army had helped to drum it out of him. It was a lesson taught on the first day and on every day after. Everyone fits into a uniform, he was taught. The exact size of it matters not at all.

He shouldered his way inside the building, alternately promising that he was not cutting to the front of the line and threatening grievous harm to those who refused to cooperate. Because of the warmer air outside, the body heat trapped in the main hall was enough to make people sweat out loud. Yesterday's stink had been surpassed and, in a way, Aaron was impressed.

Battered, bruised and now stinking himself, Aaron was finally able to work his way to the doors of the Jewish Police's offices. Fortunately, one of the guards on duty had been there the day before and recognized Aaron, saving him the trouble of pleading his own special case.

The commandant, Blaustein, was in his office when Aaron knocked, the little heater was off and the man himself was in shirtsleeves, poring over papers. He looked up as Aaron walked in.

"Have you found our killer?" Blaustein asked without preamble.

"Not yet."

"Then what the fuck are you doing here?"

"I didn't say I hadn't made progress," Aaron replied. "But I need some more information."

"Isn't that why we picked you for this case, to find things out by yourself? You're the real detective, right?"

"I appreciate your confidence in my skills, but a little help never hurt anyone," Aaron said lightly, hoping to defuse some of Blaustein's antagonism. "Just a couple of questions."

"Quickly."

"Did you know that Martin Gersh was shot outside Breslaw Hospital, yesterday?"

"Yes."

Blaustein didn't sound particularly upset about it.

"And did you know that Martin Gersh was also a Pole named Jaruzelski?"

Blaustein's eyes widened, but his voice was cool when he spoke.

"Yes," he said, and pointed to his heater. "He was a helpful guy to have around."

"Any particular reason you didn't tell me that Berson's partner was a big-time smuggler when we spoke, yesterday?"

"Berson didn't die because of Gersh," Blaustein said. "All Berson did was shut up and keep his head down. I doubt Gersh even let him know what was going on."

"That's not what Berson's rabbi thinks," Aaron said sharply. "He thinks Berson was deeply enough involved that he could feed a shul."

"And who is that?"

"Schmuel Levinsohn."

"Never heard of him," Blaustein said, and from what Aaron could tell, he meant it.

"I'm not sure that's the point," Aaron said. "The point is that Lev Berson was giving a lot of food to the shul. There's no way he was doing that on his Judenrat salary."

"Are you seriously suggesting ... "

Aaron steeled himself for the outburst to come.

"That there is a single person on my force who doesn't make money from smuggling? Of course Berson was paid off! Everyone's paid off," Blaustein said. "What possible reason could there be to take on a job like this — hated by everyone you know, front and center in the Nazi line of vision — without some kind of benefit?

"But just because he took his cut hardly means Berson was a major player. I can assure you, he was not."

"How can you possibly know that?" Aaron asked.

Blaustein stared at him.

"You'll have to take my word for it."

Creak ... Clang ... and finally, whirr. The gears came unstuck in Aaron's mind.

"And no chance he was involved in some way you weren't aware of?"

"None," Blaustein said. "What else have you found out? Maybe something I don't know?"

It didn't seem a time for the whole truth, Aaron thought, but maybe some wouldn't hurt.

"I spoke to Gersh before he was shot. He swore that Berson wasn't with him when he was injured, that they'd gone their separate ways."

"Okay. What else?"

"I also spoke with a roommate, who claimed Berson had no outside interests beyond his synagogue," Aaron said.

"And that's when you went to see Rav Levinsohn."

"Right. That was this morning."

"That's it?"

Aaron then told Blaustein about his examination of the body, neglecting to say anything about the note. He also remained silent about having stumbled across the scene of the crime before the Jewish Police.

"Shit. That's not much," Blaustein said afterward.

"Not enough. That's why I want a quick look in the files."

"What files are you talking about?"

"I'd like to see recent case reports filed by Berson. Maybe something in there will point to who would want to kill him," Aaron said.

"He wasn't an investigator, you know," Blaustein said. "The only reports he filed were from when he picked someone up off the street for something. I doubt one of the vendors he busted for blocking up the road got mad enough to crush his skull."

"That's what I've assumed so far, but it won't hurt to look."

"You know we don't have much longer before all hell breaks loose, right?" Blaustein asked.

"I understand that. That's why I need all the information I can get my hands on now," Aaron said, with exaggerated patience. "I'm not asking for anything extraordinary."

Blaustein sat for a minute, looking as if he was mustering up reasons to say no. Finally, though, he nodded.

"Fine," he said, "but be quick."

"Thank you," Aaron said with exaggerated irony. "Just one more question. Do you know if Berson spoke German?"

"I have no idea," Blaustein said. "Done?"

Aaron gave a parade-ground salute, turned on his heels and closed the door firmly behind him.

Unsurprisingly, when Aaron asked where he could find Berson's files, he was told a clerk would have to bring them. The clerk in question, of course, had stepped out of the office for a minute.

A minute became five. Five became ten. At the fifteen-minute mark on the dot, a man who could only have been a career bureaucrat — slumped shoulders, weak, watery eyes, the air of a man with few friends and many regrets — stood in front of Aaron and asked him what he wanted.

Once Aaron had explained and assured the man that he had Blaustein's approval, the clerk proved he hadn't spent all of his time among the files in vain. He quickly returned with a short stack of paper. In the stack was exactly what Aaron had asked for.

Aaron thanked the clerk. The man bowed his head slightly and slumped back to a desk somewhere to gather more dust. Aaron took the files into the police lounge, grabbed himself a cup of the worst imaginable "tea," and sat down to read.

All the paperwork in the stack had Berson's name on it, or at least in it, but it wasn't immediately clear who had written what or what was signed by whom. After a little poking, Aaron felt sure he'd identified which reports were in Berson's hand and which he had merely signed on to.

Aaron slid his hand into his coat and tried to remove the note of betrayal from his pocket nonchalantly. Two officers were in the room with him, and they were eyeing the man drinking their tea.

Aaron opened the note and held it next to a report that had been filled out by Berson. He sighed. There was no doubt.

Berson's clear, schoolboy hand was nothing like the scribbles on the torn scrap of paper.

Whether Berson had spoken German or not, he wasn't the author of the note. That left Berson the messenger or Berson the interceptor in Aaron's scenario.

So, which was it?

How big a step would it be for Berson to go from professional collaborator to outright traitor?

It was more pleasant to believe that Berson had somehow found the note and prevented it from ever reaching its intended destination. Perhaps he'd confronted the author, and the author killed him to keep it quiet.

Maybe.

Better to focus on what facts were available and gather what more he could. Aaron turned his attention back to the files in front of him. He decided to look through them all in order to rule out any other potential motives behind the young policeman's death. He took another sip of the now-cold unspeakable "tea" and dug in.

The files started back at the very beginning of the ghetto. Apparently, Berson had been an early volunteer. Aaron wondered why he'd been so quick join the force, but found no clue in the files. Nearly all the reports revolved around broken-up brawls and arrests for petty theft.

One told the abbreviated story of a 14-year-old thief who had broken into the home of a neighbor looking for anything he would be able to sell. What had happened to the boy after his detention was nowhere to be found in the report. There was no prison inside the ghetto, just temporary holding cells. He must have been turned over to the authorities beyond the walls.

Another report showcased a domestic dispute, a husband who had beaten his wife badly. The attack was attributed to a missing tidbit of gristle that the woman had apparently taken to feed a cat. The husband had been hauled off and given a chance to cool down before being sent back home with a warning. He was hardly likely to seek revenge against one of the men who had briefly detained him.

A third case was more interesting. The crime had been political. A man had stood on a street corner and railed against both the Judenrat and the Nazis. It wasn't anything that every person in the ghetto hadn't said, but most people were smart enough to say it more quietly. The incident wasn't something that could be ignored, especially as there had been a number of Germans in hearing distance. Their statements were noted in the file. Though it appeared that the man had been drunk during his rant, he had been handed over to the Gestapo for punishment.

Whatever the justice of the case, a man taken away by the Gestapo would make an unlikely suspect in a homicide that occurred months later.

It was an hour and a second cup of tea later that Aaron finished going through all the files. There seemed to be nothing that would help to solve the mystery of the murder, only a listing of human tragedy and villainy. It was nothing he hadn't seen before, which depressed him a little. Even in the midst of a larger tragedy, people were always happy to make things just that little bit worse.

As Aaron stood up, he saw that there was no one left in the room with him and that he'd stamped out several cigarette butts on the floor with little regard for whoever would have to clean it. He felt no interest in picking them up.

Instead, he dropped the files off on a convenient desk and walked out into the main hall, which he found empty. Some rules remained immutable, office hours among them. The stench of the absent crowd, unfortunately, lingered.

He'd wanted to stop for a minute and talk with his father, but Aaron knew the man as a slave to the clock. If business hours were over, he was gone.

Maybe we'll talk again, once the case is finished, Aaron thought.

The front door was locked when Aaron tried it. He knocked to get the attention of the guard outside. When he walked out, he saw there was still a little daylight left.

Offices closed early enough for workers to make it home before the curfew. Judging by the angle of the sun, Aaron would again have to hurry to reach the building where he was expecting his shipment and another chance to see his wife.

Chapter 13

The street vendors packed hurriedly, pedestrians knocked into them and each other, unheeding. All were hurrying home. If they made it safely, they would close their doors behind them, hoping to keep out the night and the Nazis. The Jewish District's curfew was descending on buyers and sellers; thieves and beggars; whores and their pimps; the religious and those who cursed God. All equally, except for the Jewish Police, whose purpose was to enforce the curfew on the rest.

Another hungry day was passing into oblivion.

Some people had been able to find warmth and food while the sun was up.

Some had been able to bathe, though nearly all in cold water.

Some had found loved ones that they had believed lost forever.

Others, that day, had lost loved ones to disease, hunger or overwork. Many of the new ghosts had marched off for the "shops" — small factories set up by German businessmen to help supply the war effort — at first light, but dusk brought them no closer to home. Families and friends would keep watch behind shut doors that the fallen would never pass through again.

Bureaucracy or fate — those who lived in the ghetto learned that there was no difference.

Aaron joined the crowd, walking back to the building where he had spent the previous night, feeling the weight of the evening to come. Every day, there was risk. Every night was darkened by it, but tonight's plan was enough to rip a man's stomach apart.

Tonight, Aaron's little crew would be giving Jews the tools to make choices that had been stolen from them in a flurry of years. With a very few exceptions, Jews hadn't fought the Nazis as 1933 had become '34 and '35, eventually reaching the untenable present. Families had resisted alone or not resisted at all. They had trusted to common sense and the good will of the neighbors who knew them so well — whom they had grown up with. They trusted the government and the law, which the Jewish community had been a part of, and which it had obeyed.

They had never learned to trust the gun.

Aaron wasn't alone in feeling the time had come — had probably come and gone — to say no and to use lead for exclamation marks. Tonight's shipment had been ordered by men who were in such deep despair that they planned a fight they had no thought of winning. They knew the eventual outcome would be the same whether they fought or not.

So, now a leap from bread to bullets, supplying death instead of life. Aaron had agreed, but what he'd agreed to scared him. He knew the punishment for smuggling an apple was death. He suspected that the penalty for smuggling guns would be the same. Still the whole thing seemed more somber and dangerous.

Every step on the leaden street was harder to take, but Aaron's feet followed one after the other until his destination was nearly in sight. When he finally lifted his eyes from his boots and saw the door ahead, he also caught a reflection flashing past a window. The shape he'd seen had been small and dun colored and was gone almost before he perceived it.

Chapter 13

Instead of turning suddenly, Aaron found one of a hundred stoops and crouched down over his shoelaces. He stayed there for a little while, making the motions of retying while slowly surveying the street.

A bundle in a doorway caught his eye. He pretended to finish what he was doing and walked in that direction. The bundle decided to run, but its timing was off. Though it darted valiantly, Aaron was too close and his arms were too long. The scrap of cloth was caught and transformed itself into a child.

It was the same girl who had stolen his food that morning in the undertakers' district. She weighed little more than her improvised clothing.

"What are you doing here?" Aaron said, his face inches from hers.

She didn't reply. Her face appeared a solid, wooden mask of fear. Her body, as he held it, was as stiff as a plank.

Intimidation seemed unlikely to get him what he wanted, so Aaron adjusted his tactics. He put the girl down on the stoop. He kept an arm gently resting on her shoulder to keep her in place when she inevitably decided to run again. He spoke gently to her, hoping to bring to mind the man who had rewarded rather than punished her earlier attempt at theft.

"I have nothing else to give you at the moment, sparrow." The endearment came without effort. She struck him as exactly that. All fragile bones and nerves and, even while unmoving, eager to be free. "But I may tomorrow. Is that what's made you follow me? You're hungry?"

His soft voice melted her slightly. A tremble rippled through her, but she wasn't yet able to respond directly to what Aaron said.

Something told him not to tighten his grip, that to embrace her would be to lose her entirely. Instead he took his hand from her shoulder and took a half step back. If she were going to run, she probably wouldn't need much more space.

She didn't run, though. Her body relaxed a bit further and she remained where she was.

Aaron pulled out a cigarette and lit it, cupping his hand around the match to keep out the breeze, though it wasn't strong. His face must have glowed for her in the dim light, and something she saw seemed to reassure her.

"May I have a bit of your cigarette?" she asked.

Aaron worked to control his face and keep his voice warm. "How old are you, sparrow?"

"I'm twelve," she said defensively.

She looked as if she couldn't have been more than ten, if that, but Aaron knew himself to be no judge. Yelena and he had no children, and had given thanks for it every day since the war broke out. He had been an only child himself, and hadn't spent any time with children since he'd been one.

He did know that many children in the ghetto had their growth stunted by hunger

He took the cigarette from his mouth and handed it to her, careful that she not burn herself.

She put the cigarette to her lips, but only puffed at it without drawing the smoke into her lungs. She was aping something she'd seen the adults around her do rather than looking for salvation through nicotine. Aaron smiled at her as a cloud quickly formed around her head.

"Is there something you'd like me to call you, other than sparrow?"

"I'm Rebecca, but I think I like Sparrow better."

"Sparrow it is."

The cigarette would soon be gone, the way she was going at it, and Aaron wasn't sure he had enough of them to light another for himself so soon.

They stood companionably while Rebecca finished Aaron's cigarette, saying nothing. When she was done, she threw it to the ground and clearly enjoyed stomping on it, though her shoes looked so worn, Aaron wouldn't have been surprised if she burned herself in the process.

And since she was done, she moved to go. Aaron gently touched her shoulder again, and she halted, though this time she didn't stiffen as much.

"So, were you following me all day?" he asked, managing to sound amused, though it wasn't how he felt.

She nodded, her face pointing toward the ground.

"All day?"

She nodded again.

"So how was it that I didn't see you?"

She wriggled. It might have been a shrug, or it might have meant something else.

"What was it that you wanted? More food?"

She nodded again.

"What happened to what I gave you this morning?"

This time she clearly shrugged.

"You can see I don't have anything else to give you. In fact, you just about took my last cigarette."

No response.

"And that's the only reason you were following me?"

A pause and a nod.

"Nothing else?"

"No."

Aaron decided he didn't believe her, but he also decided he wasn't going to start torturing recalcitrant children, either.

"Well, look. You've gotten what I have, and I've got important things to do. I don't like being followed. I'm not sure anyone does, for that matter," he said. "If I have anything for you tomorrow, I tell you what, I'll meet you here first thing. Okay? But now, Sparrow, bugger off."

No sooner had he said it than she was gone, leaving Aaron with the feeling that he'd missed something. Not that he had the faintest idea what it might have been. He turned on his heel and headed back to the building where he would be spending the night. No more restfully, he supposed, than he had the night before.

Dov was in the basement, but otherwise Aaron was the first of the crew to arrive. Rather than sit nervously, Aaron thought a twenty-minute nap might help him see the rest of the night through. He opened the room with the cots and tucked himself in, still wearing everything from his hat to his boots. His last conscious thought was for Yelena and the pleasure he anticipated from seeing her in just a few hours.

A hand woke him by grabbing his shoulder and shaking vigorously. Lech Teitel was attached to the hand. Even after Teitel saw Aaron's eyes, he didn't stop his prodding. It was only when Aaron barked at him that he finally eased off.

"That wasn't the first time I saw your eyes pop open," Teitel said. "I just wanted to be sure I had your attention."

"Yeah, yeah," Aaron mumbled, bringing his hands up to his face and rubbing it like putty to fill a crack. "Have you been here long?"

"Just a few minutes."

"You ran into trouble?" Aaron asked. What other reason could there be for traveling after curfew?

"Purely personal. My daughter got sick and it wasn't easy finding medicine for her," Teitel said. "Nothing for you to worry about."

"I'm sorry to hear it. What's wrong with her?"

"Just diarrhea. I wouldn't have been concerned, except it's been a couple of days."

Aaron frowned. Dysentery could be caused by a number of things and was serious and common behind the ghetto's wall. Sanitary conditions had crumbled due to overcrowding, inadequate sewage lines and uncollected garbage, allowing cholera into people's homes. Poor nutrition and a lack of medicine made it deadly for many. In fact, the Germans had created the very conditions they had accused Jews of causing, making the ostensible reason for closing the ghetto into a bizarre, circular truth.

Aaron reached into his pocket and pulled out the box of morphine ampules.

"You can give her one of these in the morning, if she's not feeling better," he said. "It stops you right up."

"I've always wondered why addicts look like that," Teitel said with a relieved smile. He nodded gratefully. "I wasn't able to find much."

"Have you seen Boris?" Aaron asked. Along with Dov, he would be doing the heavy lifting.

"They're downstairs, waiting," Teitel said. "Shall we join them?"

Aaron looked at his watch and saw there was still quite a bit of time before they could expect the shipment. He stood anyway.

"I'll follow you down. Let me just stop and use the bathroom," he said.

There was only one toilet and shower for the floor and Aaron fumbled toward it in the dark as Teitel made his way to the basement. When he opened the door and found himself alone, Aaron breathed a sigh of thanks. Having grown up in a building much like this one, he had memories of waiting an eternity for a neighbor to finish, sure that his eyes had turned a sickly yellow from the built up piss.

When he finished, Aaron moved to the sink and turned on the tap, happy to feel a trickle fill his hands. He sprayed his face with it, the cold water transubstantiating into coffee, bringing him back to life, or at least a formidable mockery of it. Then he shivered.

He wouldn't show it in front of the others, but he was worried, for himself but mostly for Yelena.

They'd been talking about smuggling guns into the ghetto for a long time, though they had kept it to themselves, fearing betrayal. Still, Aaron was surprised when Yelena told him that she had made a contact who could supply them. The man had claimed to be part of the Polish underground, fighting the Nazis mostly from the forests, Yelena said. His group's weapons came from a stash that had been set aside as it became clear — nearly instantly — that the Germans and Russians would quickly overrun the country.

Aaron had only a matter of days to put together the treasure that would pay for the weapons. Yelena hadn't told her men anything about the deal. Some of the people she worked with were patriots, but others were far more interested in profiteering. Yelena figured the best way to ensure that everyone kept their mouths shut was to stoke their greed. Aaron's gold Torah raiment had played its part nicely. It was unlikely the Nazis would match that kind of payout just for unconfirmed information.

Aaron was more concerned about the other end of the deal — the man who claimed he had the guns, Andrusz.

He told a good story, but was it true?

There was no way Aaron could know. He had to rely on what Yelena saw and thought. She lived in a wider world.

Chapter 13

How could a city be cut in such a way? Aaron still couldn't truly comprehend it. People, meters apart, might as well have been living in separate universes.

He stood in a building that sat on a darkened "Jewish" street. It was back-to-back with a similar one that faced onto a road where streetlights still burned and people ate their fill at dinner. That building was outside the ghetto solely because of black magic and people's willingness to believe in it.

The "wall" around the ghetto wasn't even a wall in many places — it was made from wooden fences running down the middle of a street; a row of homes turned into a palisade; newly built concrete barriers that filled gaps that had been alleys, and checkpoints that had taken the place of traffic signs.

And because of the miracle of human cognitive dissonance, it was possible to live cheek-by-jowl with those less fortunate and still concentrate on one's own affairs. How many times had Aaron walked past a beggar before the war and not thought for a second about whether the man would be eating that night? Instead, he'd probably been wondering if he had time to stop off for a pastry on the way home. If he was truthful with himself, he had to acknowledge that the beggar hadn't hurt his appetite.

And when people on the "Aryan" side heard gunshots coming over the wall, did they flinch and think about whom the bullets were killing? Perhaps a quick shiver, a second's prayer, and it was over.

He was sure people sometimes remembered a dear friend who was now locked behind the wall, or maybe thought fondly of some store that had been run by a Jewish family and a treat they could no longer get. But more than that? Well, people had their own worries. And under German occupation there were plenty of worries for everyone. The secret police didn't focus on Jews alone.

And how much more guilty of indifference was Aaron? He'd heard stories of what was happening to the Jews of Germany, his cousins, for years before the war. He'd done nothing about it, not even sending a few zloty to help build a state of Israel in what was now Palestine.

He was unimpressed with his own compassion.

He gave his face one more splash, glad there was no mirror above the sink. It was time to go downstairs.

The cellar was filled to over-capacity with smoke again. As he descended he was grateful that the lanterns at least gave his feet a target.

"Come sit, have a drink," Boris called.

Aaron pulled up a crate at the makeshift table and took a cigarette from his jacket. Dov offered him the lit end of his own cigarette to save matches. Aaron drew deep and then exhaled like a snuffed-out dragon.

"I hate the waiting," Dov said.

"That's funny, because I have to say, it's my favorite part," Teitel said. "Have some more brandy."

The bottle was passed, and when Dov was filled to the brim, Aaron took the bottle for himself. There wasn't much left. He must have slept longer than he'd thought. Or the others were as nervous as he was. Probably the latter.

Cards were dealt again, but no one played with much interest. A few times, Aaron failed to notice when he had a winning hand.

"Are they late?" Boris asked.

"Not yet," Aaron said after looking at his watch again. He was surprised that his eyes hadn't burned a hole in its face.

Chapter 13

How late had it been when Berson had died? Surely later than this, or his body would have been spotted sooner by some patrol or other. What had the young policeman been doing two nights before at this time? Had he already parted company with his partner? Was he patrolling on his own? Taking refuge from the cold somewhere out of sight?

Was he talking with the person who would soon become his killer? Maybe running from him?

Aaron realized he was ignoring his cards and made a play.

Why had Berson been carrying that note? Who was he betraying — his fellow Jews, or the man who had given him the note?

And the torn note itself, on expensive paper? There'd been no notebook among Berson's possessions. Yet it seemed to Aaron that he'd seen something similar recently. He sighed in frustration, unable to tease meaning from his thoughts.

He looked down at his cards again, but it seemed he was having as much luck there as in his investigation.

"Forget it," he said. "I'm out."

He stood and stretched his shoulders and back, his hands on his hips. But the tightness that wasn't so easily exorcised. He thought for a second and realized he'd been feeling it since the war began.

He was about to half-heartedly start some calisthenics when he heard a scraping sound that froze him. It came from the hole in the wall. Yelena was coming and, if anything, she was a few minutes early. He felt immense relief.

Still, Boris and Dov were more cautious, perhaps smarter. They picked up two of the rusty rifles that had been delivered the night before and stood in front of the hole. Aaron and Lech Teitel stood further back, both unarmed.

Teitel called out a challenge in Polish that was answered in the same language, but with an accent that didn't quite ring true. As Aaron and Teitel looked at each other to see if both had heard the same thing, a crash from above caused them both to spin around and look up.

"Drop those fucking guns!" a voice shouted from the dark at the top of the stairs.

The words were in German, but Aaron had no trouble understanding them. He was so startled that he let go of a weapon he wasn't even holding.

Dov had a different idea. He fired one bullet toward the voice. Or rather he tried to. He failed because the rifle was as corroded at its core as it looked from the outside. When the gunpowder was struck, the barrel exploded in his face, leaving him a mass of pulp and blood that slid to the ground.

However Boris might have been inclined — to fire or to drop his gun — he didn't have time to choose. His head exploded, too. A bullet had struck it from very close range.

SS men had manifested in the cellar through the hole in the wall. The sound Aaron had heard had never been Yelena.

As the German who had first spoken made his way down the stairs, Aaron realized he and Teitel both had their hands raised over their heads without having been told to put them there.

There was no question of fighting. Aaron had no impulse to do so. Fatalism and perhaps relief overwhelmed him. There was no more fear of being caught because he had been. It was over. The tension in his back ebbed.

Aaron felt no surprise at all when he recognized the Nazi who came down the stairs. The man wore the same black leather coat at the massacre in front of Breslaw Hospital. The same silver death's head was pinned to its lapel.

The man had no trouble recognizing Aaron, either.

"I told you I'd see you again," he said.

Aaron could only nod. No smart remarks came to mind. He was terrified of this man who stood a full head above him and had the shoulders to back up his height. Even when Aaron had eaten better and more regularly, he would hardly have been two-thirds of the man's width.

"Hermann Clausewitz, Section IV," the German said, now speaking Polish. He stuck out his hand as if to shake Aaron's, and when Aaron instinctively moved to reciprocate the gesture, Clausewitz twitched at the speed of lightning and smacked him with his open hand. It felt and sounded like thunder, and Aaron fell to the ground.

He had only a second to realize the man who had hit him was the man addressed in the note he'd found on Berson's body.

Someone brought Aaron roughly back to his feet. Clausewitz struck him again, and this time his hand was closed.

Aaron's eyes opened again as his feet bumped up the stairs, his shins catching painfully more than once. He tried to see around him, but all he could do was peer down between his own legs. From that view, he caught a glance of Teitel being carried up behind him. The blood that was dripping from Teitel's body showed that Aaron's friend hadn't benefited from any kind of favoritism.

Aaron tried to move a little and that was how he discovered that his hands were cuffed behind him. He tried to get his feet under him, if for nothing else than dignity's sake, but kept tripping. He had no choice to but allow himself to be muscled through the main hall and out onto the darkened street. There were three black Gestapo cars waiting with their lights on and engines running.

Clausewitz was illuminated by one of the beams and Aaron caught a glimpse of the man talking to someone who barely came up to his waist. When Aaron saw the tiny figure was haphazardly wrapped in brown cloth, he knew immediately who it was.

Clausewitz handed the girl something and even patted her on the head, though his palm could have swallowed it entirely. She took what she was given and ran off as fast as Aaron had ever seen her go.

"I was right to call you Sparrow," he muttered beneath his breath. "Look at how you sing."

Aaron was thrown into the back of one of the cars and Teitel was loaded into another. Clausewitz climbed into the front passenger seat of the vehicle in the lead and the small convoy rolled forward.

Aaron's head was swimming. Gestapo men bracketed him on either side, his hands were pinned behind him and reality was beginning to break through the shock.

He began to fear for what would happen to him, the torture he could expect and then death.

And he thought of Yelena, the broken rendezvous and where she might be. He guessed she was in a position much like his or dead already, summarily executed. But the stupidest part of his mind wouldn't let go of the hope that she had been warned somehow and had fled.

A checkpoint was coming up. Aaron first saw it through a blur. As they drew close, he realized the blur was snow. It had just begun to fall. A brief stop at the guard hut, some conversation between Clausewitz and the men on duty, a little curiosity on the faces of the Jewish policemen on guard and it was done.

The barrier lifted, the cars picked up speed and, for the first time in months, Aaron left the Miasto ghetto.

Chapter 14

The first thing that Aaron noticed on arriving at the prison/ headquarters of the Gestapo was the friendly smile on the face of the officer at the desk who welcomed him. He seemed genuinely pleased that Aaron had been able to spare the time to become a prisoner of the Reich.

It was clear that the man had a sense of humor, as well.

"The name on the reservation?" he asked.

"Goering, Hermann," Aaron replied, hoping his own humor would be appreciated.

"Ahh! Reichsmarschall! I can't say we've been expecting you, but a pleasure, nonetheless."

"Cut the shit, Himmelfarb," Clausewitz, the Gestapo officer who had captured Aaron, said. "Just get the fucking paperwork filled out and get him in a cell. We can all have our fun, later."

"Ja vol," Himmelfarb replied, the smile still on his face, though not quite as bright.

Aaron handed over his papers and the ritual began. All the various boxes had to be ticked. Even if Aaron were going to disappear, the event would need to be properly recorded.

Seeing the process was well in hand, Clausewitz shrugged his massive shoulders, rubbed the top of his bald head for a second and announced he was leaving.

"But don't worry," he said. "I'll be back to speak with you much sooner than you'd like."

He didn't laugh like a villain in the movies as he walked off. Aaron had half expected it, but supposed the gesture would have been gratuitous.

Shortly thereafter, the proper forms were filled out, Aaron's identity papers were filed away somewhere — forever more out of his reach — and there was nothing to keep Aaron from becoming one more wretch trapped in the stone hell around him.

The door that opened to Aaron's right had always led to the cells, as far as Aaron knew. The complex hadn't been built by the Germans, but rather taken over by them. It had been a place of fear long before they came. Common criminals, thieves and murderers had been kept here by the Poles, as had political prisoners, including some of note over the past century. Aaron felt their collective fear radiating off the walls. He could smell it wafting down a stone-lined corridor with few lights. He could hear it coming from cells downstairs.

A young, blond, blue-eyed example of perfection followed behind him. The man's face was sweet, one that invited trust, but the gun he held at the ready showed no remorse for its role in the prison's brutality.

As the two walked forward, the door closed softly behind them. The final muffled snick of the catch was definitive. It wouldn't open again, even if Aaron asked nicely.

Doors on either side of the passage looked heavy, but the third one they passed on the right did little to block out the sounds of the woman being tortured inside. She was chanting a prayer in Yiddish in between screams. The same few words were offered up to God over and over again, even as Aaron heard the sound of flesh slapping against flesh. From the rhythm of her broken voice, he was sure she was being raped. His heart shrank in his chest. He lowered his head and must have slowed until a shove reminded him of the expected pace.

A little further, Aaron saw a broken old man with a mop, working vigorously. There was a scrap of black cloth on his head in a vaguely circular shape and a white band with a blue Star of David on his sleeve. The man leaned heavily on the mop as he dragged it back and forth, staring blankly. Aaron turned his head just enough to look the man in the face and realized he'd been mistaken. The man wasn't very old at all. His mouth was puckered and misshapen because he had no teeth. His gaze was blank because one eye was swollen nearly shut. Where the other should have been, there was nothing.

Aaron doubted the poor soul was there to clean, but rather as an abject lesson for new arrivals.

Aaron turned to see how this sight affected the beautiful young man who was his Virgil through the Inferno. The guard's face gave away nothing at all. He might as well have been a clockwork figure.

Aaron shivered — as well he might. His coat, sweaters and shoes had been taken from him before his registration at the prison. He's seen no record being made that would link him to his clothes. It seemed unlikely he would ever wear them again. The floor of the corridor, and now the steps down below the ground, were colder than ice, though his breath didn't fog.

The lighting on the stairs came from a single round fixture. It illuminated hardly anything at all. Aaron's numb feet soon missed a step and he was heading toward the ground when a hand shot out and pulled him back. Aaron again turned to look at his escort, but found no new sign of fellow feeling. It seemed that Aaron's breaking his neck wasn't part of the plan at the moment.

The staircase ended at another stone corridor that felt so solid, it could only have been underground. Two guards flanked the entrance, a third man, who stank of boredom, sat at a desk. Aaron's escort gave his prisoner's name and status and was given a cell number in return.

The cells lined both sides of the hall, and each one was filled to the point where every man was pressed against his neighbors. Prisoners didn't have to stand, the pressure of each other's bodies kept them upright. Aaron saw an arm sticking out beyond the bars of one cell. The skin had a bluish tinge. It wasn't moving.

There seemed no way Aaron could be squeezed inside any of the cells, but the young German didn't try. Instead, eventually, they came to a cell with no one in it at all and no furniture of any kind. Aaron was invited in and landed on his face.

The bars closed behind him.

The smell of piss and shit and vomit enwrapped him. The cold nuzzled his cheeks, his chest, his legs, his feet. Aaron lay down and curled his body into as small a space as was possible, hoping to use his own body's warmth for comfort. He built a wall between himself and the mumbling and shrieking of the men in the other cells.

He sensed Death waiting patiently outside.

They came for Aaron after an indefinite, gray time. It wasn't that he'd slept, exactly, but for a time his conscious mind had left his body. His gauziness was aided by the blows his head had already taken. Reality, dreams and visions were sometimes hard to tell apart as he waited for his torturers.

Chapter 14

He was sure that torture would be the next step. There would be questions about his partners, his operations, his intentions, and Aaron would volunteer none of the answers.

But how long could he hold out? Forever? For Yelena's sake, he hoped so, but Aaron was in no mood to kid himself. If even half of what he'd heard about the creativity of Nazi interrogators was true, he figured it would be a matter of a few days if he were lucky, hours if he wasn't.

The blond guard was elsewhere when the cage opened. Instead, two SS privates screamed at him to get on his feet.

"Raus, Juden!"

He wasn't a man with a name in this place. He was a Jew and nothing else.

When Aaron climbed too slowly to his feet, one of the soldiers stepped forward and grabbed him under the arm. Aaron was jerked up and incidentally slammed heavily into the wall. The breath went out of him, but he didn't dare fall.

As this was happening, the other man in gray kept his machine gun pointed into the cell. If Aaron had planned to feign weakness and tackle the guard, he wouldn't have made it a single step.

Finally allowed to stand on his own, Aaron began the march back up the corridor, past the other cells and toward the stairs. The body of the man who had died was still pressed against the bars. The odor coming from the cages was hardly to be believed. Aaron thought he would have gotten used to the stench after however may hours he'd lain in it, but passing this close to its source, he retched. His stomach was empty. A thin stream of clear fluid came up.

"Stop that!" one of the guards shouted. "I'm not cleaning up after a fucking Jew."

Aaron thought of the man with one eye and the mop, shuddered and worked hard to keep his stomach in place.

The three marched down a flight of stairs that Aaron hadn't noticed on his way in, down a corridor that didn't smell like much at all, and finally into a small room with a metal chair at its center. The guards made it clear that he was supposed to sit in the chair by pushing him down into it and tying him there. Then they left.

There were bright lights shining in Aaron's eyes. Sounds of torture filtered through the heavy door and softened Aaron for what was coming next.

He tried to look beyond the light, and by squinting his eyes just so, he could begin to make out a wooden chair on wheels, like a secretary might use in an office. He could also see a table that sat near the wall. As there was little else to do, he spent some time imagining what might be on the table.

Were those things on the right pliers? If so, how would they be used?

And next to them, what else? Ah, perhaps a hammer? Nails beside it? That didn't seem right, but then, who knew?

He was stumped for a while by a box with a crank attached to it. Would a limb — or something else — be placed inside the box, to be ground up? But then what were the strings that dangled from it for?

Strings …

No! Of course not strings. Wires! Electrical wires, and the box with the crank would have to be a small generator.

Something about it broke through Aaron's haze of detachment and he began to grow very afraid.

Still, the door stayed shut. No one came.

As the time passed, boredom and terror fought a war for his soul. Neither had won a decisive victory when, finally, the door to the room opened and, to Aaron's complete lack of surprise, Hermann Clausewitz walked in.

He was in the uniform of the SS, but there was an unadorned black patch on the right side of his collar instead of any identifying mark. Of course the absence was identification in itself. Only the Gestapo wore that patch.

Before he spoke, Clausewitz sat himself on the rolling chair and pushed off in Aaron's direction, spinning to face him with a bit of a flourish. He took the damaged side of Aaron's face in his hand, cupped it and then squeezed until Aaron shouted out.

"I think you know already what I'm going to ask you," Clausewitz said, removing his hand. "But there's no harm in setting out some specifics and ground rules. First rule, when you understand what I'm saying, nod your head. You understand?"

Aaron nodded.

"Good. Let's begin with who you were planning to meet last night?"

Was this a trick question? Did Clausewitz know or not know? Was Yelena in custody, or still unknown to the Gestapo?

At least Clausewitz's question gave Aaron back some sense of time. No more than a day had elapsed since his capture.

"We weren't there to meet anyone," Aaron said, reaching for the ring of truth. "We were there to escape."

"No," Clausewitz shook his head. "No, that's not a good place to start at all."

He stood and used his arm as a piston.

Aaron collapsed around the fist, which struck him in the abdomen. He was lucky that some of the force was absorbed when his chair fell to the floor. He was less lucky that the back of his head also absorbed some of the energy when it struck the ground. He blacked out.

Or perhaps that was a blessing as well.

Aaron was woken by ice-cold water that first dripped onto his head and then came down in a rush, choking him. The man who was pouring the bucket wasn't Clausewitz. In fact, Aaron didn't recognize him at all.

It took Aaron a minute to realize that he was no longer sitting in the metal chair. Instead he was lying on some kind of plank, his head slightly lower than his feet. He was still tied up, unable to move much beyond his neck, his toes and fingertips.

He looked left and right, and lifted his head the little bit he could. There was little to see in the room other than bald, grinning Clausewitz.

"You're weaker than I would have guessed," Clausewitz said as a greeting.

Aaron said nothing.

"So, no more punching."

Clausewitz nodded to the man who stood over Aaron.

Aaron felt his head sinking, and realized his feet were also rising. Then frigid liquid grasped the back of his head. Then his ears, his eyes, his nose and, finally, his closed mouth.

His eyes shut against the liquid, but they soon popped open against his will. He looked in the face of the man who was holding him under. There was no sign of physical strain on it. Aaron attributed that to how thin he had become.

Enough of the liquid got into Aaron's mouth for him to realize it was simply fresh water and, as he had received nothing to drink, he swallowed some. It was then Aaron realized that the cold water had led him to expel his breath.

Chapter 14

There was nothing in his lungs and time was passing.

The urgency for air took a few more seconds to realize, but when the realization came, Aaron knew he wouldn't be able to resist for long. His body, somewhere above him, struggled and scraped itself against its tight bonds. Pointlessly.

It was done. Aaron tried with all his might to breath water, failed and began to convulse.

He fell out of the water as the man above him lowered his legs. He retched, coughed, spluttered, turned his head and drooled, too. The water didn't want to come out. He wasn't able to curl up around his middle and use that pressure to push the water from his lungs.

His torturer bent over and helped by pushing down hard on Aaron's ribs and belly. The water — not all of it — came out and air took its place. Aaron could do nothing other than breathe and choke for a while. Clausewitz gave him that time.

The Gestapo man then spoke casually.

"Whom were you waiting for?"

Yelena.

"We weren't waiting for anyone. We were waiting for the right time to escape," Aaron said through a gasp.

"I see. And the treasure you were found with?"

Clausewitz spoke like a snake hissing to a mouse.

"We were going to use it to buy our way out of Poland," Aaron said, his voice coming nearly under control.

"And the guns?"

"The guns?" Aaron answered stupidly.

Clausewitz again nodded at the man who was still hovering over Aaron, and again Aaron felt his feet lifting.

"Wait! Wait!" Aaron shouted, not even knowing what he would say.

His words had no effect.

This time, Aaron was able to get a breath before he head was entirely covered.

It made no difference, other than that the drowning took a bit longer. Apparently, the Germans had time.

Aaron tasted death. It had practically no taste at all.

Then, once again, he was brought out. He retched, choked and gasped again. The nameless German did his lifeguard routine. Aaron lived a little longer, if only to answer Clausewitz's questions.

"The guns, I assume, were meant for some kind of pointless resistance?" Clausewitz asked now. "Let's talk about that. How many people are in this resistance?"

"I don't know," Aaron said.

"So there is a resistance, then?"

"I don't know," Aaron said again, though he yearned to say something else.

"I don't know! I don't know!" Clausewitz shrieked in a horrible falsetto. Then, in his normal voice, "Oh, Aaron. I'm not a stupid man, and you're not even a man. Not really. Just a Jew, that's all. Just a Jew.

"Are you scared Aaron?"

Every time Clausewitz spoke his name, Aaron felt it was a little less his, that his identity became a little more tenuous.

But he said nothing.

"Whom were you waiting for?" Clausewitz said, changing the subject again. "What was the delivery supposed to be? More guns?"

Yelena.

No. Instead, silence.

Clausewitz himself edged over, grabbed the foot of the plank and lifted.

"This time, you're not coming out," he said.

Chapter 14

Aaron screamed. He hit the water so fast there was no time for another breath.

He thrashed his head, he flapped his fingers and feet.

Time passed.

He drowned.

Aaron awoke in a cell, but this time he wasn't alone in it. He was on the floor with a man's crotch at eye level. His back was to the wall. Aaron reached up and weakly tried to push the other man further away, but instead received a kick. It was half-hearted.

After a few minutes of consciousness and the passing of several waves of nausea, Aaron wedged his back against the wall and slowly pressed his way upward, until he stood face to face with the man whose crotch he had become so intimately acquainted with.

"I thought you were dead," the man said.

"Yes, nearly," Aaron replied.

"It's a shame," the man said. "Would have been nice to have a little more room."

"Thank you for your concern," Aaron said weakly, "but I'm quite all right."

The man was dressed much the same as Aaron, which is to say ravaged pants and a shirt. On his feet were holes with a little wool to bind them together. When the man tried to shift away from Aaron, he couldn't get very far. There were at least twenty-five men in the cell with them. Aaron doubted it was supposed to hold even ten. Certainly in Aaron's time in the Zendarmerie, he had never seen so many crammed together in a space this size.

Still, it appeared to be a little better than the pens he'd passed on the way to his first cell — however long ago that was. There was room to sit, as Aaron had, and the air was comprised of something more than his neighbor's exhaled breath.

Aaron allowed time to pass, feeling his wounds, uncertain about the prospect of living; certain that Clausewitz wasn't done with him. Not by a long shot.

Finally, the man who wished Aaron was dead needed some conversation, some contact beyond the mere pressing of flesh.

"What's your name, then?" the man asked.

"Kaminski."

"I'm Hirsch." He tried out a grim smile.

"Okay," Aaron said.

"I broke curfew," Hirsch said. "That's why I'm here."

"Okay."

Hirsch frowned. He must have hoped for something more revealing — or at least friendlier — in response, but Aaron was in no mood or shape to make friends. Instead, he stared dully around him.

Every age was represented in the cage, from the oldest grandfathers to boys hardly ready for school. He wondered what the old men could have done to attract the attention of the authorities. Were they guilty of curfew violations, too? Had the religious among them been caught praying where they could be overheard? Were they thieves, or even rapists?

And the men of his own age. Aaron could imagine them guilty of any of a hundred crimes. The fact that he knew none of the faces didn't mean that they weren't fellow smugglers. Smuggling was the art of survival in Miasto.

The worst, the saddest, Aaron thought, were the younger men, the boys. One in particular caught Aaron's eye. He was stick-thin, with the luminous eyes of malnutrition. He looked neither Jewish nor Aryan. He was brown haired and simply Middle European, unremarkable. Except for the fact that no 10-year-old should be in a cage such as this one. No 10-year-old should be so frightened, so drawn into himself or work so hard to avoid the gaze of the people around him. If a boy could will himself invisible, the boy would have gone unseen.

Aaron's heart yearned to reach out, but he knew he wouldn't be able to speak the words of false reassurance. His own despair was so deep that he had lost the power to lie to a child. The world was simply as he saw it. His eyes were clear. Nothing would be changed. At least not by anyone in his cell.

Aaron closed his eyes and shifted to lean his head back against the wall. He wasn't yet ready to lie down in the filth at his feet, so he took what rest he could standing up.

He heard a rustle in the crowd and felt bodies shift around him. He opened his eyes, and now in front of him was a man who topped Aaron by perhaps an inch. His eyes were narrow and peeked out of a narrow mind.

"My turn," the man said.

"Your turn for what?" Aaron asked, politely enough.

"My turn against the wall."

It took Aaron a second to realize what the man meant. He wanted to lean his back against the wall and take some of the weight off his feet.

Aaron was conflicted. It wasn't such an unreasonable request. There were essentially no resources in the cell and so the walls of the cell had become a resource. There was a finite supply of wall and Aaron had a piece of it.

Okay.

On the other hand, Aaron had been beaten, drowned and would soon be dead. The tall man had been rude.

"No."

Aaron's voice was gravel and he spoke from somewhere beyond the cell.

The other man reached out a hand to shove Aaron, expecting no resistance from the shade in front of him. Aaron grabbed that arm and used it as a lever to spin the man around, kicked the man's knees out from under him and then kicked him in the back of the head, planting him facedown on the stone floor. There was just enough room because the sudden violence had sent everyone else pressing back against the iron bars of the cell door.

The extra weight caused the metal to groan audibly, but no guards came to take a look. As long as no one escaped, it seemed like the Germans didn't very much care what went on in the cells.

The young boy Aaron had noticed squeezed through the crowd. He looked down at the man below him and spat, but said nothing. Then he turned and wormed away, deeper into the press of bodies.

It was feeding time at the zoo. One by one, the men were allowed to come up to the front of the cell and receive a cup of broth from the same metal mug. There was a lot of pushing and shoving and men trying very hard to steal a second helping by taking their comrades' place.

As Aaron made his way to the front, he found himself looking for the boy. He wasn't visible until Aaron ducked his head down below chest height. All the men seemed to be treating him like an obstacle to be gotten around. The boy was getting no closer to the broth, nor would he without help.

Chapter 14

Aaron swam through the crowd until he reached the boy, bent down and somehow lifted him. With the boy hugged to his chest Aaron waded toward the broth.

And men moved. The crowd parted.

Broth for both of them, and then Aaron put the boy back down, and resumed his own place along the wall. The boy had no words of thanks, but stayed at Aaron's side.

Aaron shook his head and closed his eyes, leaned back in the spot he'd earned and made the world go away.

For less than a minute.

He heard his name called from outside the cell. At first he didn't move.

He heard his name again.

He knew the guard would offer him nothing that he wanted.

The third time the guard asked it was by turning a hard jet of water into the cell. Spraying up, spraying down, spraying from one side to the other. The water was deadly cold and the men tried their hardest to get away from it. Aaron felt ever-increasing pressure on his chest. The boy had slipped out of sight, trying to take refuge below the crowd.

It was hard to speak and harder to be heard above the general roar, but those nearest Aaron must have figured out what he was saying because suddenly they did everything they could to let him through. It wasn't long until Aaron was vomited up and stood at the front of the cell, admitting whom he was.

The door opened. Aaron was taken. The trip was a whirl of gray stone and institutional paint but, in the end, he found himself in the room with the metal chair, the bright lights, the pliers and the hand-cranked generator.

Here, too, was Hermann Clausewitz, infinitely patient.

Aaron was again put roughly in the metal chair, his arms tied ruthlessly behind him. He slumped as much as he could, enjoying the weight of his body resting comfortably on his ass, as God had intended.

"Better?" Clausewitz asked, seeing Aaron's posture.

Aaron said nothing. If he began to talk, where would he stop?

"They fed you?"

No reply.

"You know when I said I'd see you again, that first time we met at the hospital?" Clausewitz asked. "How did I know such a thing?

"I have to admit, I didn't. It was simply an effort to intimidate you. It worked, didn't it?"

Aaron kept his face blank.

"I know it did," Clausewitz said. "It always does, especially with you people. Even if you did serve in the Zendarmerie and the army."

So, Aaron was more than a name, a man in a basement. He was a file now, with "facts" and details.

"I'm sure you led the retreat. You Jews are always the first to run, if you can be made to fight at all."

Was Clausewitz going to insult him to death, Aaron wondered? It would make a nice change from physical injury.

"You know what? I'm just going to stop talking," Clausewitz said.

Aaron couldn't help himself.

"That would be nice."

Clausewitz actually laughed.

"Well, you're not going to like what I do instead any better."

"I suppose not," Aaron said.

He didn't know why, but he was talking, and now it was all just a matter of time.

Chapter 14

There were electrical shocks, punches and kicks, there was diesel fuel to drink and even breathe. There were fingernails slowly extracted.

Aaron worked hard to be somewhere else, but this time there was nowhere to go.

And this time he talked.

Some of what he said was even true.

Chapter 15

"You've just had an enormous stroke of luck," a voice in Polish said to Aaron. He was lying on the floor of another crowded cell, bleeding from cuts above his eye, lashes to his back and a gash in his thigh uncomfortably near his scrotum — not that it would have been comfortable anywhere else. The other prisoners had given him some room in order to let him die in peace.

"How so?" It was a faint croak, but it still surprised the men in his cell that Aaron could make any sound other than moans.

"You've just been shot trying to escape," the Polish speaker said cheerfully.

Aaron summoned enough energy to point an incurious eye at the man. It was the eye that could still open at all.

"So, get the fuck up! Don't just lie there like a dead man," the Pole, who was wearing the uniform of the Blue Police, said.

Aaron said nothing, nor did he move.

The man and his partner opened the door to the cell. They were large men with no inclination toward mercy in their faces. They reached down and grabbed Aaron under the arms, turning him into a grotesque marionette, unable to either resist or cooperate.

The rest of the men who shared Aaron's cell cowered, clambering on top of each other in their effort to get as far back from the open door as possible. Standing in each other's shit and dying slowly of starvation, dysentery and a lack of oxygen was better than the only other alternatives they knew of, being beaten or shot. There was no one to defend Aaron, no matter how helpless he appeared, and soon there would be no one to remember him.

Aaron was dragged in front of the German who was in charge of the floor. There was an exchange of words — perhaps an envelope? — and soon the journey continued up a flight and then down another corridor of the prison. This hallway, too, was lined with closed doors. Here, though, the sounds of horror were mixed with those of administration, including clattering typewriters and endlessly ringing telephones. The walls were lined with the grime of a million hands over a thousand years. The smells ranged from vomit to disinfectant and back again. The light that came down from the fixtures was itself a shadow.

The little troop pulled up in front of no door in particular and the policeman who had spoken opened it. Instead of a torture chamber, an office desk and chair were revealed. The telephone that sat on the desk was silent. On the visitor's side of the desk, was something that could only be called a chair by convention. It looked more uncomfortable than a church pew.

"Put him there," the man waiting in the room said, pointing to the guest "chair."

Aaron's ass met metal with surprising speed. He grunted and was still.

"Go," the man said, speaking to the two guards. "If he attacks me, I'll call you."

The two officers glanced down at Aaron who appeared catatonic and, laughing, left the room. Even the sound of the door slamming behind them elicited no response from the prisoner.

"Aaron. Aaron!"

Nothing.

Chapter 15

The man whose office it was pulled a small first aid kit from a drawer in his desk and locked the door. Before bandaging any of Aaron's wounds, he brought smelling salts under the helpless man's nose. Aaron jerked back in the seat and his one eye opened. The other man spoke softly and quickly.

"I've got good news and bad news. Your mouth looks really painful so I won't ask which you'd like to hear first.

"The good news is you're not going to be executed tonight."

"Okay," Aaron managed, not sounding like he cared very much.

"The bad news is that you're going to a camp."

Aaron stared, unblinking, but with a dawning recognition and more than a little surprise.

"Don't look at me like that!" the main said fiercely, but without raising his voice. "You're only getting this chance because I had you shot trying to escape. At great personal risk, I must add."

Aaron worked his jaw and felt it loosen a little beneath the bruising.

"Your man said the same thing, Novak. What the fuck do you mean?"

Aaron's voice was akin to a rusty saw cutting through particularly dry wood. If Novak, once Aaron's partner in the Zendarmerie, hadn't been trying to patch him up, he wouldn't have been close enough to pick out the meaning in the mumbles.

"You really are a lucky bastard," Novak said, attending to the gash in Aaron's thigh. "They must not have wanted you dead, yet. They didn't quite nick the artery."

Aaron grunted interrogatively and insistently.

"I had a man who was scheduled for the labor camps shot and he's in the record books as you. So, now you are going to the labor camps in his place."

Novak smiled benevolently at Aaron, and then shouted as the wounded man used his bare foot to smash down on his shoe.

"You killed someone for me?"

This time his voice was clear enough to be easily understood.

Novak was hopping and grabbing at his foot.

"What did you want me to do? What was your idea other than being beaten to death or shot? I'm your friend!"

Could that last part be true? Was Novak still a friend?

The two men had met shortly after Aaron had joined the Zendarmerie. Novak was one of the few officers who had shown Aaron any kindness. Or at least no derision. The Pole was from cosmopolitan Warsaw. He saw no reason to object to Jews, and he enjoyed a good fight. Novak had helped to beat off the men who Aaron couldn't take care of himself.

When Aaron was posted to the town where he would eventually meet Yelena, Novak had gone with him. They had been fixtures at each other's dinner tables, and liked to think that they were the scourges of the town's criminals.

Aaron had been swept up into the Army after the bombs began to fall, while Novak had disappeared, leaving Aaron with no idea what had happened to him.

But here Novak was, in the heart of Nazi Miasto, saving him one more time.

Aaron began to weep. It was all far, far too much: his pain, the ruined plan, Yelena gone. And now a man sentenced to death for no other reason than to let him live? Covered with wounds both psychic and physical, he wasn't sure how much farther he wanted to go.

There was no way to communicate all this to Novak, and little chance that a man who was able to commit murder so lightly would understand. Aaron didn't try.

After a minute or so, Novak was back on two feet. Seeing Aaron's tears and hearing his sobs, he pulled a flask from his jacket. He tipped it back, drinking deeply, and then put it to Aaron's lips. Despite their soreness, Aaron was able to seal them around his salvation. He drank.

"You know, there's nothing really so serious about your wounds," Novak said, with false cheer and a smile intended to win his friend back.

Aaron said nothing.

Novak became serious again.

"It doesn't matter how you feel now. You're going to live — at least for a while longer. From what I've heard about the camps, there's no guarantee of longevity, but still … Life is life. Isn't that what you people say is important?"

"You say that after what you just did?"

"I didn't say all life is equal," Novak replied. "If the war has taught us one thing, it's that. I killed a man who was going to die anyway so that my friend could live. We all have to make choices. What's changed is that every little choice we make today is between life and death."

"We aren't supposed to make those choices for others."

"But we do," Novak said. "If you keep a crust of bread for yourself in the ghetto, some child dies somewhere. But I know you eat, otherwise it would have been you who died. You chose yourself. You're lucky today, because I chose you, too."

"It isn't supposed to work like that." Aaron's tears were back.

"No, it's not," Novak agreed.

Finished with the bandages, the Pole returned to his side of the desk and picked up his phone. It only took a few seconds for the person on the other end to answer.

"What time does the train leave for the camp, today?" Novak asked. "Good. Then send someone to my office in five minutes to pick up Rosen."

He listened for a second.

"Good," he said again, and hung up, turning to Aaron. "You may live to thank me, yet."

Aaron sat quietly, downcast.

"Here, you'll need this," Novak said, passing Aaron a stained but very heavy coat from a hook. Then, from under his desk, he pulled out an old pair of warm boots.

Aaron found both a little large, but still he was grateful — especially as the boots had already been broken in. He remembered the pair he'd been given when he'd first joined the army. He still had scars from where they'd cut into the backs of his ankles.

Within a few moments of Aaron's dressing, there was a knock on the door and Novak rose to open it. Two Blue Policemen that Aaron had never seen before came in.

"Take Mr. Chaim Rosen here to his train," Novak said.

Aaron was again jerked to his feet. He turned with a question to Novak.

"Yelena?"

"I don't know," Novak said brusquely.

Finally, it dawned on Aaron to ask the most obvious question of all.

"How did you find me? Why are you here?"

"Don't you people believe in luck?" Novak asked, his eyebrows raised.

There was no time for Aaron to say a final word to his cruel savior. He was quickly out the door, through the corridor and down several flights of stairs. Every time he tried to stand on his own, he had his legs knocked out from under him by the pace.

He wasn't strong enough to keep up, though the vodka from Novak's flask helped somewhat with the pain.

However long it felt, it must have only been a few minutes before Aaron found himself without his guards in a sort of pen alongside other prisoners. Some displayed cuts and bruises, but nothing as severe as what Aaron had suffered. Most looked away from him. Aaron, knowing he stood in another man's place — that he had cost that man his life — was unable to look anywhere but the ground.

Outside the pen he saw many black uniforms with the death's head insignia, very few blue Polish jackets. Wherever his group was going, there was to be no thin veneer of Polish authority.

"Do you see over there?"

One man had jabbed another with an elbow.

"Where?"

"To your left," the older man said.

Aaron looked, too. He saw a line of women being herded into an adjacent enclosure that was similar to his own.

A voice only a few steps away from Aaron called, "Rachel!" The man who owned it ran toward the fence.

The woman turned to meet him. The two locked hands through the wooden boards that separated them and quickly had their heads down, speaking intimately to each other.

There were a few other such reunions, leaving the rest of the men grimmer than before. They stamped their feet to keep warm and tried to reassure themselves that wherever their loved ones might be, they were safe.

Aaron scanned the group of women again and again, but saw no sign of Yelena's bright hair. There was no one he knew in the group.

"I guess Novak couldn't find anyone to kill for her," he said to himself. Prisoners nearest to him tried to edge just a little further away, hearing the bitterness and rage, though not the words.

Everyone stood in the open air for first one hour, then two. The weather, unseasonably warm for much of the day, began to cool. People unconsciously began to huddle together, the women and the men. The few couples, mothers and sons, fathers and daughters who had found each other, had to pull their hands back from the fence to put them in their pockets. There was little chatter now. The words had been said.

Light was dimming as both the cloud cover thickened and the sun sank. Train sounds were heard and then drew closer. A metallic whistle cut through the cold air. People began to talk again, speculation rife on where exactly they were going.

Now the gates of the prison were rolled back, revealing rails and an impromptu platform.

A man with a religious beard turned to another who looked much the same.

"I'm sure that it won't be so terrible. After all, the women are going to the same place."

The other nodded. The assumption of gallantry wasn't dead, Aaron thought, even if the thing itself had galloped away long before.

A locomotive chuffed into view but behind it weren't coaches. Instead, the cars were made up of wooden slats spaced fairly close together with big doors in the middle. Clearly they were used for freight.

They weren't empty. It was possible to hear voices calling out from inside some of the cars, and to see limbs waving. Some voices demanded to know what was going on, why the train was stopping, what the final destination was. The wind was blowing from across the tracks and struck the faces of the waiting men and women with the smell of an open sewer. Some turned their faces away. One woman retched thinly.

The train finally came to rest. A few guards swung down from their places between the cars, machine guns pointing toward the waiting crowd. Doors were thrown open on empty compartments and the prison's soldiers began to shout.

"Raus! Raus!"

The gates of the pens were pulled wide and the men and women, terrified by what they'd seen, heard and smelled, slowly began to walk toward the train.

"Raus!" Move it!

Rifle butts struck backs in the rear of the crowd and the pace began to pick up somewhat.

Suddenly, a woman broke out of the crowd and ran toward an officer.

"I can't leave! I have a baby! She'll die without me."

"Back in line," said a soldier who had stepped over to protect his officer.

"Please! This isn't right!" She was crying, yelling.

The officer looked away as if bored. Seeing this, the woman began to shriek.

"You must listen to me! *You must!*"

She threw her fists against the soldier, who pushed her to her knees. The officer calmly pulled his sidearm and walked over to point it at the woman's skull.

"Please!" she screamed.

The shot silenced her.

The shot silenced everyone in the courtyard.

The woman's body slumped and then fell to the side.

Still, the officer said nothing, just calmly put the gun back in its holster and returned to where he'd been standing. He nodded to the soldiers who again began shoving the Jews toward the train.

“Raus!”

When it was Aaron’s turn, he put up no more struggle than anyone else. He climbed over the lip of the doorway and then made his way toward the back where there was already a group of men sitting. They weren’t able to sit for long. More and more men followed them into the car. Soon it was crowded and the men tiredly got to their feet. It became more crowded, and more. Fifteen minutes after he had boarded, Aaron was trapped, breathing in the breath the man in front of him had just exhaled.

“It must be nearby, wherever we’re going,” an optimistic voice said.

The door of the car slammed shut. The locomotive’s wheels began to turn.

Chapter 16

No matter how far the train traveled or how cold the Polish countryside became, there was little fear that most of the occupants inside the cattle cars would freeze. All were packed together so closely that body heat made up for the frigid winds — at least for those in the middle of the car.

Those closest to the center of the pile were the children, shielded by their fathers when it was possible, or by strangers when it was necessary. Some men had tried to take the warmth for themselves, but were severely discouraged by the rest. Many of those who had tried, in fact, were now pressed against the wooden slats that made up the walls of the carriage. There they could enjoy the freshest air and the coldest winds. The air further in had been cycled through too many pairs of lungs, and there was little nourishment in it.

The people were not fed, nor were they given water. Several times along the route, the train stopped for one reason or another. German and Polish guards would climb down from their posts to stretch their legs, warm coats comforting them as they stood about. They would smoke cigarettes, make jokes and a great show of eating and drinking in front of an audience that wished them nothing but death and dismemberment. The guards knew it, and it made them laugh all the harder.

If they became bored, the guards would sometimes throw snowballs at the cars, watching the Jews scramble to grab whatever ice came through the slats and shove it into their mouths to melt as if it were the sweetest ice cream.

The Jews themselves were often bored. Aaron spent some of his time eavesdropping on conversations between neighbors who were searching for small commonalities and temporary friendships.

"You grew up on Krasno Street? I lived just a block away for years," one man said to his thinner comrade. "Funny we never met. Did you ever go to Weiss' bakery?"

"I loved that place. When did it close?"

"Oh, some time before the war. I think that's actually one thing we can't blame the Germans for."

The men gave each other faint smiles.

A corner of Aaron's mouth quirked, too.

Aaron didn't participate in much of the talk. His body and soul were in no shape to reach out. He was trapped upright, pressed against a changing cast of fellow travelers. He had no doubt that several of his ribs were broken. Each breath was a source of shocking pain that was becoming familiar.

He was tortured by his inability to sort his memories from his nightmares. Sometimes he couldn't see any difference between the two.

What had he told Clausewitz? Who had he betrayed? Were his friends being tortured, were they dead because of what he'd said as he wept? Were they meeting Clausewitz themselves and giving up other friends in turn? Would it stop before the entire fabric of the ghetto had been torn apart like so much tissue paper?

But Clausewitz had spoken, too … Had given Aaron a piece to his puzzle … To Berson's death.

What the hell had he said?

The answer was drowned in Aaron's immediate misery, the swaying of the train, the pressing of the bodies around him, each breath that he struggled not to take. He didn't sleep, but he did pass out.

Chapter 16

He woke as the train slowed. Inertia caused his fellow passengers to squeeze harder against his rib cage, bringing on fresh pain. It was nighttime and snow was falling heavily. People muttered that they hoped the weather wasn't the reason for the stop. No one was exactly sure how much longer they could survive on the train. A number had fallen, and efforts to wake them had come to nothing. No one wanted to admit that they were dead.

Aaron squinted to see beyond the flakes and the darkness. There was something nearby. He was sure.

A harsh beam of light proved him right and blinded him at the same time. A second spotlight quickly followed. When Aaron could see again, men with dogs and guns were coming to meet the train. The guards on board jumped down to meet their relief.

The commander of the train, his face and breath visible in silhouette, spoke with a man who carried himself as if he were in charge of something. There was paperwork exchanged and full-armed salutes. Aaron could only guess that heels were clicked. The snow would have muffled the sound.

One by one, the carriages were emptied. Most of the passengers could walk, albeit stiffly. Others, alive and dead, were carried out by their fellow Jews. On orders from the commandant, the dead were thrown into a waiting ditch. Those alive but unable to walk were shot. The ambulatory were again made to throw the bodies into the ditch.

Aaron's car was the third to be unloaded. Even those who couldn't walk did. People lent one another a shoulder, an arm or a hand. The dead, however dear they had been in life, could not be helped.

For a moment, Aaron wasn't sure how he was going to leave the train, on his feet or back. A youngish woman who had come aboard to clear the dead slipped him her hand to clutch. Whatever deprivation she had lived through since the invasion, she had a reserve of strength Aaron felt flow through him. As they strode together, Aaron stood taller and took more weight on his own feet.

At last, the ten cars of the train held no one else. Hoses were turned on them to flush out the excrement that had covered the floors in noisome mud. One soldier playfully squirted a Jew, adding a deeper cold to his misery.

The guards formed the Jews up into squares of sixty-four, dividing men and women into separate columns. Temporary reunions were broken up. Sons were taken from mothers, daughters from fathers. The shrieks of both parents and children filled the night until a gunshot silenced them. An example having been made, the Nazi soldiers marched the survivors into the compound. Everyone was given "soup" made out of warmish water and God alone knew what else, and then were marched further, into barracks.

The barracks contained nothing more than floor-to-ceiling rows of bunks comprised of rough wooden slats, like the walls of the cattle cars. The beds were stacked so tightly they resembled nothing more than bookshelves. To husband resources, the builders — slave laborers — had used as few boards as possible, making the gap between them dangerous for a man who rolled onto his side.

As each new trainload of workers arrived, the barracks filled beyond capacity. Men were forced to share shelf space with two or more companions. There were few blankets, so in the winter the warmth was much appreciated, if not the company.

The overcrowding wasn't a permanent condition. Over the days, bunks emptied as those who had been using them died from starvation, exhaustion or other forms of cruelty. Each train's arrival began the process anew.

On Aaron's first night at the camp, he found himself a place with three other men who had lived there for weeks or months. They were in no better shape than he was himself, perhaps worse. Looking at them, the word that popped into Aaron's mind was "wraith." Their clothes were so tattered that even in the darkness, he was able to make out skin stretched thin over ribs, and limbs that looked more like bare bones.

Aaron begged their pardon as he joined them, explaining that their bunk seemed the least crowded of the accommodations available. There was grumbling, but no energy for a fight. The man nearest the wall edged closer to it and the others closed ranks behind him. Rags that appeared to be made from a mixture of old sweaters and coats were the only covering available. The men Aaron had found were even gracious enough to share with him. He added his own coat to the pile and found his eyes welling up at the small, unnecessary kindness the men had offered.

Only lovers and small children with secrets should have their mouths as close to another person's ear as Aaron's was to his bedmate. The uncomfortable intimacy allowed Aaron to talk in a whisper barely above silence.

"Thank you," was where Aaron began.

He could feel the man nod in return.

"Where are we?" Aaron asked.

He could feel the breath of the man's answer.

"Kronberg Labor Camp."

"Are we near Miasto?"

"I don't know."

"How bad is it here?"

"Bad."

"The food?"

"Food?" The man's chuckle was a wheeze. "Please, now, be quiet. There are only a few hours of the night left. We must sleep."

"What's your name?" Aaron asked.

"Kaczynski."

"That's not Jewish," Aaron half asked, half said.

"No. Sleep."

That was all Aaron could get. It wasn't long before his own exhaustion made the splintered boards feel like a featherbed. He slept.

Dawn had not come, but that made no difference to the sounds and sights that woke Aaron. Men were shouting, dogs growled. A horn sounded somewhere. Before Aaron's eyes had opened to more than slits, his friend from the night before was trying to edge him out of the bunk.

"We have ten minutes to present ourselves," Kaczynski said. "Move it."

The ten minutes included the time needed to use the latrines and wash as well as they could in near-frozen water. There were a lot of men who had to go, and it didn't take Aaron very long to realize that not everyone was going to make it through in time. As he was new, he was stronger than those who had lived on the camp's rations for any length of time. With regret, he took advantage of that fact and found himself facing the open latrine before many others.

Men stood and squatted in full view of each other and also of two amused guards, who laughed as one man shat blood.

Chapter 16

"Not much longer for him," said the Nazi who stood to Aaron's right. He spoke in a Polish so perfect he could only be a Pole, despite his SS uniform.

The other man answered in the same language.

"I'll bet you a reichsmark he doesn't even make it back to the barracks tonight."

"I'll take that bet. I think there's a little more life in him." The guard leaned down toward the trench. "Isn't that right, my little Jew? In fact, you better make it home tonight, otherwise I'll kill you!"

Both guards laughed hard.

The man with the bloody diarrhea slipped and fell into his own shit.

The guards laughed harder.

Aaron said nothing, but he leaned over and took the man's flailing, shit-stained hand and pulled him up.

The shitter tried to thank him, weakly. Aaron said nothing, didn't glance at him, and moved on to the frigid water where he tried, inadequately, to wash his hands.

Aaron moved toward the front door of the barracks as he saw others doing. The ten minutes were apparently up. Guards started to file in and club anyone who wasn't moving fast enough.

"Schnell!" they shouted, sweeping their arms side to side, showing no concern for where the truncheons fell. Some who were hit cried out, others didn't bother, either knowing there was no mercy or because they didn't have the energy to waste.

The inmates were marched to the spacious central parade ground of the camp. The camp itself, Aaron could now see, was a rectangular structure that seemed made entirely of raw timber and barbed wire, with floodlights mounted all around. There were occasional towers with spotlights and men with machine guns at the gates and at numerous other spots along the wall. Guards roamed the grounds with dogs that were clearly better fed than the prisoners.

Men who knew better than Aaron lined up shoulder-to-shoulder, eventually making ranks ten wide and deep. He picked a place next to Kaczynski, who Aaron had decided to make a friend.

When he looked over to say something to the other man, though, Kaczynski gave him a warning look that bottled the words deep in Aaron's chest.

They stood there, all the men, all the women, even the children who had spilled out of the barracks and into this open space. They observed silence. The cold became ever more intense. The sun refused to rise.

Aaron could see knees buckling, people who were beginning to crumple in on themselves. It wasn't a question of who would fall, but rather who would fall first.

Finally, someone did.

The man may or may not have been dead when he fell, but he certainly was by the time the guards had finished beating and kicking him, shouting for him to get back in line. An officer came by, made the pronouncement of death and pulled two prisoners out of line in order to carry the body to an open pit that must have been dug for the purpose. The man wasn't big enough to fill the hole, but Aaron was sure the hole would be filled by the end of the day.

At the first glimmer of sun on the dull horizon, the guards moved men and women into new lines to receive their breakfast. Aaron's line was long, but the rules seemed a little more relaxed than on the parade ground. People spoke quietly to each other while they waited.

Chapter 16

"Does that happen all the time?" Aaron asked Kaczynski, referring to the casual beating and death of the unknown man.

"All the time. The only way to avoid being beaten is to avoid being noticed," Kaczynski said. "And, truthfully, that's hardly a guarantee. The secret of the camp is that you're not here to work, you're here to die. If they can get something out of us first, that's fine. But it's not necessary."

"But what's a Pole like you doing here? Did they make a mistake?"

"Not at all. Actually, I'm not the only Pole in here. You can tell by looking at the little patches on people's clothing. Yellow means Jew. Red," he pointed to his lapel, "means temporary resident."

Kaczynski grunted a laugh.

"In fact, all I have to do is make it another week. If I do, I get to go home."

"But how did you get here?"

"Me? I've made my living as a small-time thief since I was a boy. Nothing big, but a burglary here, a burglary there. I made the mistake of thinking it would be business as usual after the Germans came. Still, that isn't why I'm here," Kaczynski said, laughing again. This time he choked on it. It was a while before the hacking stopped, and when it did, there was blood on the ground.

During their conversation, the two had moved to the front of the line where they were given a cup of "coffee" and a slice of brown bread.

"You might want to save your bread for later," Kaczynski said. "There's no lunch and the days are long."

There was little time to suck down the dirty water — which was all Aaron could imagine the "coffee" to be. Chewing would have to be done on the run.

The one hundred men of Aaron's barracks were arranged in two lines and ordered to select heavy shovels or hammers from a stack. Once they were equipped, the march began. Guards kept pace, leading them out of the gates of the camp and onto a path that had been cleared of snow.

There was no talking on the march to the worksite. After the first kilometer or so, no one would have been able to talk, anyway. The tools' wooden shafts bore down on the men's shoulders, adding to their exhaustion. The guards weren't happy to be on this walk either, and from the looks on their partially covered faces, they were becoming more dangerous the farther the detachment went.

A man stumbled in front of Aaron. The column stumbled with him. There was no way to get around him. Without thinking, Aaron grabbed him off the ground and swung the man's shovel over his own shoulder. By the time the guard came to the spot where the hiccup had been, all he saw was a steady stream of shuffling men. Still, the SS private noticed that Aaron was carrying two shovels and had a comment to make.

"We'll see how you feel about your kindness later in the day." The guard smiled. It wasn't a smile Aaron wanted to see again.

It could have been two hours — or possibly just one — when the column finally arrived at a fenced-in area filled with partially cut stones and broken up rocks. A guard unlocked the gate to the quarry and everyone else filed in behind him.

Men took up various positions, immediately beginning to dig and crush. There was no pause between the march and the start of work.

Aaron found, like everyone else, that his coat quickly became an encumbrance. He removed it and let his work with the hammer keep him warm. He smashed rocks in the name of the German war effort and when the pile was large enough, he borrowed a shovel to load them onto a wheelbarrow that another slave then pushed somewhere else. Aaron didn't know where. He didn't give a shit, either.

Aaron had no idea why he was breaking rocks, or why someone else was carting them. Perhaps it was simply a way of working men to death quickly. Aaron shook his head. No, it didn't seem nearly efficient enough, and the world knew the German devotion to efficiency. At a natural pause, Aaron stuck his hammer in a pile of rocks that were waiting for the wheelbarrow and turned to Kaczynski to ask what they were doing.

"I think the stones are for roads," the man said, his face red, his wheeze pronounced.

"Ah," Aaron said, idly wondering where the roads would go and what unfortunate people the Germans planned to visit at their ends.

The day passed, rocks were broken and men died. Some died for the guards' amusement, others because they'd reached the end of their strength. As the sun was going down, one died because of a watch.

He was a youngish man, but he looked worn to a nub. He made the mistake of looking up from his digging. The guard above was wearing a watch that the prisoner's mother had given him as a birthday present a few years before.

It wasn't the smart thing to do, but perhaps the young man's smarts had gone with his old life. He called out to the guard.

"You're wearing my watch!" he shouted.

"Could be," the guard said, amused. "I have so many watches nowadays."

All personal items were taken from prisoners as they entered the labor camp, though Aaron and his trainload had already given up theirs at the prison in Miasto.

"Is that what it was? Just theft? Not part of your great 'war effort?' Just good, honest theft?" The prisoner's voice rose in both pitch and volume.

"So, what do you need it for, anyway?" the guard asked. "We tell you when to get up, when to eat, when to march, when to work, when to walk home, when to sleep.

"And frankly, it's so much easier for me to keep it all straight now that I have this nice watch. Swiss, isn't it?"

The prisoner's curses were as creative as they were pointless.

He kicked the ground at his feet, scattering small bits of granite and other stones only a geologist could identify.

"How about these pebbles that we're making, that we're dying to make for you?" asked the Jew. "Do they go anywhere? Are you even building roads, like you say? Or is that just another lie? You steal from us, you kill us, and it's for nothing at all?"

Several of the other guards had gathered. The more angry the man got, the more they laughed, poking each other in the ribs and making little comments that led to great guffaws. The other prisoners continued to work as if nothing was happening, or at least did their best to give that appearance. Everyone understood that there were no excuses for stopping work.

Now there were no more words, just an inhuman screech. A face that had recently seen no color except from frostbite was now full red with rage. The slave reached up to grab the guard, pulling the man down into the pit beside him.

In seconds, the guard was bloody.

Seconds later, the prisoner was dead, blood pouring from where the back of his head had been. A small cloud of smoke wafted from the Luger of another guard standing just a few meters away.

Chapter 16

This time, Aaron was on the detail that took the body outside the quarry's fence, dropping it into a deep depression that was already half filled.

Soon, but not soon enough, it was time for the survivors to head back to Kronberg. Despite their exhaustion, the prisoners walked with a will. Even the promise of a cup of something called soup and a cold bed was enough to motivate them after a day playing at quarrymen. Looking at the faces and skeletal bodies that made up his column, it was hard for Aaron to imagine them as fit for any job other than invalid.

Aaron could only assume that he looked no better, but a day of hard labor had shown him that his injuries weren't quite as bad as he'd first supposed. While his chest still felt as if it were in a vice, he had to acknowledge that there was no way he could have lifted a hammer, let alone swung it, if his ribs were truly broken. He was also getting the sight back in his left eye, which had swollen shut thanks to Clausewitz.

Sticking a hand into a pocket for warmth, he discovered yet another reason for unreasonable optimism: he had forgotten to eat his slice of bread during the day, meaning that he now faced the happy prospect of bread to lap up his soup.

Yes, things were looking up.

At the front of the line, a man stumbled and was pushed off to the side without comment. It mattered to nobody if he was alive or dead. The cold would finish him if nothing else did.

Two steps ahead of Aaron, a man lunged out of line and went to the prisoner who had fallen. Aaron was touched by the sentiment. The brave soul would surely be beaten for his act of kindness.

If that was what it was.

As the apparent hero leaned over the maybe corpse, he pulled and struggled, finally coming away with the fallen man's coat. The guards were on the scavenger seconds after and he was beaten bloody.

But he kept the coat.

Numbed feet and minds were finally roused by the sight of harsh floodlights ahead. The camp was near and the men's steps quickened to a shuffle. Aaron could see that his wasn't the only group returning. There were other squads of men and also women. God alone knew where they had been or what they had done with their day.

Inside the grounds, everyone was forced into lines again. Vats of something steamed under the lights. Jewish trustees were stirring the "broth" and serving out the mugs. Aaron found Kaczynski in the line, which was only possible because his position in it was *behind* Aaron. If Aaron had tried to cut *ahead* in the line, there was no doubt in his mind that he would have sparked a riot, no matter how tired everyone was.

"How did you enjoy your first day?" Kaczynski asked tiredly.

"I'm lucky it wasn't my last," Aaron said.

"I say that to myself every day."

"There's no way to survive this place, is there?" Aaron asked. "The man who owned the watch was right, wasn't he? They couldn't give a shit whether we work. We're just here to die."

"Yes, I think so," Kaczynski said solemnly. "Even those of us who are only supposed to be here for three months, six months. As you can see, we're all treated the same."

The mug that Aaron grabbed was cold in his hand, but the woman with the dull eyes and the ladle poured in wonderful warmth.

The two men took their steaming soup and stood apart. Aaron brought out the brown bread and broke it, careful not to let a crumb fall to the ground. He passed precisely half to Kaczynski. The two men dipped the bread and brought it to their lips slowly, savoring the moment and the most simple of pleasures, now a treat.

The taste was terrible, the broth mostly water, some beets perhaps playing a peripheral role. The bread was rough-textured and Aaron wouldn't have been surprised if sawdust had been stored too close to the flour. But hunger and cold were the only spices the meal needed, and those were available in abundance.

"I wonder what my wife is eating tonight." Kaczynski said, as he chewed slowly.

"Hopefully it's better than this," Aaron said.

"Perhaps."

"Even in the ghetto, I ate better than this," Aaron said.

"It's bad there?"

"Yes, it's bad. Not much for anyone to eat. Not much medicine, warm clothing, fuel. Not much of anything, really."

"I'm not sure there's much of those things anywhere. Outside of the German storerooms, I mean," Kaczynski said.

"No."

Aaron didn't want to argue with his new friend, or compare suffering with a man who had lived in Kronberg for more than a few days.

The two men shared a bit more of their lives with each other, but were cautious lest they reveal anything of interest to the guards.

More shouting. It was time to head to the barracks. No one minded. There wasn't any food left, anyway. There hadn't been for a while. The men and women brought their bone-dry mugs back to the tables. People in different barracks nodded to each other as they passed. A man saw his wife, their hands touched and then both were forced to turn away.

In the barracks, Aaron saw the man who had taken a beating for a coat. He was curled up in it, and though his lips were split, he was smiling.

At least someone was warm, Aaron thought wryly.

"Six days," Kaczynski said as he turned away from Aaron, positioning himself for sleep.

They were the last words spoken that night.

Chapter 17

Aaron was woken by dreams of Yelena and the erection they brought with them. He was astonished to find that his body was capable of such a reaction and relieved to find himself lying on the outer edge of the bunk and facing out as well. As knowledge of his surroundings returned to him, he wondered at his unconscious mind's ability to feel lust for anything other than food or warmth.

Aaron still had no idea what had happened to Yelena on the night that he was captured. Much of his interrogation by the Gestapo was fog. The pain and exhaustion had melded days and nights together, along with conversations and waking dreams — nightmares rather. Still, one name had never come up. Aaron had never mentioned Yelena and neither had his interrogator, Clausewitz. If Clausewitz had her — or even knew about her — he would have used Yelena ruthlessly, and without hesitation. She would have become the primary implement of Aaron's torture.

Still, it spun and spun in Aaron's mind. Why had she failed to make the rendezvous? Had she seen the Germans readying for the raid and held back? Had she been killed without the Germans ever learning who she was, or her relationship to Aaron?

Had she faced her own betrayal? Aaron had never been happy with bringing in Andrusz, the gunrunner. He'd only agreed because there was no other way to get the weapons.

But a necessary risk wasn't necessarily a smart risk. While Aaron had reasons to believe that Andrusz had nothing to do with his own capture, none of them was a guarantee of the man's fidelity. Just because he hadn't betrayed Aaron didn't mean he'd kept faith with Yelena.

The need for answers had helped keep Aaron alive in both frying pan and fire. The answers lived in Miasto and Aaron was going back to find them. Soon.

It had been seven days spent in Hell. Aaron had used that word indiscriminately all of his life, but now it was more than a mild expletive or even an abstract notion. Aaron had grown to know Hell intimately, along with its demons, devils and the condemned. He knew which guards killed for pleasure or caused pain to pass the time. He knew which of the other prisoners were still capable of compassion and those who had turned feral in their time at Kronberg labor camp, stealing what they could and informing for the slightest imagined infraction.

Seven days had been enough for Aaron. It was time to go, and he knew how he would do it.

Contemplating his task kept sleep at arm's length. An extra dose of exhaustion would be no help, but there was nothing he could do about it.

Aaron listened to the sounds that filled Kronberg's walls.

Within the barracks were the snorers, the moaners, the night farters.

Generators pounded, keeping the spot and floodlights on, perhaps creating heat for someone.

A little further out, a dog was barking, a guard was cursing, complaining about the cold. Further yet, a scream, its cause unknown.

Night.

Aaron saw no hint of a sunrise, had no watch to check, so he took the word of the bugle and the hollers of the guards as proof of approaching dawn. Kaczynski stirred next to him.

Chapter 17

Everybody groaned and turned, stretched as they could and climbed down from the bunks. As always, the guards urged them to move faster.

On the way to the latrine ditch, Aaron noticed a bunk with a solitary, unmoving figure on it.

Isaac, Aaron said to himself, putting a name to the body. A hint of guilt tickled the back of his mind when he realized he'd already assessed the dead man's possessions before remembering his name. But Isaac's rags had become shreds. Aaron had no need of them.

He passed on and did what was necessary, making it out to the parade ground to stand pointlessly without being hit. He stood with everyone else, slumped at attention — if such a thing was possible.

A slow hour passed. A woman in some other group fell, as someone seemed to do every morning during this assembly. Maybe that was the point. No other reason had ever been given for the time they stood every day in freezing inactivity.

The woman's friends — comrades? bunkmates? — gathered her up quickly and there was no punishment meted out.

Nothing else happened. Then it was time for breakfast and a grateful sigh swept the open place, unheard beneath the morning's wind.

Kaczynski looked particularly weak to Aaron. He'd been watching his friend closely. In the week before his scheduled release, the man had grown sicker and more frail. The bloody cough was more frequent and Aaron had seen more blood in the man's urine.

After they had received their breakfast Aaron gave Kaczynski half of his bread, though he knew it wasn't going to make a difference. Both welcomed the warm water flavored with just a touch of dirt and remembered coffee.

The two men returned their mugs, picked up their heavy tools and joined the march to the quarry. As the sun finally rose, the air changed. The edge seemed to have fallen off the wind. It was blowing from behind for once, making the walk a little easier. Aaron wondered, looking around, if maybe the snow was melting a little? Was water streaming at the side of the road?

It would be a good day to go home.

Kaczynski stumbled ahead of Aaron, his feet crossed up. His shovel fell to the ground with a clang. Aaron sprang into action, grabbing his friend under his armpits, desperately trying to get him back on his feet and in rhythm with the rest of the line. Kaczynski had already called attention to himself, which was dangerous enough. Falling out of line might have been the end of him.

The man behind Aaron also did his part to save Kaczynski, grabbing up the shovel as he passed it with a quick bobbing motion. The man passed the shovel forward to Aaron; Aaron passed it forward to Kaczynski, who took it up as if he was bearing a cross to Calvary.

"Thank you," Kaczynski breathed and immediately started coughing, blood flecking the ground.

One of the guards opened the gate to the quarry as usual and the men took their places, with the exception of a few prisoners who had arrived on a train the night before. There was little to teach, and in a few minutes the new men were situated and could hardly be told from the old, except by their strength.

In his week breaking rocks, Aaron's hands had grown callused and the tools he used familiar. Today they were heavier than yesterday, when they had been heavier than the day before. He became lost in the rhythm, left himself behind.

Around him, people worked, they fell, they were beaten. The guards laughed and tried to keep warm by stamping their feet and drinking brandy. They drank through every day and their amusements turned darker the drunker they became.

Aaron needed the guards to get good and drunk today and they were happy to oblige. As the sun — which, in a break from Eastern European tradition, was visible today — began to lower itself toward the far horizon, the SS began to sing a sentimental favorite. A few swayed slowly back and forth, arm in arm. A Jewish man in his pit made the mistake of looking up at the guards with an expression of disgust. A guard who wasn't singing looked down and saw him.

"What do you think you're looking at?" the guard shouted. "And what's that look on your face? You don't appreciate a little patriotic signing?"

It was time for Aaron to move.

Kaczynski was working next to him. Aaron grabbed his arm and dragged his friend against the wall of their own pit, into the shadows.

"I'm sorry," Aaron said, and grabbed Kaczynski by the throat. He squeezed the thin reed that supported the Pole's gaunt head. Kaczynski's arms flailed feebly at his unimagined attacker. His eyes bugged out, but still they managed to ask, "Why?"

Aaron knew this wasn't a moment to listen to his conscience, but he couldn't finish what he was doing without trying to justify himself.

"Every day that we've been here, you've been sicker and sicker. You can hardly lift your shovel. You cough blood in the day and it's worse when I'm lying next to you at night.

"But you don't die!" Aaron hissed. "You won't die!

"You won't last two days after they let you out, but they're going to let you go any hour now. You keep saying so yourself! What choice do I have? I need to live! I have to find my wife! I can't die now!"

Kaczynski's head began to slump, finally falling to the side and still. The eyes remained open. Aaron denied the urge to close them. Dignity had no place in what had happened. Instead, he kept Kaczynski's body standing against the wall by leaning his own body in. He reached down, fumbling with numb fingers at the buttons of his own coat, followed by Kaczynski's. He struggled, tugged and pulled. He felt the air on his sweating skin as his coat came off.

In a second, he was wearing his friend's jacket with the crucial red patch on the lapel. It took longer to get Aaron's warmer coat unto Kaczynski's uncooperative body, but then it was done.

Aaron put his arms under Kaczynski's, holding him up as he had on the morning march. This time it was no kindness. He did it only to drag Kaczynski back into the light and lay him down. Aaron picked up his shovel and went back to work, trying very hard not to look around to see if he'd been observed. He kept his back to where Kaczynski's body lay.

Finally, Aaron reached up to wipe sweat from his forehead. He used the motion to surreptitiously check if anyone had noticed the dead man. No one had. The guards were still busy with their fun. The man who'd dare disapprove of their antics was screaming in a way Kaczynski had never had the opportunity to. Finally, Aaron couldn't take it any longer.

"A man's dead here, I think!" he shouted.

That got the attention of two of the guards. In no rush, they ambled over to confirm what Aaron had said.

"You think?" one of the guards asked. His name was Weber and he was known for his particular sense of humor. "I would imagine you'd be able to tell by now."

The other guard laughed.

"Yes," Aaron said. "He's dead."

"Good, good. A little more for the rest of you on the chow line tonight!" he said, and both of the Germans laughed. The joke was so funny because no matter how many slaves died in a day, the portions at breakfast or dinner never changed.

When Weber had recovered himself, he turned back to Aaron.

"What was his name? I'm sorry, but I can't keep track of all of you. You never seem to last long enough. It's not that the name matters, really, but we have to keep the paperwork straight."

Aaron looked Weber in the eye, on the edge of impudence, but lowered his gaze before he crossed the line.

"Chaim," Aaron said, "Chaim Rosen."

"Not Rosenstein or Rosenberg, or one of those other names you all have?"

"Rosen," Aaron said, once again skating the edge of defiance.

"Good, good."

Weber was quite cheerful.

"So, what are you waiting for?" the Nazi said. "Don't just leave him there!"

It was grim duty, but Aaron had done it before. Kaczynski was so thin that dragging him to the pit outside the fence was easier than lifting a shovel. A guard opened the gate and followed Aaron out to the shallow burial ditch. Aaron laid Kaczynski down and pushed a few clods of dirt on top of him while saying the Kaddish for a Catholic Pole he had killed with his bare hands.

No one at the quarry had bothered to glance closely enough at Kaczynski's body to see the obvious cause of death.

The walk back to Kronberg took years. Aaron felt trapped by the pace of the column. He needed to get away from Kaczynski, he needed to get back to the camp so that he could be released. He had no time for the walking corpses who were plodding in front and behind.

An unexpected kink in the line, caused by someone's attempt to remove a rock from his shoe without entirely stopping, caused Aaron to hit his nose on the top of another man's head. Aaron cursed, but not loudly.

With the sun sinking, the water on each side of the path was slowing to syrup. It would be frozen before Aaron had finished his evening soup. He turned his thoughts from what he'd done and tried to imagine where he would be when all of Poland's snow had melted. Feverish daydreams of Yelena and a cottage in a world turned green distracted him from the march and helped him finish it.

The camp, when he got there, was the same, but the soup tasted more wholesome. Neither the guards, nor the loudspeakers said anything about an impending release of prisoners. Aaron was not worried. After all, it was only the sixth night since Kaczynski told Aaron that he had a week left on his sentence. The announcement would come in the morning.

As the curfew descended, Aaron shared his bunk with the two men who had always lain beside him and Kaczynski. If they noticed there was a different man wearing the red patch on his coat, they said nothing. If they noticed anyone was missing at all, they asked no questions. By the end of the day, exhaustion had dulled the eyes of the keenest observers and starvation lulled the senses.

How could one tell the difference between two men with light-brown beards, dirty blond hair and muddled blue eyes? Dirt and a beard could hide a multitude of sins.

At first Aaron slept badly, and then he slept worse. A shout in a dream became a squeal in the dark that woke no one, except himself. For a second night in a row, sleep wouldn't return. For the first night since his arrival, Kaczynski's body offered no warmth.

Aaron lay and listened again. He heard the winds wake up and saw the first new snowflakes landing, obliterating yesterday's promise of warmer weather. Kaczynski's face covered the walls, but Aaron tried to focus on his freedom, on the fact that he wouldn't have to carry a hammer or shovel a thousand miles out in the snow and crush stones until his back was broken. Even if he had to wait for every second to pass, the morning and freedom were coming for him, he told himself. He brushed away voices telling him that he didn't deserve to see either.

Somehow he dozed. Not for long, but long enough for the guards to start another day. Aaron fled his bed and was the first to the latrine, thinking that it would be the last time he used it. That fact didn't make it smell any better. Nor did it make the stares of the guards and their heckling easier to take.

Aaron took his place in the pointless parade in the camp's central square, the filthy red patch on his lapel there for the guards to see.

Time froze. The men and women in the square froze.

And then it was breakfast. No one was called out of line, no one was exempted from duty.

Aaron drank his coffee alone, though he nodded to a few others. He told himself that the guards would stop him before he picked up a shovel.

Then the ten minutes of breakfast were over. Aaron returned his mug. He'd eaten his bread. He had no one to share it with, and what reason was there for hoarding it?

The line for the tools formed and Aaron hung back. Not in the line, not separate from it. The men inched forward and the distance between Aaron and his nearest neighbor grew. The man behind gave Aaron a little shove. He refused to be beaten just because someone else was half asleep. Aaron moved forward a step, then another. Finally, he had no choice but to grab a shovel.

The line of march was beginning to form up, and again Aaron held back. He was carrying a shovel but surely it was a mistake. He would be stopped before he marched out the gate. Aaron joined the others when the guard — Weber again — swatted him playfully and painfully on the back of his thigh with a truncheon.

It must be some kind of mistake, he said, I'm supposed to go free today.

But he'd been in the camp too long to speak the words aloud. Whatever was going on, he knew there was no chance of mercy from the men who would lead him to the quarry, and he saw no officer to ask.

The labor crew that he had done murder to leave filed its way out the gate, with Aaron last in line.

Aaron had no idea he was marching, that he was carrying anything, that he waited or that the gate was opened. He had no awareness of breaking rocks, carrying rocks, shoveling rocks or clearing rocks. His conscious mind had completely deserted him. There was no room for it in his body.

Chapter 17

He had killed a man who had shown him kindness for nothing but false hope. For something that he thought he knew, but knew nothing about. There was no way for Aaron to keep both who he knew himself to be and the knowledge of what he'd done in the same skull.

So he went away.

And worked.

And men suffered.

And men drank.

And men sang.

And men were beaten.

And men died.

And the day passed.

The march "home" — what else to call it? — began. Aaron's body got into line and fell in step with the rest.

When there was less than a third of a kilometer to go, Aaron's feet tangled themselves, his legs buckled and his face hit the ground. A guard was on him almost instantly, shouting and brandishing a club. There was no one to hear the threats.

The club swung down and blood spurted from a gash near the crown of Aaron's head.

A hand reached out and gently restrained the arm holding the club.

"Ah, let him live. This one's going home tomorrow."

"That's hardly like you, Johann. Such sentiment!"

"I'm feeling sentimental. It's my anniversary today, and Gretchen is so far from here," Johann Weber said. "Maybe this guy has a wife, too."

"And he's not a Jew."

"Exactly."

Aaron heard none of this. The blow to his head had brought back his wandering mind and extinguished it. Two Jews, newly arrived, were forced to carry him the rest of the way back to the camp, where he was put in a bunk and given no further attention.

No one tried to wake him, so he missed his dinner. No ghosts visited him during the night. The shouts of the guards and the shaking of the bunks finally brought him back to earth. Another morning had begun before sunup.

Aaron's mind and body occupied the same bunk, though neither was happy about it. Remorse filled every fissure in his soul. And as he got up and felt the pain that the guard had left him from the day before, he resolved that he would die before he left the camp for the quarry. He was done and the only marching he would do today would be straight to Hell.

Still, he got up. He took a leak. He ached and found his place in the parade. And then he stood, working up his courage for a leap at one of the guards — Weber if he was lucky. He would take Weber with him, either killing him with his hands, as he had Kaczynski, or placing the guard between himself and the bullets that would come.

He waited.

No Weber. No announcements, either. Aaron decided he might as well have breakfast before committing suicide, so he joined the queue, drank his coffee, pulled at the hard bread and tried to grind it into pieces small enough to swallow.

Men were grabbing heavy tools and Aaron decided taking out a guard or two would be much easier if he had a weapon in his hands. He waited his turn and was able to secure a pick. He followed the others and joined the line as if to head for the quarry.

He could make out Weber coming down the line.

Wait, wait, he told himself. *Be sure. Let him come close.*

As casually as he could, Aaron lifted the pick from his shoulder, readying to swing. A few more steps. And now the column was moving forward.

Chapter 17

Ready, ready …

"Kaczynski? Stefan?" Weber called out, looking Aaron in the eye. "Today's the day!"

The strength went out of Aaron's arms. The pick fell and hit him a glancing blow on the shin on the way down. Aaron grabbed his leg and hopped. Weber guffawed.

"Good news, bad news, I guess!" Weber said. He took Aaron by the shoulder and began pushing him toward the administrative hut. With a limp, Aaron let himself be pushed.

Once inside, the warmth shocked Aaron. He hadn't felt the cold when he was swinging his shovel in the quarry, but had felt no other kind of warmth in days. He looked through tear-blurred eyes at the young officer with the death's head on his collar. The man was poring over some papers, content to let Aaron stand.

A dismissive hand flicked out, Weber clicked his heels and removed himself. There were other guards in the room.

"Stefan Kaczynski, Lucknow, Poland, correct?" the officer asked, still staring at his forms and files.

"Yes, sir," Aaron said.

The officer finally looked up, his gaze flat.

"I assume you've learned your lesson?"

"Yes, sir."

"The Reich will not tolerate drunken displays from our new citizens!"

The officer warmed to his work.

"In the future, you will show the proper respect to your superiors. And we are all your superiors."

"Yes, sir!"

"If someone tells you to toast the Fuhrer's health, that is what you will do!" the officer ordered.

"Yes, sir!"

"Now get the fuck out of here! If I see you again — ever — you are a dead man."

Aaron knew that to be true. He glanced down at the officer's desk and saw Kaczynski's papers, including the photo. It had been taken in better times but, as Aaron had bet his life on, he looked enough like Kaczynski's desiccated, bearded corpse to pass. He'd also gotten lucky — the photo was awful and the paper it was printed on had been folded and crumpled so many times that the face was obscured by creases and streaks.

The officer folded up the identity papers and handed them to a guard.

"You'll get these when you are released in Krasno. You can make your own way home from there."

Aaron was marched out of the office and onto the back of a truck where he was joined by three men and two women who also had red flashes on their lapels. Two guards climbed up after them. None of the people who were being released seemed to have had an easy time of it, and Aaron looked as bad as any of them. The others may have spent more time in the camp, but none of them had started off as beaten, malnourished or exhausted as Aaron.

The gate opened and the truck shuddered as it searched for its lowest gear. A woman smiled tentatively at Aaron, but there was no way he could answer it. Seeing how grim he was, she looked away.

Aaron tried to see his cohort as it marched toward the quarry, but they were already beyond the horizon.

Chapter 18

The town of Krasno might never have drawn many tourists, but under Nazi occupation it appeared completely drained of life. If Aaron hadn't seen window curtains twitch as the truck bulled through the medieval streets, he would have guessed it had been evacuated.

Thick fog rose from the mouths of everyone on the vehicle's back. Nazis and their prisoners alike worked hard to warm their hands and feet; stamping and slapping at themselves, even jumping up and down as the truck swayed violently on the unevenly paved streets.

Aaron almost made himself laugh by thinking how all the rocks he'd broken as a slave could have been used to ease his trip to freedom. But thoughts of the quarry meant thoughts of Kaczynski. He shook his head violently to rid it of the connection. To continue to dwell on what he'd done could only lead to moral madness. In less than fifteen minutes, he would be free — if being outside of a jail in German-occupied Poland could be called that — and Aaron had to believe that was worth any price.

His priorities needed to remain clear.

First, he would find Yelena. He didn't know if she was in German custody, dead or in hiding, but he needed to go back to Miasto and find answers.

Second was revenge on the man who was responsible for both Lev Berson's death and Aaron's imprisonment. Aaron was now ninety-five percent certain the men were one and the same. Aaron swore to himself that no one else would suffer as he had because of the alliance between a Jewish traitor and the Gestapo.

If, impossibly, he succeeded in both of his tasks, he would find his way to the resistance and do what damage he could to the Nazis until they killed him.

Aaron's thoughts were interrupted by the sound of the truck grinding down through its gears. It finally came to a stop in front of a building that was perhaps a third bigger than its neighbors, probably the town hall. Like the buildings on either side, it was old without being historic, showing no sign of having played a role in great events.

No one was on the street, likely due to the Germans and the cold. It didn't seem like much of a day for walking. Unfortunately, the freed prisoners seemed unlikely to have a choice.

The truck stopped and once again Aaron heard the familiar sound of German voices shouting, "*Raus! Schnell!*"

Aaron rushed to jump down. He was half-convinced the whole episode was a nasty prank and that he would be taken back to Kronberg to the sound of German laughter.

Instead, the former prisoners were told to form a line while one of the guards walked in front of them, handing out identification papers to each. They were given nothing else. No food, no money, none of the personal possessions that had been taken from them when they'd been arrested. Everything the Germans stole, they kept.

With a final, "*Heil, Hitler!*" which the Poles were forced to ape, the Germans clambered back aboard the transport, returning to their regular jobs of spreading fear and death.

Chapter 18

As the truck drove off, the four men and two women turned to look at each other, their expressions a mix of joy and uncertainty. Where should they go now? And how would they get there? Should they go alone, or stick together?

"I'm going to Krakow," the fittest of the men said. "Any of you are welcome to come with me. Truthfully, though, I'm not sure how I'm going to get there."

"I think we need food before we can really make any other decisions," the younger of the two women said.

The reminder of their shared hunger brought an end to any feeling of euphoria.

"Shit," someone said.

"Does anyone have any money at all?"

"Where the fuck would I get money from?" asked the first man. "Where would any of us? They took every groczy. Even if I'd shoved a few up my ass for safekeeping, they would have found them."

It was soon clear to Aaron that no one in the little group had a single idea worth listening to.

Okay, then, Aaron thought. *Every man, woman and child for themselves.*

"We're going to have to beg," Aaron said aloud. "What else can we do? And I don't think we should do it together. Who's going to open his door to a whole gang of starved, ragged strangers?"

The others nodded grimly but didn't seem inclined to separate.

Aaron wasn't feeling sentimental and there was little time or energy to waste.

"Good luck to you all," he said, then set off down the street alone, looking for a likely door to knock on.

None opened for him.

Aaron lay under a bridge thinking of the irony of escaping from the cruelty of the Germans only to die from the indifference of the Poles. He was at least as cold as he'd been in the camp and, having had literally nothing to eat, he was even hungrier.

Aaron cursed at the coat that had gotten him out of the camp but was now taking his life. It was less than half as thick as the one he'd been given by his friend in the Blue Police.

Maybe its poor quality was Kaczynski's revenge, Aaron thought, then giggled. He stopped himself after catching a glimpse of the delusion and hysteria that were building inside. He could let himself go, but knew he wouldn't come back once he did.

Aaron began to gather himself for a final push. He would not allow whoever found his body to believe that he was just another vagrant who had died of drink and bad weather. He wanted a better legacy than that.

He braced himself against the ground with his hands and slowly began to push himself up, first onto his knees and, finally, sweeping his legs beneath him, onto his feet.

"One foot and then the other," he said, hoping that the sound of his own voice would give encouragement to the rest of his body. "Let's move. We have places to go."

He felt the wind as if he were a ghost. It passed straight through his skin, freezing his insides directly. Kaczynski's face visited Aaron again and again. It was sometimes replaced by a shadow that represented the man who had died in his place at the police headquarters in Miasto. Both visions gave him motivation to keep on his feet. He wanted to meet neither spirit in the afterlife.

Perhaps half a kilometer from the bridge, Aaron reached his end. He had nothing left. He stumbled and fell. Hitting the ground was painful, but lying still was bliss. His eyes closed. He had no expectation that they would open again.

Light swept the road and fell on Aaron's closed eyelids. He hoped it would pass on. He could imagine nothing good coming from it.

But the light persisted and was joined by a rumbling that grew closer until it could only have been a few meters away. Against Aaron's conscious will, his eyes opened. What they saw was a pickup truck that looked as old as Aaron himself. It seemed to be made almost entirely out of rust, with just enough glass to provide the driver with a peek of the road.

Aaron wished it away and its driver dead.

Neither happened.

Instead, the driver's door creaked open and a booted foot stepped out, followed by another. The vehicle rocked on its springs as the owner of the boots pulled himself up. He looked at Aaron from where he was standing. Aaron couldn't make out more than a shadow. He was blinded by the headlights.

"Are you all right?" the driver asked in Polish.

Aaron thought it was probably the stupidest question he'd ever been asked, but he was in no position for a snappy reply. What energy he had was entirely invested in his next breath.

Not getting an answer, the driver came into the light and bent over Aaron. When he finally occluded the headlights, Aaron could make out a look of deep concern on the man's face. Aaron then felt warm arms wrap around him, carefully lifting him from the frozen ground and the winter's banked snow. He could feel his raggedly shod heels drag on the ground as he was brought over to the passenger's side of the truck.

He was so light that his apparent savior was able to shift him to one arm while he used the other to open the door. The man had no more trouble in sliding Aaron into the seat. He then climbed in from the other side. With both doors closed, Aaron felt himself slowly thawing as the warmth from a small gas heater at his feet spread into the cabin.

He gasped as if he'd been rescued from drowning.

"That's better, eh, my friend?" the stranger said.

"Whh-ho are you?" Aaron's teeth began to chatter again. Outside, they'd lost the knack.

"Here, have some tea first."

A warm container was passed over. Aaron took it with shaky hands. He couldn't get the lid off and, seeing him struggle, the stranger reached over and opened it. He then gently tipped it so that Aaron could get a sip and then another. It was like nothing else Aaron had ever experienced. It was life itself. Warm, not hot. Sweet like the best parts of childhood with a hint of adulthood's lingering bitterness.

A little more and Aaron was able to take the container for himself. The warmth it brought to his hands was as welcome as the sirocco that was washing over his body. Another drink and he felt just enough strength return to allow him the luxury of worry.

"I don't mean to be rude at all," Aaron said. "I'm incredibly grateful, obviously. But it's been a while since someone has done me a good turn for no reason."

"We can talk about my motives later, but I'm not planning on hurting you. That I can promise," the driver said, putting the protesting pickup into gear.

Aaron had to take the man's answer on faith. Whatever was coming next, there was no way he was going to climb out of the warm car at anything less than gunpoint.

"Sit back. I know you're hungry. There's no other way to come out of a German camp," the man said. He reached down next to where Aaron was sitting and pulled out a cloth bag. He put it in Aaron's lap. "Eat."

Aaron wanted to be cautious. He wanted to be careful and shrewd. He didn't want to put himself so deeply in the debt of a man he didn't know, but there was so little resistance left. So little left in him at all.

Still.

"Your name, at least?" Aaron asked, trying to insist.

In reality he couldn't wait anymore. He could smell onions in the sandwich and nothing had ever smelled so good to him in a lifetime of eating. If he'd been able to stop for a second, Aaron might have remembered that he'd never been very fond of onions. After the first bite, though, he would also have sworn that the onions he tasted in the truck and the onions he'd eaten before the war must certainly have been different species.

The rough brown bread alone, unadulterated by sawdust, talc or any other foreign substance, was a pleasure so overwhelming, Aaron temporarily lost his ability to speak or pay attention to his surroundings.

If his benefactor had wanted to hide their destination, a blindfold wouldn't have done any better.

A few minutes, a few kilometers must have passed before the stranger turned to Aaron and said one word: "Tadeusz."

In his ecstasy, Aaron had completely forgotten the question he'd asked, or even that he'd asked one. He was baffled for a minute before he understood the driver was offering his name.

"Aaron," he replied, completely forgetting what his identity papers said.

"A pleasure," Tadeusz said. "We'll be there soon."

If "there" was the place the sandwiches came from, Aaron was willing to wait for more information.

"Would you like your tea back?" Aaron asked, desperately hoping the answer would be no.

"You're welcome to finish it." The man then reached into his jacket and pulled out a flask. "And feel free to add a little flavor."

Aaron reached for the flask the same time the truck must have hit a deep pothole or God knew what else. Both men were lifted off their seats. Aaron bumped his head on the roof, though not hard. The truck continued to bounce for quite a while longer. Its springs were shot.

Aaron laughed. At first it was a rough sound, almost a grunt. But it swelled and turned into something nearly recognizable for what it was. Tadeusz finally succeeded in passing over the flask and joined Aaron with a chuckle.

The feeling was nothing like the near hysteria that had gripped him just a short while before, and though it didn't last long, the laughter was almost as welcome to Aaron as the food. The only laughter heard at Kronberg was the product of someone else's sorrow.

In less than five minutes, the truck pulled off the road at an unmarked gap in a fence. The path it proceeded down was made of mud, ice and holes. If the truck had jumped and rolled on the paved road, it became a ship caught in a typhoon on this trail.

They hadn't traveled far when Aaron made out a farmhouse that looked likely to fall down onto its foundation in the next storm. The roof was made of thatch and hung down far over the eaves. The house itself was stucco and timber with what appeared to be undressed stone adding support in key places. Smoke rose from the chimney. Aaron fell in love.

Tadeusz pulled the truck to a stop with a heavy application of the brakes. He then turned off the engine, which came as a relief to all involved.

"Come," Tadeusz said, and nothing else. Aaron heard it as a warm invitation.

Inside, the house was as homely as on the outside. There was nothing beautiful to be seen, but the rough wood furniture was well made, cushions and hand-knitted or crocheted blankets were bright and promised warmth and comfort. Aaron guessed that nothing in the house had ever seen the inside of a store. Perhaps a smithy for the pots, pans and irons for the fire. Homely. Home.

"This is my wife, Lucja."

Aaron hadn't even noticed there was another person in the room. Like her husband, she appeared to be in her late fifties or perhaps early sixties, with few teeth — she was smiling — but she differed from him in other respects. She was short and as fat as a person could be during a war with the Germans. A kerchief covered her hair, but what he could see beneath it shone silver. She also had glasses. The overall effect was of seeing one's mother, whoever one's mother might happen to be.

"Be welcome," she said.

"Thank you," Aaron managed. He felt unsteady on his feet. Too much had changed too quickly: a shift from death to life in less than an hour. The heat suddenly became intolerable and Aaron began to sway.

He had no memory at all of hitting the floor.

For an uncountable amount of time, Aaron woke only in nightmares. Terror of what had already happened to him plagued his dreams. Horror redounded from what he had done. He swam in a lake of fire and ice, looking for a foothold, a handhold and drowning instead.

Later, moments of lucidity began to work their way into the routine. He found his blankets soaked. He found straw beneath him. He found himself naked and was ashamed.

He ate borscht with a touch of sour cream. He drank water. He slept again, if that was the right word for it, and whenever he woke the face he saw was Lucja's — his mother, everyone's mother. He never saw Tadeusz, but was in no position to wonder about his absence or even why the couple was sheltering and nursing him.

Another wave of oblivion washed over him and this time it brought no dreams.

"Time to wake."

An insistent hand shook Aaron's shoulder and the rest of his body shook with it.

"Wake up!"

Aaron's eyelids lifted a crack.

"I said, wake up!"

There was enough urgency in Tadeusz's voice to penetrate Aaron's muddled skull. He tried to sit up, and was able to move himself a little. His eyes, though, were now fully open.

"Your fever is broken, and you can't stay in my house forever. And if you're going to leave, you'll need to get some of your strength back."

Chapter 18

Aaron nodded and the man handed over another bowl of borscht and more brown bread to sop it up with. It was as delicious as anything Aaron had ever tasted.

"I've gone through your papers."

Aaron nodded again, taking a break from sipping directly from the bowl.

"They say your name is Stefan Kaczynski."

The way the man said it gave Aaron grave doubts that he believed it.

"When I picked you up on the road, you told me your name was Aaron. That's a Jewish name. The papers say you're not Jewish."

The bowl was now in Aaron's lap, with the bread sitting in the middle of it, like a shark fin sticking out of the ocean. Aaron wasn't feeling particularly clever and Tadeusz didn't look to be in the mood for awkward lies. His fate was already in this man's hands.

"Yes, those weren't my papers, originally," Aaron said, his voice creaky from disuse.

Tadeusz looked at him, waiting for more.

"My name is Aaron Kaminski. I am a Jew."

The words were out. He wanted them back, but there they were.

The other man stared at Aaron for a few seconds more, but seemed satisfied.

"Good. We've always had Jews in our village and they never seemed any different to me than anyone else. And who's Kaczynski? You look quite a bit like him."

"Someone I knew in the labor camp. He was being freed soon."

"And how did you end up with his papers?"

"He died, so I pretended to be him," Aaron said.

Tadeusz was silent again. There was something about the way the words were said that troubled him. He sat for a minute, deciding whether to let it go.

“Right,” he said, finally. It could have meant anything.

Conditions in the labor camps weren’t a secret, or at least not inside Poland. Many Poles had been worked to death, and others who escaped had either told their story or their bodies had borne testimony to what the camps were like.

Tadeusz had lived through times of great hardship, even famine, but no one he had ever known had looked as Aaron did now. Seeing the Jewish man naked had been close to an anatomy lesson. Tadeusz would never forget it.

He found he was impressed by Aaron’s ability to survive, even if it had been by a thread. The farmer decided that how Aaron had managed it was his own business.

“And no one’s looking for you?”

“There’s no reason they would be.”

Tadeusz decided to take that at face value, too.

Aaron’s face screwed up in a question. Tadeusz nodded encouragement.

“Why did you save me?” he asked.

“I’d seen you and the others the Germans dumped in town. I saw you begging, but I didn’t do anything.” He paused. “When I caught a glimpse of you by the side of the road, I was ashamed.

“My wife and I have stayed here, trying to keep away from the war, but it comes to us. A German patrol. A summons into town. Forms and papers. Most of our crop was taken to feed the damn Nazis.”

His eyes lit and his voice turned fierce.

“But some we hid. They didn’t get everything and they won’t!

"We've been able to help some of our own people. Not much. But people who are resisting, they know they can find a place to stay here, for a day, two. Not longer, though. Every day is more risk. A patrol comes by, word gets out. We can hide someone, but not if the Germans are searching too closely.

"You've been here for four days," Tadeusz said. "I'm sorry, but this is pushing our luck. I will have to ask you to leave tonight."

He sounded regretful, but Aaron heard there was no room for negotiation.

"I understand. And thank you," Aaron said, bowing his head. "Four days!"

"Lucja didn't think you were going to make it, frankly. Figured we'd have to bury you, which isn't easy with the ground so cold."

Aaron nodded, having become something of an expert in digging graves.

"Since you don't seem like you'd be able to walk far on your own, I'll take you where you want to go, if it's close. Or maybe I can find someone who can take you a little further."

"Where are we?"

"A little town called Lublin is the closest."

"Is it anywhere near Miasto?"

"Actually, it's not far. There are patrols everywhere, though, and I'm not willing to bet on your paperwork. If that's where you want to go, you'll have to take that risk yourself. I'll drive you to the outskirts. From there, you're on your own."

"I couldn't possibly ask for more than that," Aaron said. "There are no words to thank you, thank your wife … "

He began to cry.

The farmer didn't want to see it. He turned away.

"You have a couple of hours before I'm ready to leave. My wife will bring you more food, and we'll give you some to take with you," he said over his shoulder and left.

Aaron was able to collect himself in a minute and he began to take stock of his situation. Cautiously, he reached down under his blankets, afraid of what he might not find.

Thank God! Clothing!

The room was very small and there was no window. The floor was dirt. His comfortable pallet was placed directly on it. The room was exceptionally quiet. He could hear his own breathing, which seemed a little loud. Perhaps the room was underground?

A familiar flash of hunger struck Aaron, but joy filled him as he realized he could actually do something about it. He finished the soup and bread in front of him. He put the bowl aside and decided to try to stand.

It was a process.

Standing is always a process. It involves many different muscles working together in ways specified by God and nature. But this time nothing wanted to cooperate. Aaron had to convince each fiber to go along with the overall plan. He kept at it and soon he was upright, if hanging on to a wall.

He couldn't be sure if he'd been sick for the last four days or just exhausted of all of his resources. He listened to his body now and felt a surprising strength below the surface.

Maybe not so surprising, he reflected. For the first time in months he'd slept undisturbed in a warm place for more than just a few hours. Lucja — that was what Tadeusz had called his wife? — must have turned him over and fed him, even in his delirium.

He stood, stood straighter, took his hand off the wall and took a few steps. Yes, he could do it. His gait was a little uncertain, but pacing seemed to help. He made the trip from one side of the room to the other many times before the door opened without a knock.

It was Lucja, carrying another plate. She seemed surprised to see him out of bed, but she quickly smiled.

"Feeling better?" she asked.

"Yes. Thanks only to you and your husband," Aaron said with such warmth that she blushed.

"I'm very glad to do it," she said. "We're glad to be able to do it."

"Well, thank you."

He wasn't going to start crying again.

"Here, why don't you come up to the table?" Lucja asked.

"I'd enjoy that. Thank you."

He'd been right that his room was underground. It was a clean space that had been carved out of a root cellar. A brief flight of stairs led to the main room of the house above. A carpet waited to be rolled back over the opening after the floorboards had been replaced. It wouldn't take much of a search for the hideaway to be found, but Aaron guessed the disguise would work well enough to fool more casual visitors.

He sat down on the bench that ran alongside the table and Lucja placed the plate she'd been carrying down in front of him. That gave him his first glance of what was on it: Meat.

Meat had been rare, even for smugglers, in the ghetto. What little was available came in cans or had been carved off the carcass of a starved horse or donkey. The random bits of fat or gristle that were occasionally found in bowls of soup could hardly be said to count.

Unfortunately, Aaron recognized, the piece of meat in front of him was ham.

He shook his head against the habit of a lifetime.

I've done murder to survive. Ham isn't likely to be what condemns me, he thought.

Still, he hesitated. He was not religious. He had chosen to live as a gentile among the gentiles, against the wishes of his family and to the disgust of some in his community. He had married a woman without a drop of Jewish blood ... but this he had not done. He had never chosen to eat pork of any kind, however tempting the aroma had been when he'd come across it. Not bacon, nor ham, nor a roast. It was a line he had never willfully crossed, though God alone knew what had been in some of the cans of German military rations.

He smiled ruefully, cut into the slice of pink flesh, brought it to his lips with trepidation and chewed with a slight queasiness that was generated by five thousand years of ancestors turning uncomfortably in their graves.

Eh, he thought. *A little salty.*

As he swallowed he laughed a bit to himself, causing Lucja to give him a strange glance.

His laugh died down to a smile. His hostess continued to clean things, and in a short while his meal was finished.

"Delicious," he said. "Like everything you've served me."

Lucja blushed again.

"Thank you," she said, "but I doubt it's very hard to please a starving man."

Aaron didn't argue the point.

So, he sat and drank tea while she cleaned, and neither of them said a word for nearly an hour. Then both heard the truck springs creaking down the long lane that led to the house.

Tadeusz opened the door, stamped his boots and looked slightly surprised to see Aaron outside of the basement. He said nothing about it, though. Instead, he motioned that it was time to go.

Aaron nodded. He was ready. There was nothing for him to pack. As far as he knew, he had no possessions at all. He imagined the clothes now on his back must have belonged to the farmer at some point, or perhaps a son. He walked over to Lucja, and — to her pleased embarrassment — kissed her on the cheek and embraced her firmly.

"Thank you," he said.

They were all the words he had.

Tadeusz held open the door and Aaron headed into the cold. He was climbing into the truck when Lucja ran out of the house.

"Wait. One second," she shouted. She was carrying a winter coat with a scarf tucked into a pocket, as well as a haversack. She presented them to Aaron.

"We had to burn your clothes," she said. "The moths have had this coat for a long time, but it'll have to do."

Aaron thanked her again, knowing he was completely undeserving of any of the couple's kindnesses.

He shrugged into the coat. Inside the haversack were sandwiches and also Stefan Kaczynski's papers.

Aaron closed the door of the truck. There was a final wave good-bye. The trusty rust bucket was reluctant to fall into gear but, with some softly spoken curses, it was subdued. Tadeusz said the drive would take about three hours.

Aaron fell back to sleep almost immediately.

Chapter 19

Tadeusz's pickup carefully navigated through a warren of small, industrial buildings on the outskirts of Miasto. It was dark because it was night, but Aaron suspected there was so much soot in the air that it would have been the same with the sun high over the horizon. Even now, a few of the factories were up and running, smoke belching from rooftops, undoubtedly producing items the Nazis wanted.

Aaron thought of the workers inside and wondered how many of them were Jewish slaves like he'd been so recently. Were they eating any better than he had? Were the guards any less sadistic? Would all of them go back to their homes and their loved ones after the night's work was over?

He hoped it would all be so, but believed in none of it.

"I can't take you any farther," Tadeusz said. "We've been lucky so far with checkpoints, but I can't imagine that lasting much longer. You'll have to find your own way into the city."

"I understand. I agree that we've been very, very lucky so far," Aaron said. "I've been much luckier than you, though. I don't have words to thank you, and I don't know what I can do … "

"Kill one of those fucking Nazi bastards for me," Tadeusz said with surprising vehemence. "If you're really all that grateful, kill two! Kill a dozen!

"That's what you can do for me."

Aaron nodded solemnly.

"We'll be more than even then," Tadeusz said. His smile wasn't very nice at all.

Aaron picked up his haversack. It was lighter than it had been only three hours before. One of the sandwiches had proved irresistible, despite the ham at its center.

As he left the car, Aaron felt a strength that he hadn't for a very long time, caused by purpose as much as by rest and food.

He closed the door behind him and offered a quick wave that wasn't returned. The pickup was already on its way out of Miasto, probably back to the farm. Aaron faced into the city and took his first steps toward home.

It was only then that Aaron realized he hadn't had a cigarette in many days. He shrugged to himself and realized that torture and starvation were a sure way to kick the habit, though he wouldn't recommend it as a course of treatment.

His plan, as far as he had one, was to head straight to Yelena's apartment. Even if she wasn't there, it was an area he knew well and where he could hope to gather information rather than the attention of the authorities.

He judged that he was less than five miles from where he needed to be. The only obstacle he foresaw was the Miasto River, which he needed to cross. The Germans would be watching the bridges, which provided a natural choke point, making it easy to monitor the whole town's movements.

Aaron's eyes were now perfectly adjusted to the dimness, but he could still see little. The factory windows were all blacked out and there were no streetlights. Everything was shadows and outlines. As he walked past the chain-link fences and barbed wire than protected the factories, he tried to use his ears as much as his eyes. There would be patrols, complete with dogs, to safeguard whatever it was that the factories were making and to prevent any of the workers from escaping.

One dark block, another.

A sound from up ahead. Drunken laughter.

Chapter 19

He could hear the men getting closer. They certainly weren't trying for subtlety.

Aaron was alongside a fence that protected nothing more than a vacant lot, and therefore wasn't in great repair. He reached down to see if he could lift it from the bottom and felt some give. A little more, he thought, just a little more.

I'm thin enough, this should hardly be an issue, he thought. *I should be able to squeeze through anywhere.*

But when the fence was barely six centimeters off the ground, he couldn't lift it any further. There was no way to burrow under it. He'd have to rely on Stefan Kaczynski's paperwork again to see him through. At least it was dark enough that the photo would be hard to make out, Aaron thought.

Rather than wait for the patrol to come to him, Aaron decided he would walk to them. Perhaps if he walked like a man who had every right to be on the streets, they wouldn't even stop him.

Sure.

Louder and louder — and drunker and drunker from what Aaron could tell — but now they were close enough for him to realize the jokes were in Polish, not German. That didn't mean he was safe. After all, many Poles who traced their ancestry back to Germany had joined the Blue Police or even the SS itself. Still, Aaron felt himself relax the least little bit.

Finally, Aaron was able to see the men fairly clearly. They weren't moving fast and what little light that had escaped from one of the factories was enough to present them in fair detail.

They were Poles. They looked like they had come off shift at one of the factories and were on their way to or from a bar. From their state, Aaron guessed it was from.

So, he picked up his pace further and walked past the men, on the opposite side of the empty street. He didn't look at them, just kept moving, his eyes down. A turn around the corner, and they would be gone. Aaron felt eyes on his back.

Then he heard the words, “Too good to drink with us?”

He kept walking and hoped the man wouldn’t feel the need to follow up on his dig.

One breath. Two breaths. One step. Ten steps.

Nothing.

Aaron felt his muscles pop as the tension eased. The Poles were back in their world and he was alone again in his.

Within a quiet hour, he was in sight of the bridge he needed to cross. The neighborhoods that surrounded it were bathed in light from street lamps and a sliver of newly risen moon.

The illumination showed him that, as he’d feared, checkpoints had been set up at either end of the bridge, complete with sandbags and soldiers. Aaron wasn’t thrilled with any of his choices for getting past.

He could present his papers and brave it out, but Aaron was loath to put himself in the hands of German soldiers again, especially alone and at night. He would try it only as a last resort.

All he needed to do now was think of other resorts.

Swimming was out of the question. The river wasn’t wide, but it was cold and the current strong. His coat would instantly become waterlogged, dragging him toward the bottom. Even if he made it across, he’d have no way to warm himself again.

A boat? The problem there was that he’d have to find one to steal and then take it across the river unobserved. Besides, he knew little about boats and had trouble believing he’d be able to make the trip silently.

That left only one option that Aaron could think of, and he wasn’t fond of it.

Below the level of the street, a quay ran along both sides of the river. It met up with the foundation of the bridge, which was constructed of brick and ornamented stone. As a child, Aaron and a few of his friends would climb up and try to make it across the bridge by scaling its outer wall. They used only the handholds unintentionally created by the architect in designing its elaborate façade. It was possible — though not likely — that Aaron could get across using the same method now.

There were a couple of facts that discouraged Aaron:

First, when he'd played there as a boy, it had been midsummer and the water was warm. Since the bridge wasn't particularly high, the price for falling was mainly embarrassment. That and a bath his mother would have made him take in the evening anyway.

Second, he'd never made it across. He'd seen it done by others, but he'd always had trouble finding his next handhold. He'd had the courage but not the coordination he needed. After he'd endured enough laughter, he'd gone on to other things.

Aaron stood for a while, hoping a workable fourth option would come into his mind. It didn't.

He'd have to try the circus act, he decided. Without a net.

Shit.

In order to approach the bridge, he first had to get farther away, walking far enough from the guard posts to climb down to the quay without being seen. He walked briskly and in the shadows, pausing in doorways to make sure the next little patch of road was safe.

It took ten minutes to walk three hundred yards, but Aaron was able to find a spot where there were no lampposts to give him away as he climbed down the embankment. There he removed his boots, tied their laces together and strung them around his neck. The quay was stone and he wanted to make no sound as he neared the bridge.

The walk back was faster, even though each step was precisely calculated before Aaron took it. The light was uniformly dim on the quay and there was no sign of anyone else. Aaron assumed it was now long past curfew on the Aryan side of Miasto, though he had no watch to confirm it.

The bridge loomed ahead, a single span no more than one hundred meters long, built where the river was narrowest.

How hard could it be? Aaron asked himself.

Every sense in his body and his powers of reason had a single answer to that: *Very.*

No matter how revived he felt now that he'd eaten and slept, four days was barely a start on his recovery. When he'd tried to cross the bridge like a circus performer as a teen, he'd been something of an athlete, always strong, if not particularly agile.

Aaron shook his head. He decided to be done with doubt because he had to be. He'd made it to the bridge without drawing attention, now it was time to climb. He'd heard of a little lizard once that walked up walls and even on ceilings. A gecko?

Be a gecko, he told himself, and reached up with a hand, finding a space in between the bricks. He was then able to lodge his foot a little less than a meter off the ground. He pulled with the hand and pushed with the foot and found himself a little closer to his goal. As he reached around for the next foothold, he realized his decision to remove his boots was helping him to get and keep a grip. He'd always had long toes, showing off for friends by picking things up and throwing them with his feet.

He made better progress than he'd expected and, when he next reached up, he felt the stone carving of an ancient king's crest. The sculpted relief was deep enough to give Aaron a chance to rest and see where he was.

Chapter 19

He'd climbed level with the bottom of the roadway, making it time to start the trip out over open water. He could hear it running below him and it wasn't enticing. Aaron paused for a long minute. He didn't want to let go of the — what was it? — dove he was holding and take the next step into space. He felt the cold of the water enveloping him, even though it was still far below.

Fuck it, he thought, and stepped sideways on faith.

His long, cold toes found a chink in the bridge's armor that allowed him to take another step. He worked slowly, feeling his way. What had been a mere hundred-meter span when seen from the ground was clearly more than a kilometer long from where Aaron stood.

But perhaps because he was more careful as an adult than he'd been as a child, or because he had so little bulk to carry, he came close to death only once as he inched his way across.

When he had only ten meters left to go, a solid handhold metamorphosed into a chunk of ice looking to break free from the wall. His toes became his savior, keeping their grip just long enough for Aaron to fall forward and find a new gap to jam a hand into.

On the far side, Aaron climbed down as quietly as he'd crossed, jumping the final half-meter and absorbing the force with his knees. There was no sign that anyone had noticed his act of lunacy. He heard nothing from the guards.

For a fleeting moment, Aaron wished his school friends had been able to see his feat. As far as he knew, no one had ever made the trip in the dark — certainly not in the dark in the winter. Aaron could now claim bragging rights for all time.

If there was anyone alive for him to tell.

Aaron turned left up the quay, in the direction of Yelena's apartment. As he walked, the river kept him company.

Chapter 20

The neighborhood that surrounded Yelena's apartment was similar to many parts of the ghetto in outward appearance. Brick- and stone-fronted buildings of three and four stories, most with narrow doorways. It was a cozy, residential area with cafes nestled on every block. None were open and there was no sign of nightlife.

Perhaps because of that, Aaron had seen no German or Polish patrols for quite some time.

Aaron had never visited Yelena's flat. She'd rented it after his capture and confinement to the ghetto, but he had no trouble finding it. Miasto was his city and he knew it like he knew how to breathe.

There were no lights in the building's windows, but it was late enough that he hadn't expected to see any. If Yelena were inside, she'd likely be asleep. Aaron hoped she might be dreaming of him.

He needed her to be alive. He needed a reason to live beyond simple revenge. Without her, all that would be left was hate for the people who had tortured him and self-loathing because of what he'd done to survive.

Everything else had burned away. His concern for his people — even his father — still suffering only miles away, meant nothing. Yelena was his only buffer against the blackness.

Aaron tried to shake all these thoughts away, as he had a thousand or million times before. He stared up at the building in front of him, suddenly hesitant.

What if Yelena wasn't upstairs? If the apartment was empty? Would it mean that she'd reached safety? Or that she'd been tortured and was now dead?

He almost walked away then, giving in to cowardice. It was only the distance he'd already traveled that led him to take the final steps

Aaron entered the building's entryway and was confronted by a single line of buttons, one with Yelena's name on top of it. A deep breath. A pause. He reached out the quivering index finger on his right hand and pressed. There was a buzzing somewhere between the lobby and the flat upstairs. Aaron hoped the noise wasn't enough to cause some insomniac tenant to get curious.

The buzz was followed by silence. After more than a minute, Aaron tried another, longer push. That, too, was followed only by silence.

Unless Yelena had gone deaf or the buzzing hadn't made it up to her apartment, she wasn't home.

Yelena and he had always known that Aaron might have to flee the ghetto someday. Both thought it would be a pretty sad end if he was shot or captured simply because Yelena was out at the store. She was supposed to have hidden keys in a window box on the ground floor. He hoped to God she'd done it.

In less than a minute he was back outside leaning precariously off the front step and into a window box that was filled with nothing but brittle stalks and hard dirt. The digging wasn't easy and he was worried that the person who lived behind the box would see his shadow through their curtain and figure him for a burglar. How far could he push his luck in a single night?

At least this far.

The sleeves of both his coat and shirt were literally soiled but a small ring of keys dangled from his fingers. Aaron took a second to do a sloppy job of smoothing over the dirt in the box. He didn't figure anyone would notice the mess he'd made, but it couldn't hurt to make it look like he'd never been there.

The door to the building opened easily and with only a whisper once he found the right key. He didn't dare turn the switch for the light over the stairs, so he felt his way to the bannister and then carefully up each step. The staircase was made out of wood and wasn't new. There was a creak with each step that made Aaron wince.

It was a long, slow climb. When he reached Yelena's landing it was so dark that he was forced to feel the letters on the doors to distinguish unit B from the others. He was deeply grateful that the letters weren't simply painted on.

It took an eternity to find the proper key for each of the locks and turn them the right way. He got none of them right the first time.

He opened the door in stages, hoping to catch a glimpse inside the flat before giving himself away. He didn't expect anyone to be inside, but caution was a habit that had saved his life more than once.

Once the door was open wide enough, he slipped in quietly. Enough light came in through the window at the end of the long, narrow hallway to give him a sense of direction. The hallway itself was filled with peeling paint and items in need of throwing out, including refuse, a bicycle and several bits of machinery. It was all roughly strewn about and Aaron had some trouble picking his path through.

A tiny kitchen was at the end of the hall and in the sink was nearly everything from the few cabinets, which hung open above. Many of the plates, bowls, glasses and teacups were shattered. Shards of ceramic and glass covered a floor made of tile.

He touched his boots to the ground as lightly as he could with each step, not wanting to hear crunching china. He hadn't found the bedroom, yet, and there was still the possibility that someone was asleep in the flat.

The silence was broken when he missed a step, crushing a wineglass under his boot heel. It shattered loudly, and if his boots hadn't been as thick as they were, he probably wouldn't have been able to walk again for weeks.

Aaron heard the sound echo off the hard walls of the tight space, but nothing stirred. He told himself it was impossible for the noise to have been as loud as he'd heard it. It wasn't a gunshot or a bomb blast, after all.

Finally, he was through the kitchen and into what appeared to be the living area, complete with a daybed. This room wasn't large either, and every inch of the floor was taken up by what appeared to be the contents of a smashed dresser that leaned against the far wall. The bedclothes were torn and on the floor near the mattress. The mattress itself had been slit and was on the other side of the room from its cheap iron frame.

Surveying the damage as best he could, Aaron was sure of one thing: Yelena wasn't here. He had no idea how long she'd been gone, or whether she'd been taken or had left voluntarily. Until he had sunlight to work by, he was unlikely to figure it out.

Aaron decided the best thing he could do was rest. Dawn was close and his trek across the city had been exhausting. He knew if he lay down for a while, things would become clearer.

He bent down and picked up what was left of the mattress and placed it on the frame again. Much of the stuffing was missing from it and the blanket he grabbed was in tatters, but after the week he'd spent in Kronberg, Aaron didn't think he'd ever be tempted to complain about sleeping conditions again.

Chapter 20

He closed his eyes as his back hit the mattress, pulling the blanket's remnants over himself. Not quite as comfortable as the warm basement at Tadeusz and Lucja's farmhouse, he thought, but not bad at all.

He expected to fall asleep quickly, but didn't. Instead, he found himself thinking about his time with Yelena before the war. Their little house. Her cooking. Their lovemaking. Somehow, every day of that life had been sun-filled. Everything after the German invasion had turned gray.

Aaron tried to imagine a life after the war, but couldn't. He wasn't even sure what after would mean. Could the Germans lose? They had most of Western Europe, too. He knew Poland's government was in exile in Britain, but never heard anything more about them.

Britain itself was still fighting, but it was so far away. The diplomats' pretty words about friendship with Poland had turned into the purest bullshit. It had been no secret the Germans were coming, but the British and French sent none of their promised aid.

And the Americans, of course, dithered and dawdled, crying out against evil but doing little to fight it.

No, Aaron was afraid the war would end only because the Nazis had won, when the world's other nations agreed either to surrender or let the Germans keep whatever they could grab.

What then for Poland? Aaron knew that it wasn't just Jews that the Nazis hated. They didn't think much of the Poles, either. Unless they had German blood in their veins, Poles counted as Slavs. Not as low on the scale of sub humans as Jews, but no prizewinners, either. Would the Poles be turned into slaves when the supply of Jews dried up? Would they slowly be starved the way the Jews were being starved now? Jews headed the shit list, but they didn't make up the entirety of it.

Aaron again wished for a cigarette, but he wasn't likely to find anything except splinters and glass in the dark. He let that thought go as he let go of all the others. He reached for clarity, briefly finding oblivion instead.

Yelena's window faced east, so the sun wasted no time in filling the room. Aaron felt its caress and his eyes twitched open. He'd woken in so many different places recently, he was completely baffled by which one it was today.

What brought him back to the flat in Miasto was a faint smell of Yelena in the mattress. He was surprised he hadn't noticed it before. Her scent was one of many things he'd always loved about her.

He sat up and rubbed his eyes, surveying the damage to the room. Books had been pulled down from the single shelf and their spines had been slit. The dresser must have been disassembled in an effort to find any hidden compartments. It didn't look like any had been found.

A small bathroom was attached to the living space. A medicine cabinet had been pulled from the wall. Behind it was a rectangular hole, large enough to store a pistol and perhaps some ammunition but little else. The toilet bowl itself had been cracked. With few options immediately available, Aaron used it anyway.

Back to the kitchen and a quick sorting of the debris. Aaron found nothing of interest. The Germans — he assumed it was the Germans — had even thought to check the pipes, with the one leading from the drain sitting out on the floor. Whatever water had dripped out in the process had long since dried, but that wasn't nearly enough to give Aaron an idea of when the search had been conducted.

Nothing that he'd seen gave him any idea of where to go next in his search for Yelena. The fact that the apartment had been ransacked might mean that she was in German custody, or even dead at their hands, but that wasn't the only plausible explanation.

The Germans could have searched the apartment because they were looking for Yelena but hadn't been able to find her.

Or maybe none of this had anything to do with the Germans. Yelena had been in business with some pretty rough people, some of whom Aaron had never trusted, like the gunrunner Andrusz.

With Aaron's capture, Andrusz hadn't gotten his hands on the gold Torah vestments. Would he be looking to Yelena to make up the difference?

Aaron decided that if there had been a clue to find, whoever tore the apartment apart had taken it with them.

Aaron took one last look around the flat. He'd hoped to find a keepsake of some kind but was disappointed there as well. Other than torn clothing, anything personal — photographs, jewelry — was gone or had never been in the apartment at all. Aaron turned his back on the wreckage and fought his way down the hallway to the front door.

Once on the street, Aaron was uncertain of what to do next. There was a cafe a few doors down. He wondered if Yelena had ever been there. Would someone know her, or have an idea of where she'd gone? He wouldn't mind something warm to drink, either, but he hadn't found any money in the flat and wasn't sure how he would pay for it.

He did have something to eat, though. He huddled in a doorway and opened his haversack. Inside was Lucja's final sandwich. Ham again. God's little joke.

He lifted out the sandwich and a ten-zloty note came with it. If he ever saw Lucja again, he would bring her diamonds, Aaron promised silently.

He took a minute to eat the sandwich. He had no idea how far the ten zlotys would have to carry him and wasn't going to waste it on a breakfast he didn't need. He did, however, buy himself something called tea when he sat down at the counter of the café. He would have been hard pressed to say what kind of tea it was.

At this early hour, the only others in the place were a pair of bald old men talking about better times and current events.

Aaron listened with half an ear as he considered how he wanted to frame his questions to the proprietress.

He caught the words, "in the paper the other day. Do you remember Radislaw, the poet?" one of the men asked.

"I think so. He was pretty good, right?" asked the other.

"He was terrible, but my daughter really liked his stuff. But she was always dreamy. She loves romance and horses and such," the first man said. "Radislaw used to write about them all the time."

"Yeah, I'm pretty sure I know who you're talking about. I think you're being a little too hard on him."

Aaron, now caught up in the conversation, remembered he'd disliked Radislaw's work intensely.

"Well, doesn't really matter if you like him anymore. He's dead."

"Dead how? Writer's cramp?"

The first man glared.

"Not so funny, actually. It was the Germans. There was some kind of writers meeting. The Germans came in and took them all."

Chapter 20

Aaron must have sighed aloud. He hadn't meant to.

"Exactly," said the man who'd been telling the story. "It seems like anyone who can put a pen to paper is being arrested these days. It's the stupidest thing I've ever heard. Who ever heard of a dangerous poet?"

His friend agreed and Aaron held his tongue.

"More tea?" the woman behind the counter asked. Aaron's cup was empty.

"Please. And perhaps you could give these two gentleman a refill of whatever they're having, too."

"Actually, we're having coffee," said the man who had spoken first.

"Real coffee?" Aaron asked with a smile.

All three laughed and the proprietress poured.

"I'm Stefan," Aaron said, remembering to introduce himself by the name on his papers.

"Andrej," said the first man. "And this is Karol."

"Pleased to meet you both."

"No offense, but you look like you just got out of a hospital, my friend," Andrej said.

"Not a hospital, exactly."

"Well, you certainly don't look healthy."

"You may not believe it, but I looked worse just a few days ago," Aaron said.

"Jesus," Karol said. "What the hell happened to you?"

"Nazis."

"Oh," Karol said. He couldn't think of anything else.

"If you really want to know, I just got out of a labor camp."

"You look it," Andrej said. "Shit, are they really that bad?"

"They're not good," Aaron said.

The men and the woman behind the counter asked for details. It seemed everyone in Miasto had heard rumors about the camps, but nobody in the café had met anyone who'd been inside. More people were disappearing every day. How many were being sent to places like Kronberg? Aaron could hear the anxiety in their questions.

Aaron told them what he'd experienced, leaving out only what mattered — that he was a Jew and had murdered a man to escape.

After he was done telling his story, it was they who bought him a drink — stronger than tea — adding on a pastry as well.

"Jesus," Karol said again. His tone said he meant it.

Silence filled the café for a time.

"So, do you live in the neighborhood?" Andrej asked. "I don't remember seeing you around here."

"Would you recognize me, now, if you had?"

Aaron smiled to show he was kidding — sort of.

Andrej offered a strained grin.

"No, probably not."

"Actually, I'm here because an old friend lives on the block. Yelena Gorska," Aaron said, using the last name she'd never changed. "You don't happen to know her, do you?"

The men shook their heads, but the proprietress asked, "Is she a small blond woman?"

"Smallish," Aaron said.

"I know her. She had her breakfast here, most days."

"You mean the tasty little dish who always takes a table at the back?" Andrej asked.

The proprietress gave him a nasty look, but nodded.

"I knocked on her door this morning," Aaron said, "but she didn't answer."

"No. The last time I saw her was a little more than a week ago. She was carrying a small bag and looked like she was going somewhere, so I asked."

"You've got to be kidding me! She took off when she knew I was locked up? How am I supposed to find her?" Aaron asked, sounding like a jilted lover. "What did she say?"

"I'm really sorry. All she said was something about Gradno being nice this time of year. I thought she was kidding."

Gradno was an ugly little town of old smokestacks and grinding poverty.

But it was also the name on the door of a mountain cottage that Aaron and Yelena had shared during a blissful summer.

Every muscle in his body melted. He had no idea how, but she'd gotten away. Even if the Germans had asked everyone on the block where she'd gone and gotten the same answer as he had, they would have been none the wiser. It was a message — if it was a message — for him alone. He couldn't help but smile.

"Yeah," the proprietress said. "I thought it was funny, too. But then I saw the Gestapo in front of her building. We could hear things breaking all the way down the block. Everyone else is okay, so they must have been looking for her."

"Jesus," Karol said for the third time.

"But they didn't find her," Aaron said. "At least not here."

"No, not here."

"Well, that's something at least."

He changed the subject.

"Have you seen or heard anything from the Jewish District? I have a few friends there," Aaron said, hoping that they wouldn't find that odd.

"I do, too. Or at least I did," Karol said. "People I did business with before the war. I haven't heard from them in more than a year, now."

He frowned.

"I don't think anyone's heard from anybody for a while," Andrej said. "I've wondered what's going on in there, but

I haven't wanted to ask. Frankly, I haven't wanted to think about it.

"I was never very fond of them — kept too much to themselves for me — but there's no way to believe everything the Nazis say. It's not like the typhus situation's gotten any better since the Jews were locked away."

Karol nodded.

"I've seen a lot of trucks heading to and from the ghetto, recently," the proprietress added. "They're empty when they go in, but they're crammed with people on the way out."

"Well, they've done that before, I guess," Aaron said.

"This seemed like more trucks than usual," she said. "But who can tell?"

"Well, I can't tell about anything, anymore," Aaron said, sighing again. "Thank you all for your kindness. I guess I'm off to Gradno."

There was just one stop he had to make along the way.

Chapter 21

Aaron felt lightheaded from relief as he left the café.

He still had no idea what had happened to Yelena on the night he'd been taken, but at least she had left Miasto under her own power — if not necessarily by her own choice. He would follow her out of the city as soon as his other tasks were done, hoping to find her in a place where they'd been happy a lifetime ago.

Soon.

Back on the sidewalk, Aaron turned in the direction of the ghetto. It was the place he least wanted to go, but he felt compelled to complete his journey. The man he'd been tasked with finding, the murderer of the Jewish policeman Lev Berson, was still there. Aaron was sure of it. Perhaps he would even be able to prove it.

Getting in would likely be much easier than getting back out. And to be stranded in the Jewish district was the same as to fall off the icy bridge he'd climbed the night before. It was death.

Aaron didn't want to die.

He'd seen death and torture. He'd seen children take their final breaths in the arms of their mothers, and children pulling at their mothers' limp arms. He knew starvation from watching its slow progress in others and from feeling his body begin to eat itself for lack of other nourishment. He'd seen man's inhumanity to man and the banality of evil. He understood that what was best in man was the merest glimmer held up against the infinite night of what was worst.

He'd proven that truth by becoming a murderer himself, killing Stefan Kaczynski — a man who had befriended him — in order to escape the Nazi camp. Aaron tried to rationalize it by telling himself a soldier did the same — killing men to avoid dying himself. It rang false. He'd regretted the few men he'd killed in September and October of 1939, though as he'd gotten to know the Germans, he'd come to regret it less. Kaczynski had seemed a decent man and, even if he'd been dying, he deserved to do it in peace as much as anyone.

The Nazis had stolen everything from Kaczynski and Aaron had stolen the rest.

Still, despite what he knew, despite what he'd done, Aaron wasn't interested in atoning with his life.

As he drew closer to the outer boundaries of the ghetto, his hands shook and his teeth began to chatter. His muscles tensed. He felt nausea hit him, wave after wave. He knew he should turn away, should follow his wife. His papers could, possibly, get him on a train. If he needed money, he could steal it. He'd learned to be an excellent thief.

Instead, he kept walking, eyes front.

Aaron wasn't returning to the ghetto to solve the murder of a collaborator. Fuck him. Besides, it was far too late to save anyone from whatever German reprisals Berson's death would have brought. Whatever the Germans would do in response to finding out the young officer had been killed had already been done. In that sense, there was no longer a promise for Aaron to keep.

The Judenrat's threats were equally pointless. There was no longer any smuggling operation to shut down. Aaron didn't know what had happened to his partners — Teitel, Dov, Boris — or the brave men who'd planned to use his smuggled guns on the Germans — but he assumed they were all dead. He'd miss Lech Teitel, a man whose good humor was unshakeable. Aaron felt sorry for Lech's wife, too, for whatever good that did.

There was nothing noble in Aaron's motivations. He wanted to prevent Berson's killer — his own betrayer — from offering up any new sacrifices to the Nazis, yes, but he wanted revenge more. Aaron felt the need for it pulse through him like a second heartbeat.

The little girl, Sparrow, might have told the Gestapo when and where to make the arrests, but Aaron had no interest in hurting her. She hadn't acted on her own behalf. A hungry little girl would hardly have tracked him for days hoping that he would do something worth informing about.

The timing gave the truth away. Aaron had first felt his shadow's presence on the afternoon when he took the case — an unlikely coincidence. He'd first seen her clearly when he was following a lead. He could only assume it was she who had been behind him — just out of sight — as he went about his business for the next forty-eight hours. It was certainly the little girl who'd signaled the Nazis when all was ready.

But the man who showed up at the denouement had been Hermann Clausewitz of Section IV — the same man addressed in the conspiratorial note Aaron had found on Berson's body. The man who had killed Berson was the same one who had destroyed the ghetto's chance to resist the Nazis, killed Aaron's friends, and exposed Aaron himself to torture and the camps.

Aaron put his thoughts away as he neared one of several checkpoints into the ghetto. He could see German soldiers, the Polish Blue Police, and officers of the Jewish Police working together to monitor the traffic flowing in and out. At the moment, their attention was focused on an oxcart, the barrels of German weapons rifling through the straw that filled it. The guards would be done with their inspection soon. Aaron felt exposed on the street this close to the gate. He wasn't in the mood for questions.

On his right, though, was his destination. The building had once been an enormous city library. It took up most of a block. What had been its grand front entrance opened onto the Aryan part of the city. The back door faced the ghetto. Before the war, it had been possible to walk through the library from one avenue to the other. While the building had been shut tight long before, it still was.

Aaron needed to reach a short staircase that ended at a door below street level. He took one last glance at the checkpoint. Some kind of argument had broken out, giving Aaron a gift. He didn't jerk into motion, thinking that would be more likely to catch someone's eye. Instead, he looked serious and moved as if he had a job to do but wasn't looking forward to it. Which wasn't far off the mark, he realized.

Down the staircase and out of sight. He moved with urgency, now, checking the door. It was sealed with a heavy padlock and even the keyhole had been filled in, making it impossible to pick. Aaron didn't have anything to cut the lock with, but he wasn't the first person looking to get past the door. What looked solid had, in fact, been jimmied. A quick yank and the lock was open, the thick chain swinging free.

Aaron opened the door just enough to get through, then turned back and grabbed the chain. Pulling its ends together in one hand, he replaced the lock with the other. From the outside, it would look as if the seal on the building still held.

It was time to move. Aaron felt his way through a cinderblock hallway that led to the building's boiler and other maintenance facilities. The dark spaces he was passing through were often narrow and awkward, rarely used for large-scale smuggling. Instead, the route was primarily used by people who were willing to emerge from the ghetto right in front of a checkpoint. That is to say, it wasn't used often.

There were no lights to help Aaron find his way, making him grateful for his one previous visit. He had an idea of what he was stumbling over as he ran his hands along the wall to keep oriented. He also knew where to look for the staircase that led upstairs to the library proper.

He swore constantly, if softly, as he made progress. He barked his shins every few steps. Detritus such as broken tables and chairs had been abandoned every few feet and always in his path.

"Fuck!" he shouted into the black. He'd both winded himself on the edge of something and found his turn at the same time. Underneath so much stone and cement, there was little fear of being heard.

Aaron took a minute to get his breath back and then climbed twenty steps to an open door. His eyes hurt as they adjusted to the light that filled the hall above him.

It was a grandiose space built by someone trying to impress. The ceiling was nearly as high as a cathedral's, with windows that ran up and up. Even on the cloudiest days, there was no need for artificial light to read even the smallest print.

Marble covered nearly every surface, and was itself marbled with other stones in different colors in beautiful patterns. Partisans had added new decorations, most of which condemned the Nazis, though swastikas were represented, too.

The bookshelves were made from thick oak and stood tall where they hadn't been felled, smashed, or broken up for firewood. The books had been stolen, hidden away or ruined. There were signs of water damage everywhere, but what struck Aaron like a blow was seeing a rough circle in the middle of the main hall, filled with scorch marks and rubble.

Books had been burned, and it hadn't been done to keep someone warm. What Aaron saw were the remnants of a bonfire intended to destroy what little was good about humanity: hard-won knowledge and the ability to transmit it through generations.

Though he wanted to reach his next stop before dark, he couldn't help walking over to the pyre and flicking at singed spines and random pages. The majority of what he saw was in Yiddish, books that had never been published in runs of more than one hundred, often far fewer. Libraries had burned all over Europe. It was possible that Aaron was seeing the last physical evidence of an entire stream of Jewish thought. The legacy of a thousand years — more — desecrated.

Aaron stood for a moment in silence.

Another moment.

He chose a single page at random, carefully folding it into his coat. He headed toward the far side of the room. There he found another staircase. This one led to the lower stacks.

Aaron was again forced to feel his way in the dark. He was seeking a fire exit, surely unused during the great burning upstairs. He felt along shelves, finding them empty for the most part, though touching the occasional volume that had been missed. He regretted that he could take none of them along.

If I can, I'll come back, he promised himself.

Aaron found no hazards to his shins in this passage, though he nearly slipped several times on loose pieces of paper. In five minutes, he reached the door he wanted. The arrangement for opening it was the same as on the Aryan side. Aaron pushed the door gently, slowly, and saw the chain with its false lock.

He reached his hands through, hoping that no one would be watching his magician's trick. The chain rattled and Aaron paused, fearful of the noise. It had sounded like thunder to him. He began again and slid the chain carefully through his hands until he could feel the lock. He jerked down on it, expecting to hear a click. All he heard was the rattling of the chain, louder this time.

Shit.

He tried again, this time twisting the padlock in both hands to wrench it. The effort was quieter, but no more effective. He decided he needed leverage to pry the hinge open. Perhaps it had rusted, or worse, been replaced. He couldn't tell. It was hard to see clearly through the narrow opening, so he worked by feel.

Aaron turned his back on the door and began searching for a metal bar of some kind. He touched everything around him, hoping to find something he could pull loose. Ten more minutes passed in the dark as Aaron was lapped by waves of frustration and worry. He could go back the way he'd come and find another route into the ghetto, he supposed, but that would mean delay and danger. He kept searching.

After twenty minutes, his hands felt a tiny pipe running up the wall, perhaps for electrical wires or gas. It was too small for steam. He estimated it was narrow enough to fit into the hasp of the lock, so he pulled, putting all of his strength into the effort. First the pipe moved an inch, then a second inch. Eventually, Aaron was able to pry a two-foot stretch away from the wall. He took a firm grip and began to twist, hoping to unscrew a single section.

The metal began to turn, but Aaron could feel his strength ebbing.

Come on, you piece of shit!

When the pipe came loose, Aaron fell back against a shelf that tipped, but not far enough to fall. He stood stunned for a second, gathered himself and headed back to the door. No gas smell followed him.

The pipe fit into the hasp. Aaron pried and twisted. With a flake of rust, the lock fell to the ground. Aaron cringed at the metallic clang it made.

He peered cautiously out the door and saw that there'd been no one around to hear it. The exit he emerged from was in a narrow alley. Today it was empty of vagrants.

Aaron reached the corner, turning to look both left and right before he took another step. He saw no one. The guard post at the entrance to the ghetto looked small and far away. He decided he might as well chance exiting the alley.

Neither the Germans, nor the Poles, nor the Jews noticed as he walked away from them and down the street, sticking close to the buildings that lined it.

It was more than a block before Aaron began to see what was obvious all around him. Stores appeared open, but no one was in them. No one was selling anything on the streets, not bread, not sweets, not used clothing. There were no knots of men gossiping, pretending that they were speaking of important things. He could see no children begging. He saw neither the religious nor the profane.

What he did see were signs of life interrupted. There were carts lying on their sides, though their spilled contents were nowhere to be seen. The shutters of some shop windows were partially drawn, as if caught in the act of opening to welcome the day's customers. A child's stuffed toy, the worse for its wear, stared up mournfully from the paving.

All Aaron could hear was a biting wind and a rustle of random objects caught up in it: a newspaper page, scraps of wrappers, leaves that should have flown away long before.

And his own footsteps. His heels rudely struck the cobbles and startled the near silence. He walked on, but more softly, as if the ground had suddenly been sanctified.

From an unknown distance, a child's laugh broke through. Aaron's neck nearly snapped as he tried to pinpoint the sound, which was followed immediately by an adult's shushing.

He wasn't entirely alone. It only made sense if the gate was still manned and carts were still making deliveries. Still, he saw nothing as he passed through one block and then another.

On reaching the ghetto's main boulevard, Aaron faced a choice. He could carry out his original mission or check in with his father at the Judenrat. The old man would be able to explain what had happened.

Aaron turned left. He should have thought to check in with his father, anyway. The narrow scope of his bloody ambition had blinded him to everything else.

Several times along his walk, Aaron was convinced he glimpsed a small, ragged figure that ducked out of sight as quickly as a mouse diving for a hole.

Sparrow?

Whoever it was — if anyone was following him at all — they never came within clear sight, let alone reach.

The sunlight on the boulevard was winter sharp; the air possessed a fragile crispness. The buildings were bas reliefs carved out of the world's stone heart.

The Judenrat itself, though, was still a dump. It showed its age and an institutional lack of care. It was here that Aaron saw the first person that he could be sure of, a poorly uniformed member of the Jewish Police. The man was so thin that, with his cap on, he resembled nothing more than a hat rack. For all the attention he paid as Aaron walked past him, he might as well have been one.

The lobby, which had been so heated by bodies that it was the warmest place in the ghetto, was now as cold as a tomb. There were no clerks and nobody looking for them. The desks, where little had been done for people in great need of much, were entirely lifeless. No one begged and no one denied. If he'd been asked a month before, Aaron might have said the current situation would be an improvement.

It wasn't. Not in any way.

Aaron called out and heard his voice return to him, followed by an anticipatory silence. He called again and this time there was a slurred, angry reply from behind the door that separated the Jewish Police's offices from the rest of the building.

The door wouldn't budge at first, but Aaron pulled it open on his second try. The corridor behind it was, as always, dim and uninviting. Only important business would draw someone in.

Blaustein — grand chief of the Jewish Police — had his door open. From inside, Aaron could hear a buzzing. Another few steps revealed the buzzing to be an attempt at humming by the office's occupant. Blaustein was, without any doubt, truly, deeply, nearly catatonically drunk.

He managed to look up when Aaron walked in, his eyes visible through only the narrowest of slits. They widened slightly when the man behind them recognized his visitor.

"Catthh ur mudrerer, aasssole?"

Aaron spoke the language of drunks and was able to make meaning from the mangled words. He didn't answer, though.

"What happened here?" Aaron asked instead, his voice gravel. "Where the fuck are all the people? Where's my father?"

Blaustein blinked, but his eyes didn't reopen. Slowly, his head slipped toward the table. Aaron struck fast, slapping Blaustein across the face with such force that the man's head nearly spun around entirely. Blaustein's eyes flew open in shock, though not yet in pain.

"Where the FUCK IS EVERYBODY?"

"Another drink," Blaustein slurred. "Just one more ... "

The second slap was even harder. Aaron then reached down, yanked Blaustein up and punched him hard enough in the stomach to begin the detoxification process. The commandant vomited on his own shoes, barely missing Aaron's in the process.

"Can you hear me, Blaustein?" Aaron asked. He was shaking, but less so than the policeman. Aaron pinned Blaustein upright, hands on the man's shoulders. "What the fuck happened here?

"The Germans!" Blaustein blurted, with a little more clarity. "The fucking Germans!"

"Who the fuck else could it have been?" Aaron roared. "What. Did. They. Do?"

"They came for everyone. Fucking everyone. Loaded them onto trains, shot them in the streets." Blaustein exploded into tears of drunken self-pity and pure self-horror. "And we helped them do it. I helped them!"

"Not everyone. It couldn't be everyone," Aaron said. "There must have been sixty thousand people here! Sixty thousand at least."

Aaron dropped Blaustein, turned away from him. The police captain fell back in his chair, but not into sleep. He continued to cry, trying to explain what had happened in between sobs.

"The Germans came to me about two weeks ago, shortly after you and I met. They gave me no choice!"

Blaustein's story was this.

The Germans said the Jews would be removed from the ghetto. Some would go to factories. Some, if they were strong enough, to labor camps. Everyone would be much better fed when they were working and supporting the Nazi war effort. The police would keep their role and would be rewarded for their loyalty. They would have new positions of authority outside the ghetto.

"I knew that part wasn't true," Blaustein said.

"Only that part?"

Blaustein shrugged, then reached for his drawer. Aaron caught his wrist, stopping him.

"Just getting a cigarette," Blaustein begged. From his childish tone, Aaron realized Blaustein must still be drunk.

Aaron knocked Blaustein's hand out of the way. He didn't think there would be a gun in the drawer, but he couldn't be sure. Aaron reached in himself and came out with a bottle, a partially crumpled pack of cigarettes and a small box of matches.

Tenderly, Aaron reached into the pack. They were American cigarettes. Pall Malls. Even on his best days as a smuggler, Aaron couldn't have come up with them. The white cylinder he removed was dented and dinged, but still whole. To Aaron's eyes it was perfect. For a moment he saw nothing else.

Aaron ran the tube under his nose. The tobacco was slightly stale, but still incomparably better than any Aaron had smoked since the war started. He put it to his lips, drew a match from the little box, struck it with a thumb, touched it to the cigarette's tip and drew the resulting smoke deep into his lungs.

He held it in for one second, two, three. He exhaled heavily and with great satisfaction. Then he coughed … and coughed … and coughed, nearly doubling over.

Oh, it felt good.

Aaron picked a few flecks of tobacco from his tongue and turned back to Blaustein who stared knives at him.

Chapter 21

"So, what happened next?"

The Germans had come in hundreds, maybe thousands. All of them armed with pistols and machine guns. The Gestapo, the SS and the Wehrmacht were all represented. Jews were ordered out of their tenements or grand apartments, it didn't matter which. People were pulled from their businesses or places of work, and once on the street they were corralled. Children and the elderly were separated from the rest. Shortly, Blaustein found out why.

They were taken into blind alleys by the hundreds and shot where they stood. Blaustein witnessed this, but had done nothing. Jewish policemen had participated in gathering the children up, taking them from their parents. None of the policemen had participated in the shooting, but then they weren't trusted enough to be given guns.

In the end, Blaustein saw that anyone not able to work had been killed. With few exceptions, it was only the fittest that were put on the trains or trucks and taken God knew where.

The culling and sorting had taken days. Blaustein wasn't sure how many. There was little sleep and much screaming in the nights. Blaustein had spent most of the time drunk. The alcohol and a few packs of cigarettes were all he had to show for his smuggling empire and bloodguilt. That, and a stash of pointless Nazi scrip.

After the Germans had searched the obvious places, they moved on to basements and secret hiding spots that were sometimes revealed by neighbors. They searched public buildings and even the Judenrat itself. The clerks were taken — yes, Aaron's father included — but Blaustein and Zimmerman had been left behind.

Many, many of the Jewish Police who had helped organize the killings and deportations found themselves on those last trucks out, all signs of rank stripped from them. Those who objected were shot just like all the rest.

Then one day it was over. The transportations and executions stopped.

It made no sense. There were still people in the ghetto. They had hidden in the cracks and survived. Some people were still alive because they had been in one room but the Germans had only checked another. Others lived by hiding on roofs for days, despite snow and the cold. Some had died that way.

Some the Germans hadn't taken, for reasons that Blaustein seemed not to understand.

The high officers of the Judenrat were spared. Their families, for the most part, were not. Like Blaustein, many of them sat in purposeless offices now, offering up justifications and self-pity, though there was no one to listen.

"You're sure about my father?" Aaron asked.

Blaustein was very sure and increasingly sober.

The enormity of what had happened temporarily took away Aaron's ability to grieve for his own family and friends. For anyone.

He looked down at Blaustein's desk and saw the bottle the man had removed from the drawer. Twelve-year-old scotch. How the hell had that made its way to a Polish Jewish ghetto? The bottle was half-empty, but Aaron didn't mind. He lit another of Blaustein's cigarettes and took a long pull of the scotch. Fire ran down his throat and tore at his stomach. He felt nothing else.

"And our fearless leader, Zimmerman?"

Chapter 21

"Suicide," Blaustein said with a sneer. "He always thought that he could make a deal, that the Nazis were reasonable people, really. If he could just make the Jews useful enough, they'd allow us a place in the new world order."

Blaustein then took on a funny voice that he obviously intended to be Zimmerman's but sounded nothing like him.

"'We'll build factories here in the ghetto! We've got plenty of skilled workers! Hitler will see how helpful we are!'

"And the man always had plans, even up to the last minute," Blaustein said in his own voice, then switched back to parody.

"'Next week, I'm sure they'll give permission to reopen the streetcars so people can get to work. They'll build us a new bridge! The food will get better!'

"Such an optimist," Blaustein said, once again himself. "I think that's what killed him."

"It's good to see that you're made of sterner stuff," Aaron said.

Blaustein looked disgusted with himself, but Aaron couldn't be sure that some of the disgust wasn't for Zimmerman.

Aaron sighed from the bottom of his feet. His shoulders slumped.

"Do you know what happened to my people, Teitel, Boris, Dov? You have to at least know that. You know everything, right?"

"The Germans hung them."

Aaron's shoulders slumped further. It wasn't that he hadn't known, but hope isn't rational. He closed his eyes and Lech's face joined Stefan Kaczynski's — another on the list of men he'd killed. And then a terrible thought struck him. What if the woman in the café was wrong? Or what if Yelena had been captured on her way out of Miasto?

"Was a small blond woman with them?"

"Your Polish partner?" Blaustein asked.

Aaron looked surprised.

"I told you, there's nothing I don't know about smuggling here. But, no, she wasn't with them. As far as I know, she's still out there, somewhere. And don't bother to ask where, I have no idea."

Aaron silently thanked the universe for this bit of kindness.

It was time to go, but Aaron was curious about one other thing.

"What about Officer Shemtov? Is he still here?"

"Shot," Blaustein said. "He refused to put people on the trains."

"At least there was one," Aaron said, and grimaced. "Get up."

It was a struggle for the police chief to reach his feet, but he just about did it. Aaron told him to go stand by the door. He then picked up the half-empty bottle of scotch and put it in his haversack. He went around the desk and did a thorough search of its drawers, finding another bottle of alcohol — this time schnapps — and several more packs of Pall Malls. The latter went into his pockets. The bottle he broke against the desk so that Blaustein could watch his lifeblood drain away.

"I'm sure you have more somewhere," Aaron said. "But this is the least I can do."

Aaron moved to the doorway and pushed Blaustein back toward his chair.

"That's it?" Blaustein said. "That's all you're going to do?"

"Want me to kill you?"

Hesitation.

"Yes," Blaustein said, in the smallest of all voices.

Aaron hit the man in the face again, his fist clenched.

"That's why I won't," Aaron said. "Live with yourself as long as you can … Or as long as your Nazi friends will let you."

Aaron headed back toward the street.

Chapter 22

Aaron had a long walk in front of him and the streets were no more inviting than they had been an hour before. He passed more than one shop that gusted the smell of rot out its door, despite the cold. One smell that Aaron had gotten used to in the ghetto was notably absent, the miasma of unwashed bodies. Even the sewers, which had been overburdened with the doubling of the area's population, seemed to have subsided.

Small relief, but relief nonetheless.

Aaron encountered a pointless Jewish patrol after a few blocks, but knew neither of the men. No one spoke as they passed. To Aaron, the policemen's eyes looked hollow, gutted as the ghetto had been. Why they kept to their duties, Aaron could not imagine. Did they have some shred of hope that the Germans would keep their promises, even after everything they'd seen, everything they'd done?

As he moved through a neighborhood of small apartment houses, Aaron heard an engine. The streets were so silent and the buildings so close together that the sound echoed. He couldn't distinguish where the car was coming from, even as its dull purr grew louder.

Out of the corner of his eye, he saw the sedan turn a corner several blocks behind.

Aaron suddenly realized that he wasn't wearing the mandatory blue and white armband, or even a yellow Star of David on his coat. Even if the men in the car were on other business, there was no way for them to overlook such a gross violation of racial decorum.

He looked left, right, but saw no open doors or alleyways to duck into. There was nowhere to hide.

And then he noticed an overturned wooden cart. It wasn't very large, but Aaron could think of nothing better. He lay down behind it, praying that the car would go by without even slowing down. And that no one in a window behind him would signal his presence to the Germans.

The cart wasn't perfectly flush with the ground, giving Aaron a clear view of the street in front of him. As the car passed — if it passed — he would see it. If it stopped, he would have an even better vantage point.

The car was close now, no more than a block. He could feel a rumble. Aaron was seized with a sudden certainty that he would be found. That coming back to the ghetto was even stupider than he'd thought. The premonition and memory of electric shocks made Aaron's teeth chatter harder than cold ever had.

The car was a gray-painted convertible with the top up. Soldiers stood on the running boards. An Iron Cross adorned the driver's side door. It was moving at a walking pace.

And Hermann Clausewitz rode in the back seat, his face leering out the window to take in the necropolis he had helped create.

Aaron shivered so hard that it felt like a seizure. Would Clausewitz hear it? The Gestapo officer was a curious man — a suspicious one — he would make sure his men investigated.

The car slowed to a snail's pace. Aaron heard a comment from Clausewitz and then a laugh from someone else in the car.

Aaron hugged himself, dragging his knees to his chest. He tried desperately to stop his heartbeat, reverberating so loudly in his ears. He squeezed his eyes tight shut.

Chapter 22

The engine grew still louder and then began to fade away. Another minute and it was gone.

The absence of sound didn't immediately penetrate Aaron's ears.

Then it did.

I'm still here. I'm still here. I'm still here. I'm still here.

Aaron reached for the bottle in his haversack and for a cigarette. He took a long drink from the one, but stopped himself from lighting the other. If he had been smoking as the car approached, the smell would have given him away.

The first slug of scotch helped to wring out the shaking. The second finished the bottle. After waiting a careful five minutes, Aaron stood it upright before standing himself. He looked around him. A curtain twitched, but that was the only sign of life.

There was still more than a mile to walk and his progress was slow. He spooked at every sound in the wind, freezing up at the faintest susurration.

It was nearly an hour later that he found himself standing in front of a stable that had been converted into a synagogue. Lev Berson's shul.

Quietly, Aaron tried to open the small door bearing the Hebrew inscription, *Hear O Israel: The Lord is our God, the Lord is one.* It wasn't locked.

He let himself in. Where the wagons had once been kept, where the horses had once defecated, ten elaborately bearded men now stood praying. They bowed unceasingly, rocking from their hips, in the direction of Jerusalem. The men, old and young, made up a minyan — the minimum number of Jewish males required for a ceremony or a service to count in the eyes of the Lord.

They were facing away from Aaron and didn't hear him come in. He doubted they would have stopped what they were doing in any case. The men were enraptured. Leading them was Rav Schmuel Levinsohn.

Cold rage flowed over Aaron as he recalled the person he'd been before the torture, before the camp. It gave him back strength and arrogance. He became — however fleetingly — a man again.

Aaron found a wall to lean against, lit a cigarette and waited. People didn't smoke in shuls. He figured that the offense would eventually get him some attention. He didn't have all day to waste, after all.

He was right. No sooner had he lit his second from the nub of the first than the rabbi found a stopping point, quickly wrapping things up.

"Hello, rebbe," Aaron said, far too loudly for the small room. "Got a couple of minutes for me?"

One of the younger men moved toward Aaron.

"Show respect!" the man said through clenched teeth.

"Oh, no disrespect intended!" Aaron said lightly, meaning the opposite. "Just looking for a few words with the Great Man."

The first man moved closer to Aaron and another, older man with a heavy gray beard moved to join him. Aaron prepared for a fight, pleased at the prospect. The stress in his body was aching to get out and he would happily take on all ten men just for the release.

But he didn't have to fight anybody. As Aaron had suspected he would, the rabbi came up and put an arresting hand on the shoulder of the young firebrand. The rabbi then whispered a few words that only the young man could hear, calming him and causing him to take a step back.

"By all means, Mr. Kaminski, let's talk."

"Thank you, rebbe," Aaron said, taking him by the arm and pointing the old man toward his office.

That Aaron would touch the eminence brought out audible gasps from the crowd. Rav Levinsohn himself visibly stiffened but didn't resist. Not quite.

"Avraham, please bring us some tea," the rabbi called back over his shoulder. The man who had nearly assaulted Aaron obeyed immediately, hurrying off to fetch it.

Inside the small office, Aaron noticed few changes from his first visit. There were as many books as ever, sitting on shelves that sagged as if they carried the weight of the world, not just its accumulated knowledge. Added to the books were rations. Tinned vegetables and soups. Packets of cookies, even chocolate.

"Chocolate!" Aaron said. "How in the world did you manage that?"

The rabbi didn't answer directly, instead returning Aaron's question with a question.

"Why are you here?"

"Are you surprised?" Aaron asked back.

"Well, yes," the rabbi said somewhat uneasily. "So many were taken in the last few weeks."

"You're still able to put together a minyan, I see."

"The Lord has been kind. Still, we have sustained our share of losses."

The rabbi bowed his head.

"I'm sorry to hear it," Aaron said with no obvious sign of grief.

"I would be somewhat surprised to see you here in my shul again, regardless, Mr. Kaminski. When we spoke before, you showed no religious interest, and I'm uncertain what else would bring you to me."

"Well, you're right that I'm not very religious, myself. I'm afraid I see hypocrisy everywhere I look in religion," Aaron said. "But that doesn't mean I don't have an interest in religious figures."

"What does that mean?" the rabbi asked, an edge of annoyance in his voice.

Aaron pointedly looked down at the desk in front of the rabbi.

"Would it be possible to see your notebook?"

It sat quietly at the center of the cluttered rectangle, closed up in its warm leather binding.

"Why on earth do you want to see it?" the rabbi asked, seemingly genuinely puzzled.

Before Aaron could answer, Avraham arrived with the tea. He served the rabbi first, naturally, and only grudgingly handed the other cup to Aaron.

"Is there anything else I can do, rebbe?" Avraham asked, by which he meant could he perform physical violence on Aaron's person?

"No, thank you," the rabbi replied stiffly. "You may go."

Avraham exited reluctantly.

Once the door was closed, Aaron blew on his tea, acting the part of a man who had all the time in the world. The rabbi didn't wait, taking a sip immediately. It was very hot and Aaron could see the man instantly regretted it.

"The notebook, please," Aaron said. "If it makes you feel any better, I don't plan on reading it."

The temperature in the little room dropped until it was colder than it had been in the Kronberg labor camp.

"You may not!"

"You know what I'm looking for, don't you?"

"Of course not," the rabbi said with a thin veneer of indignation. "But it is private. I will not have someone as profane as yourself trying to peer into my thoughts."

"Right at the moment, I couldn't give less of a *shit* about your thoughts," Aaron said, proving his profanity.

The rabbi looked like he'd never heard the word and was shocked to hear it now. Aaron guessed it was possible that no one had ever cursed in front of him, considering his role in village life before he was brought to the ghetto. The little prince with the word of God on his lips.

"Give me the notebook," Aaron said. His voice was low but tipped in steel.

"No!" the rabbi said, beginning to sound petulant.

"I don't think it's such an unreasonable request, rebbe, considering all the trouble I've been through thanks to what you wrote in it."

Aaron smiled. It was an ugly smile.

"What could I possibly have written that would cause you trouble?" the rabbi said dismissively. "The study of God's law hurts no one."

Aaron left that alone for the moment and shifted gears.

"You remember Lev Berson, don't you? A Jewish policeman, a member of your congregation?" Aaron spread his hands in mockery. "About so tall?"

The rabbi's frown became a scowl.

"You gave Berson a note to deliver," Aaron said, "but, unfortunately for him, he must have opened it."

The rabbi stared at Aaron, eyes wide and filled with malevolent intent.

"You know what?" Aaron said, rubbing his chin. "Maybe I don't need to thumb through your notebook, after all. I'm pretty sure I know what I'd find: a ragged edge where a page was torn out. Would you like to guess where I found the rest of the page?"

Nothing.

"I saw the tear along the binding on my first visit with you, though I didn't realize that's what it was at the time," Aaron said. "I couldn't help noticing how thick and creamy the notebook paper was — you rarely see anything nice in the ghetto, anymore.

"When I thought about what I'd seen a little later, it struck me as strange that someone would rip a page out of a book like that. Still, I didn't put the pieces together — so to speak — until much later."

The rabbi still said nothing.

"I also suspect that if I saw your handwriting again, it would match nicely with what I saw in the note intended for Hermann Clausewitz. The one I found on Lev Berson's body."

"You keep talking about a note. What note? You don't have any note," the rabbi said, finally breaking his silence. There wasn't much conviction in his voice.

"How would you know that for sure?" Aaron replied. "Because you're innocent? Or because you know Clausewitz took it from me?"

The rabbi was silent, his face closing like a flower at dusk.

"Perhaps you chatted about it just now?" Aaron pressed. "I saw his car on the way here."

More silence.

"This is excellent tea, by the way. Where do you think it's from? Ceylon? China?" Aaron asked, staring into the caramel-colored contents of his cup. "But I'm not sure it's so good that it's worth betraying your own people for."

That did it.

"How dare you! You think that what I did, I did for tea? Or chocolate? Or even for my life? What I did, I did for God and His Chosen."

Chapter 22

"What do you mean His Chosen? Everyone in this fucking ghetto is one of His Chosen," Aaron snapped back.

"That is not true. You need to understand this," the rabbi said, his voice urgent but more quiet.

He leaned in toward Aaron, and spoke in a conspiratorial tone.

"Why do you think God has caused all this to happen?"

Levinsohn spread his hands to encompass the war, the ghetto, and maybe the world as a whole.

"Because His Chosen People have failed him! Have sinned, forsaken his Commandments and gone into the world as if they were ordinary men! They no longer even look like Jews. They have discarded the tallis, payos and even the keepah, baring their heads before God.

"How many have walked away from the villages and their rabbis in the last century? Into godless towns like Miasto or Warsaw or Krakow?

"Jews thinking nothing of marrying into gentile families. Some of our men have renounced God himself, worshipping the false messiah of the Christians. How can there be any wonder at what has happened? That the Germans have come?" the rabbi said, concluding his sermon and his case.

"And you, I presume, are among the righteous?" Aaron asked.

"No! I lead the righteous!"

"Are you saying you're the moshiach?"

"You have said it," was the rabbi's only reply.

"You?" Aaron said, with an unconscious laugh. "Seriously?"

"Enough!"

The rabbi slammed his desk with open palms.

A knock on the door.

"Rebbe," Avraham's voice asked. "Are you all right?"

"Does your little flock know what you've done?" Aaron asked softly.

"Avraham, stop worrying!" the rabbi shouted. "I will come to you soon."

They heard footsteps retreat.

"I'll take that as a no," Aaron said.

"What they need to know is that I've saved them. That's all." The rabbi was dismissive.

"How many Jews have you betrayed?" Aaron asked.

"I have betrayed no one," Levinsohn said. "I have only passed along God's judgments."

"And he judged Lev Berson and found him wanting?"

"Lev broke my trust and thereby God's. He was told to hand the note to the German guards unopened."

"But he opened it?" Aaron asked.

"Yes. He asked to speak to me about it. I met him and did what needed to be done."

"You killed him yourself? With your own hands?"

"As guided by God."

Aaron sensed no self-doubt, no regret coming from the rabbi. Was it pride instead?

"And when you handed me over to the Germans, that was according to God's will, too?" Aaron asked.

"I can act in no other way."

"The little girl was yours, then?"

"She worked for me, yes."

"How did she know to follow me?" Aaron asked.

"I thought someone might show up, looking for information. People knew that Berson attended shul here," the rabbi said with a shrug. "The girl's job was to look out for strangers who weren't here to attend funerals. People don't often come here for any other reason. When you and I were walking into the shul, I signaled to her."

"You must not have paid her very well. She tried to steal from me before you arrived," Aaron said.

The rabbi shrugged indifferently.

"You told her to find Clausewitz on the night I was arrested?"

"Yes. It was best to be safe."

"And my wife?"

"What wife?" the rabbi asked with blatant sincerity.

"A blond woman, Yelena Gorska? She worked from the Polish side."

"You married outside the faith?" The rabbi was horror-struck.

"Well?"

"I have no idea. All I know is that you were arrested. I assumed you would be killed. I know nothing about your 'wife,'" the rabbi said.

Thank God for that, Aaron thought.

"And the little girl? What happened to her after I was arrested," he asked.

"It doesn't matter. Maybe the Germans took her away. She wasn't a particularly godly child, just a hungry one."

"You've condemned her, too," Aaron said in wonder.

"I've condemned no one. It is God who judges. My place is merely to be the instrument of his judgment on earth," the rabbi explained. Aaron could tell the old man was trying to sound reasonable, but the ring of mania was in his voice.

"How many?" Aaron asked.

"How many?"

"Yes, how many have you saved? How many are among the righteous? How many people have the Germans allowed you to keep?"

Levinsohn sighed.

"So few have been able to keep the faith in the face of such fearsome punishment."

The rabbi shook his head sadly.

"How many?" Aaron asked again.

"We are the minyan you have already seen. We will survive all this and will find our home in Palestine, in Jerusalem itself. And God's scourge will make it come to pass."

"The Nazis are taking you to Jerusalem?" Aaron asked, incredulous. "You really think that?"

"What other purpose could they serve?" the rabbi asked with a shrug. "God would never allow such evil if it didn't directly serve his purposes. That is the role they play. And when we are in Jerusalem, their part will be done."

Aaron understood. Levinsohn wasn't the egomaniac he'd first assumed. He was simply mad. Whether or not he'd been destined for that fate all along, what the rabbi had seen over the last months had caused a complete psychotic break. Of course he would cooperate with the Germans, they were carrying out God's will on earth, serving the messiah himself, though they may not have known it.

"How did you come up with this arrangement?" Aaron asked.

"I went to the Judenrat. Mordechai Zimmerman told me that Hermann Clausewitz was the person to speak to regarding my status in the ghetto."

"That's a terrible joke!" Aaron said. "He told you to go right to the Gestapo? You must have really annoyed him."

Levinsohn continued, oblivious.

"While my first note didn't reach him, a second one did. I found him a man of understanding, even if not a Jew. He understands God's plan as I explained it to him. He is another instrument of the Lord's justice."

"And what exactly did you promise Clausewitz?"

"I promised him nothing! I provided him with names of those who had already been condemned by God for their resistance to his judgment on the Jews," Levinsohn said.

"You mean people who wanted to fight back against the Germans?"

"Some 'patriots' approached me," the rabbi said with a sneer. "They asked if I would help."

Aaron wondered if any of them had been his backers, the men who had put up the treasure to buy the guns. Could it have been that by confronting the rabbi, rather than blindly carrying out his will, Lev Berson had inadvertently tried to protect Aaron and his friends — even died doing so?

He took a breath to calm himself before asking the next question.

"So why are you still here? You may have noticed, the ghetto's empty. Shouldn't you be on your way to Jerusalem by now?"

"Soon. There are still some here who are planning to fight the Germans. I am a figure of trust and respect among our people. They will tell me everything I need to know."

"And you'll just pass it along," Aaron said. Something then occurred to him.

"What about your families? You mentioned the ten men in this building. Surely your families are coming with you."

"Sacrifices have had to be made," the rabbi said solemnly. "Some have been dreadful. Without certain knowledge of the Lord's will, I don't know if I could have made them."

Aaron snapped. He jumped from his seat and was on the point of leaping at the rabbi when he saw a small German gun in the old man's fist. It was a Walther PPK, used mainly by police and Nazi Party officials.

"Don't move," the rabbi said. "Put your hands up."

In spite of the tension, or maybe because of it, Aaron let out a sharp bark of laughter. The old man sounded like a gangster in a movie. Was it possible the rabbi went to the movies? Aaron couldn't quite picture him sitting in the dark, reading the subtitles of an American crime drama.

"Do you know anything about guns?" Aaron asked.

"I know where the bullets come out."

"Did Clausewitz give it to you? Show you how to use it?"

"I don't need lessons."

Aaron reached over and casually grabbed the gun from the rabbi. It wasn't that Levinsohn hadn't pulled the trigger. The gun simply hadn't gone off.

"You should have gotten a lesson," Aaron said. He leaned across the desk and jammed the gun painfully into the rabbi's neck. He pressed it a little harder with each passing second.

The rabbi gasped, his blue eyes wide. The old man was in pain, but most of all, he was scared. Scared enough to wet himself.

Aaron appreciated that.

"Want to know what just happened?"

The rabbi was too terrified to move.

"You're a fucking rabbi. That's what just happened. And I'm a trained fucking soldier."

Aaron pulled the gun back into the rabbi's line of sight and pointed to it.

"See here? This little switch is called a safety. You have to turn off a safety before the gun will fire. That's why it's called a safety; it keeps you safe from yourself."

Aaron toggled the little switch.

And pulled the trigger.

Again, the gun didn't go off.

"God damn it!" Aaron yelled, thoroughly disgusted with himself. Of course it wouldn't fire. What kind of Gestapo officer would give a Jew a loaded weapon?

A smile began to spread across the rabbi's face.

The butt of the gun removed it. Another blow cracked the man's skull, but Aaron didn't stop. It wasn't long before the rabbi looked a lot like Berson had when Aaron first found him.

The door rattled behind Aaron. He turned and threw it open, knocking Avraham to the floor. Blood began to well from the young man's nose, quickly covering his face.

Good, Aaron thought, *now he looks just like the messiah.*

He laughed again. It was the kind of laugh that kept the other men in the room out of his way.

As he reached the door of the shul, he could hear a keening that made him think of all the women he'd heard holding their dead children. He cursed the men making it.

Aaron set off toward his apartment. He could think of nowhere else to go in the fading light. Catching a glimpse of his red-stained coat in a window, he stopped to casually remove it and turn it inside out. He nodded to the cadaverous man he saw in the glass, reminding himself to take extra care on the walk home in case any of the fresh blood still showed.

Epilogue

Aaron hiked in clean air, a walking stick clutched in his right hand, the haversack over his shoulders full with stolen food and clothes.

He was fat by no means, but he was a good thief and the proceeds had helped him regain some weight. That, and the help of kind strangers who had fed him well over the weeks he'd trekked across the countryside.

Many had never known that he was a Jew, supposing him to be one of the hundreds of thousands who had been displaced by the war against the Germans and the Soviets and then the Germans against the Soviets.

Others had figured it out, though he didn't know how. He looked no more like a stereotypical Jew than he ever had. Light hair, blue eyes and a tall frame. He traveled using Stefan Kaczynski's identity papers.

Still, people had guessed, and it seemed as if the German lust for Jewish blood had served to calm the rampant anti-Semitism in so many Polish hearts. Aaron had found sympathy and gentle questions about his family.

The answer was that Aaron couldn't, and so didn't, think about them. His father was gone, his mother had died long before the Germans came. There had been cousins and an aunt, but they were gone, too, as far as Aaron knew. If the war ever ended with the Nazis out of Poland, he would dig graves for them, even without their bodies. He would do the same for Stefan Kaczynski.

Kaczynski was seldom far from Aaron's thoughts, and if one could feel gratitude toward a man you had killed with your own hands, Aaron did.

Aaron didn't tell the people who helped him much of his own story. Instead he told them about the dissolution of the ghetto. Of the starving children who had been shot by monsters in front of their own parents. Of the children who had watched their parents die.

The people he told nodded and said they understood, and that there had been atrocities in every town the Nazis had passed through.

No, they didn't understand, but Aaron thought it was better for them that way. He wasn't sure he could truly convey what he'd seen, felt, or heard, anyway.

During his months-long walk he heard about the final uprising in Miasto. It was a pale thing compared to what would later take place in Warsaw's ghetto, but Aaron hoped that the few rusty guns he'd scrounged over the months had seen service.

He felt guilty that he hadn't been there to fight. He could have found ammunition for the little gun he'd taken from the rabbi who thought he was the messiah. Even if he'd failed to do that, a broken bottle or a brick would kill someone just as well. If he'd taken out one German soldier, it would have left one fewer to kill Jews.

But in the end, Aaron hadn't wanted to stay or fight. He knew that any victory the uprising could achieve would be pyrrhic, without a guarantee history would even hear of it.

And, somewhat to his surprise, he wanted to live.

So, he had slipped into his old room in the district on the day the rabbi died, gathered what little he had, and left the ghetto the way he'd come in. The basement corridors were only slightly darker than the night outside; the books in the central hall were just as burnt as when he'd left them.

No one bothered him as he walked up the stairs and onto the streets of the Aryan side. He was too numb to look furtive, so maybe the guards thought he belonged there. Maybe they were just looking the other way.

Aaron knew there would be other times and places to fight. He knew there was armed resistance scattered throughout Poland. If he found it, he would join. If he didn't, he thought he might join the Soviets, though he wasn't sure they were the lesser of any evils.

But that was a decision he could make later.

Ahead, Aaron saw the outline of the little house he'd come too far to find. At this distance there was no way to see the little sign that he knew was still above the door: Gradno.

Closer to the cottage, the dirt road turned to mud. With each step it became harder to pull his feet from the muck he'd created, until he couldn't move at all.

In an instant, he became convinced that he would drown in the bodies and the blood and the terror. Drown in what he had done and what he'd been unable to do. Be swallowed up by he people he'd lost and those who he hadn't saved. Die just as those he'd killed.

The moment passed, though not forever.

Aaron looked down and saw the dirt under his boots was now strewn with pebbles and dry. He began to walk again, toward the little cottage and, he hoped, Yelena.

About the author

Jason Fields is a writer and journalist. He has worked for publications including The Washington Post, The New York Times, and The Associated Press.

His mother, Susan, was born to a Jewish family in Belgium in 1940, just as the Nazi's were invading the country. She, along with her parents, fled across Europe, eventually catching a ship for the United States.

Jason grew up with stories of the family's flight, and of the world and people that were left behind. This book is an attempt to honor them.

Jason lives with his wife and son in New York City, where he was born.

www.ingramcontent.com/pod-product-compliance
Lightning Source LLC
LaVergne TN
LVHW010603100826
845148LV00014B/2828

* 9 7 8 0 6 1 5 7 3 2 0 9 1 *